TURN BACK TIME

AN ALEX MERCER THRILLER

Stacy Claflin

www.stacyclaflin.com

Edited by Staci Troilo

Receive free books from the author: sign up here.
stacyclaflin.com/newsletter

Taken

THE LARGE DILAPIDATED building loomed in front of Lottie Mills as she hefted the bags into her arms and lumbered up the cracked walkway. Glowing rays from the setting sun behind her made it seem even more ominous than usual. She carefully avoided the raised areas in the cement where tree roots had long ago destroyed the path. A faded sign welcoming her to the Meriwether complex had profanities spray-painted across it and the scent of marijuana hung in the air. Shouts of an argument came from an open window inside the old apartment building. A baby cried somewhere. Glass shattered not far away.

Lottie picked up her pace and pushed open the chipped, muddy glass door. She passed the long-broken elevator and hurried up two flights of stairs, stepping over a young man who passed out just before the second level. The hallway on the third level reeked of dirty diapers. She made her way to unit three-thirty-two. The two hung upside down, as always. Lottie knocked with her elbow, not wanting to set the bags of food on the ground.

Shrieks from excited children sounded from inside the apartment. The door opened, and Sydney Kelly appeared with a frazzled smile. The dark circles under her eyes had gotten worse, and she had what looked like a bruise on her cheek underneath makeup. The younger woman pulled some light brown hair behind her ear and adjusted the toddler on her hip. "Thank you for bringing the groceries."

Lottie stepped inside and set the bags on the table between fast food wrappers and some half-eaten candy. "It's not much, but I hope it helps."

Sydney put the child on a chair. "It always does. Thanks again. I wish I could do something to repay you."

Lottie glanced at the makeup-covered bruise. "You could let me help you with that."

"I can't. I need him."

A boy and a girl ran into the room and chased each other around the adults.

Lottie smiled at them and turned back to their mom. "Someday when you're able, help out someone else in need."

"I can't see that day ever coming, but okay."

"I'd stay and help with dinner, but I have some more food to deliver."

Sydney sighed. "How is it you're the only one who's made anything of your life since—" She glanced at the kids playing happily. "—well, you know?"

"I'm not the only one." Lottie thought of her son and daughter-in-law, who were doing even better than she was. "But I'm glad to help if you want to look for a better job."

"I'm not sure Joey would..." Her voice trailed off for a moment and her hand rested on the bruised cheek. "I should get this food put away. Thanks again."

"Always glad to help."

Sydney grabbed a bag. "Come on, Trula, help me out."

"Aw, do I have to? I..." The girl trailed off after looking at her mother's face and picked up a bag to carry.

Lottie waved and headed out, closing the door behind her. In the hall, she was hit with the stench of dirty diapers again. She held her breath, hurried down the stairs and out the building, and gulped in the air outside. It wasn't much better with the weed smoke drifting from somewhere. Yelling sounded from inside.

Hurrying, Lottie made her way to her little sedan across the street. She drove just a few blocks before stopping again to hand out some more food. Her stomach growled since she'd yet to have her own dinner.

"Just a few more minutes." Lottie patted her belly and then pulled her messy, graying golden-copper hair into a loose bun. She topped it with an old, stained sun hat. There were many ogling eyes where she was going, and far too often her locks garnered her unwanted attention. It was best to get in and out as quickly as she could.

She got out, pulled some more plastic grocery bags from the trunk, and headed down the alleyway between two abandoned shops, now overrun with squatters. Once she reached the alley, the odors of alcohol and urine made her gag.

It saddened her that these people had to live like that. If only she could do more, but she already gave them more than she should. She was fortunate that her son and daughter-in-law were so generous with her, or she could never afford to help Sydney or any of the others.

Lottie stepped over a puddle of she-didn't-want-to-know-what, since it hadn't rained recently. Laughter roared down an alley to her right. A scuffle sounded on the left. She took a deep breath and quickened her pace. As nervous as some of the homeless made her, they weren't the ones she truly feared. Wherever Lottie went, even in her safe little backyard, she watched for them. She would never stop.

Finally, she made it to the old department store, where some of the families lived. It hurt her heart that children lived here. Some people had suggested she report them to family services, but tearing those precious little ones from their loving parents would shatter her heart to pieces.

Once inside, Lottie headed for the back of the building, smiling at all the children who crossed her path. She slid them packs of fruit snacks until she had no more.

"Thanks, Miss Lottie." The little girl in loose, dirty pigtails who'd gotten the last pack smiled at her. She showed off a gap in her front teeth.

"Did you lose another tooth, Reyna?"

She nodded, but her smiled faded. "I wish the tooth fairy came here."

Lottie set down a bag, dug into her jeans' pocket, and pulled out a quarter. "I found this outside. Maybe she dropped it on the way in here."

Reyna's eyes widened. "You think so?"

"I do." Lottie put the quarter in the girl's palm and picked up the grocery bag. "Don't lose that."

The little girl rubbed it between her thumb and first finger. "I won't!" She scampered away, giggling.

Lottie stepped over a broken, grimy mannequin and made her way to the back where the three families she visited weekly lived. She gave each family one overstuffed bag, made some small talk, and rushed outside, eager to get to her clean, safe home before her own groceries went bad in the trunk.

Just before she came to the street, a man holding a half-empty booze bottle stepped out in front of her. He smiled, showing more missing teeth than little Reyna.

"Excuse me." Lottie stepped to the side, careful not to make eye contact.

He moved in front of her again. "Up for a good time?"

She glared at him. "My burly son is expecting to hear from me. If he doesn't, he's coming right here to find me."

The man held her gaze for a moment, but then stepped to the side.

Lottie hurried out to the street and breathed a sigh of relief. Her car was only a block away. She turned toward it, and a stocky, dark-haired, bearded man just taller than she was stepped out from behind a faded blue van.

Her blood ran cold. "I-I thought you were in jail."

"I was. Thanks to you and your brat."

She struggled to breathe normally. Her car wasn't far. She needed to make a run for it.

The man stepped closer. Two more jumped out from behind the vehicle.

Lottie recognized them, also. She spun around and bolted away from them and her car. Multiple hands grabbed onto her, squeezing. She screamed. A large palm covered her mouth and nails dug into her cheeks and under her jaw. They dragged her toward the van and opened its side door.

The men shoved her inside. A rough, unfinished box resembling a coffin sat open on the floor. She fought harder, but they forced her inside. Someone hit her on the head. The lid came down over her, shrouding her in darkness.

She yelled and pushed on the lid with all her strength, using her hands and feet.

A lock clicked into place.

Family

ALEX MERCER READ over his blog post one last time, checking for errors. There were none that he could see, but then again, his grammar sucked. Luckily his readers weren't usually worried about that. He pressed publish and waited until it went live. One quick glance showed everything looked good.

His new blog had really taken off thanks to his dad's help. Dad's blog had come a long way from its early days. It had started out as a humorous sports blog, but had morphed into so much more, gaining popularity over the years until it had earned him a book deal which had turned him into a *New York Times* bestselling author.

With Dad's expertise and some shout-outs from his blog, Alex's had taken off quickly. People had really responded to the topic, and now he had multiple emails daily from people asking him to post for them to get the word out about their missing friends and family.

It felt great to help, and now the blog was even starting to bring in a little extra money. Ideally, between that and being Dad's assistant—Alex was working on a better title—he would hopefully be able to get his own place soon. But if his parents had their way, he'd never leave.

He stretched and stood up. Ariana should be getting home from her soccer practice soon. The squealing of bus brakes sounded outside. Perfect timing.

Alex hurried downstairs and threw open the door before she got there. Ari faced the bus and waved to her friends, her dark ponytail bouncing back and forth. She turned around and her face lit up when she saw Alex.

He'd been meeting her after school for almost six months, but it still felt like the first day.

Ari ran up the driveway and threw her arms around him. She clung to him, and he swung her around.

"Did you have a good day?" He set her down.

"I made two goals!" She squealed, and her entire face lit up with excitement.

"You still won't let me watch you practice?" Alex took her backpack and moved aside for her to come in.

Ari kicked off her shoes. "Not until our first game, Daddy." She poked her head down the stairs of the tri-level. "Hi, Grandpa!"

"Hey, honey! I'll be up in a few."

"Okay!" Ari turned back to Alex. "Can we have a snack? I'm starving."

"Anything you want." Alex ruffled her hair. "Sorry, I think I just messed up your ponytail."

Ari shrugged, obviously not caring. She threw her bag in the family room and ran up the stairs, skipping every other step.

Alex's mom stepped out of the kitchen. "Just a small snack. We're having dinner soon."

"Aw," Ari complained, but she gave her grandma a hug when she reached the top of the stairs.

She kissed the top of Ari's head. "Dinner's more important, sweetie. Do you have homework?"

"Always."

They all went into the kitchen. "Alex, why don't you get her some fruit and water while she gets her homework set up?"

"Sure." He grabbed an orange and a banana from the hanging fruit basket and put them on the kitchen table before filling a couple glasses with water.

They settled in, and Alex helped Ari with her math. The aromas from dinner smelled delicious, and Alex realized how hungry he was. His stomach growled loudly. Ari looked at him and giggled.

He leaned over and kissed the top of her head. "Let's focus on your equations."

She made a noise imitating his stomach and laughed again.

His mom turned to him. "You definitely have a mini-me."

"I wasn't *that* bad, was I?" Alex teased.

"Hey!" Ari exclaimed.

"Don't worry," Mom said. "He was worse."

"Hey!" Alex said in the same tone Ari had.

She scrunched up her face at him, but then grinned.

Alex's heart warmed. Moving back home to be close to Ari had been the best decision he'd ever made. Spending every day after school with her was so much better than his previous twice-yearly visits. Now he couldn't imagine ever going back to his old life.

Ari made faces at him, trying to get him to laugh. She had him wrapped around her finger, and she knew it.

He gave her a quick hug. "Let's finish up this assignment, and then hopefully we'll have time to play before dinner."

Her eyes widened. "Video games?"

Alex nodded. "If you hurry."

She turned back to the math book.

Dad came into the kitchen and turned to Alex. "Did you talk to my editor?"

"Yeah, but he couldn't move the deadline."

He frowned. "And you told him about—?"

"I brought up everything. Still no. Sorry."

Dad raked his fingertips through his hair. "Looks like I'm going to have to pull some all-nighters to get this done on time."

"Want me to brew some coffee?" Mom asked.

He kissed her on the lips. "Did anyone ever tell you that you're the best wife in the world?"

"I think someone might have mentioned it once." She gave him a teasing glance and grabbed his butt.

Alex looked away and shook his head. Some things never changed, and he had a feeling they never would. He could picture them white-haired and wrinkled, and still grabbing each other and flirting shamelessly. That would be many years in the future, though. Still in their forties, Mom had her long auburn hair and Dad his full head of dark hair. They shouldn't have been grand-parents to an eleven-year-old, but Alex had only been fourteen when she was born.

Alex tried to ignore his parents while he looked over Ari's homework. He pointed at one problem. "You need to carry the one over here." His phone rang. It was his sister. "Hi, Macy. What's up?"

"She and Luke are still coming for dinner, right?" Mom asked, finally removing her hand from Dad's jeans.

Alex got up and went into the living room. "What did you say?"

"Can you tell Mom and Dad that we can't make it tonight?" Her voice sounded tense.

"Sure. Is everything okay?"

"Yeah, it's fine." Her tone said otherwise.

"What's going on? Are you okay? You didn't get into another accident, did you?"

"No, no. It's nothing like that. Luke and I are both safe. I have to go."

"What's wrong?"

"Just tell them something came up. Hopefully it turns out to be nothing."

Alex took a deep breath. "You're starting to worry me."

"I'm sure it'll be fine. Look, I have to go. I'll tell you later.

Promise."

"Okay, but if you need anything, let me know."

"Thanks, Alex. Love you."

"You too."

The call ended, and Alex stared out the window at their front yard. It was hard not to worry, given the things that tended to go wrong in their family.

Concerned

LUKE WALKER PACED the length of the family room, phone to his ear and thoughts far away. When the voicemail message sounded again, he pulled it away and ended the call in frustration. His brows came together as he pressed call again for what had to be the tenth time. Something had to be wrong. He couldn't drop the nagging feeling.

Macy came into the room. "I just called my brother and told him we can't make it."

He nodded and put the phone back to his ear. "It's not like her to not answer."

"I know." Macy's eyes reflected the same concern he felt. She came over to him and put an arm around him. "Let's go to her house and make sure everything's okay."

His mom's cheerful recorded voice sounded again over the phone.

"I don't know if you got my other messages, but we're coming over. We're getting worried." Luke ended the call and stuffed the phone into his pocket. "What could be wrong? Is she sick? Did she get hurt?"

Macy kissed his cheek. "Maybe she lost track of time gardening and left her phone inside."

Luke frowned. "She keeps her phone on her—and she should have called us yesterday. She calls every couple days, and now she's not answering. I should've gone over there last night."

"I'm sure she's fine. Maybe she's volunteering at the shelter. If someone is having a hard time, she's probably listening to them, not wanting to let the phone interrupt."

He frowned. "Maybe."

"Let's check her house. That's at least a start. Come on. I'll drive."

"Thanks." He took a deep breath, trying to calm his nerves. If something was wrong, he wasn't sure he could live with himself. They'd gotten busy the previous night, and he hadn't noticed the missing phone call. Mom lived alone and often called to chat with either one of them. Over the years, she'd grown just as close to Macy as she was with Luke, and that really said something considering everything Luke and his mom had been through.

"Luke?" Macy's voice broke through his thoughts.

He shook his head to clear it. "Right. Let's go."

They grabbed their things and headed for Macy's car. The short ride to Mom's little rambler was quiet. His mind went over everything she'd said the last time they'd talked. He couldn't remember her mentioning anything going on that would require her to miss calling him. She was like clockwork with her calls. Every other day so as not to be overbearing, but just enough to keep in regular contact with her only two family members.

"Her car isn't out front," Macy said. "Do you want to swing by the shelter?"

Luke shook his head. "I want to look around. She might've left a note or something."

Macy cut the engine, took his hand, and squeezed. "Whatever you want to do."

He nodded and studied the little rambler. From the outside, everything looked as it should. Pristine. Not a spot of peeling paint, the grass cut short, and all the shrubs and flowers pruned to perfection. The gnawing feeling that something was wrong was suffocating, and he wasn't one to worry without reason.

"You have your key?" Macy asked.

"Yeah." They got out of the car and headed across the short walkway. Luke dug into his pocket, pulled out his keys, and found the one for Mom's house. When he tried to shove it in the lock, his hand shook, and it took him several tries before he got the door open.

The sparsely decorated front room was bright from partially open blinds. Just like the outside, everything seemed to be in its place. They walked through the house. Everything was tidy, bright, and dust-free.

"Lottie!" Macy called. "Are you in here?"

Luke's stomach twisted into a tight knot, knowing Mom wouldn't respond. She wouldn't be there without her car. He went over to the back door and looked outside. Her garden that took up half the backyard was beautiful, but she wasn't out there. He frowned and walked through the kitchen, again finding nothing out of place. If only she'd left out some dishes to give them an idea when she'd last been home.

Macy came into the room. "Everything looks normal back in the bedrooms. She even has a baby blanket in the sewing room."

Of course she did. Luke and Macy were trying—so far unsuccessfully—and Mom obviously wanted to be prepared with a gift as soon as she heard the good news.

"Anything out here?"

Luke shook his head, his worry starting to head into the territory of fear.

Macy put an arm around his waist. "Do you know the shelter's number? I can call and see if she's there."

"Check her address book." He nodded to the phone on the counter. The same black leather-bound book she'd had for years sat next to it. "I'm going to see if I can find anything on her computer."

She kissed his cheek and picked up the book. Luke headed to

his old bedroom, which was now Mom's office, and powered on her desktop computer. It opened to her desktop without needing a password. He clicked around, finding nothing. The mouse hovered over her email icon. He didn't want to invade her privacy, but she would understand. She'd do the same if the roles were reversed.

Luke opened her email program and read over the subject titles. Most everything looked like broadcast emails—announcements for the women's shelter Mom volunteered at and other similar items. Not many looked personal, and nothing seemed to indicate why she might be ignoring her phone.

Footsteps sounded. Macy stood in the doorway, her forehead wrinkled. "They said she hasn't been to the shelter this week. The woman thought she might have helped out at the soup kitchen since they're understaffed this week, but I called there and they haven't seen her, either. Did you find anything?"

He shook his head. "Something has to be wrong."

She sat on his lap and leaned her head against his. "What do you want to do?"

Luke laced his fingers through hers. "I don't know. Can we file a missing person report? Doesn't it have to be forty-eight hours? I have no idea how long she's been gone." He sighed. "I'm the worst son ever. I should've known something was wrong when she didn't call last night."

Macy ran her fingers through his nearly shoulder-length hair. "You're probably the *best* son ever, babe. Let's just focus on finding her. I could call Alex. He's practically besties with the captain."

Luke closed his eyes and nodded. He couldn't think of anything else they could do.

Interrupted

ALEX SWALLOWED HIS last bite of roast beef and turned to Dad. "Do you need me to make any calls tonight?"

He shook his head. "Just because I have to work twenty-four-seven doesn't mean you need to. I'll let you know if I need anything other than time and silence to get these final chapters finished."

"I'll make sure the coffee pot stays warm all night," Mom said.

Dad kissed her cheek. "You're the best, hon. Don't worry about me, okay? You need your sleep. Isn't tomorrow your busy day?"

Mom nodded. "Fridays and Saturdays, I'm always swamped. That's when everyone wants their hair done."

"Then you worry about getting enough sleep. Don't give me a second thought."

"Right, that's going to happen." She yawned. "Maybe I do need to go to bed, though."

Alex's phone rang.

"You're popular tonight," Dad said.

He checked the screen. It was Macy again. Something had to be wrong. "I'll be right back." Alex accepted the call as he ran to his room and closed the door behind him. "What's wrong? You can't tell me nothing is."

"How long do you have to wait to file a missing persons report?"

Alex's stomach dropped. "Who's missing?"

"Can you just answer the question?"

"I don't think you're supposed to wait. From everything I know, the first forty-eight hours are critical."

"So, we don't wait at all?"

"No. What's going on?"

"I hope we didn't miss the forty-eight-hour period."

Alex felt like pulling out his hair. "Would you tell me who's gone?"

After a couple beats, Macy finally spoke. "Lottie."

"What?" Alex exclaimed. Luke's mom was the nicest person he knew. "Are you sure?"

"We talked to her neighbor. He hasn't seen her car since at least the day before yesterday. She also didn't call us yesterday, and she calls every other day like clockwork."

"You've got to be kidding me."

"I wish I was."

"Do you want me to call Nick?" Alex asked. "He's on duty today, and should still be there."

"No, we'd better call him."

"Let me at least get you his direct line. If you just call the station, they'll give you the runaround. Trust me."

"Thanks, Alex."

"I'll text it to you. Let me know what he says."

"Okay."

Alex ended the call, copied the number, and pasted it into a text to his sister. If they couldn't find Lottie soon, he'd definitely write up a post on his blog to let people know to look for her. So far, he'd only posted about missing kids and teens, but that didn't matter. A missing person was a missing person.

He went back to the kitchen.

Mom arched a brow the moment he walked in. "What's the matter?"

Alex glanced at Ari. He didn't want to upset her by saying anything. "I'll tell you soon."

"What is it?"

He put a hand on Ari's shoulder. "Are you done eating?"

She frowned. "You can tell me. I'm eleven, soon to be twelve. That's practically a teenager."

Alex thought about everything she'd been through, and how far she'd come in the meantime. "It's best that you don't worry about this for now." With any luck, Lottie would show up soon, and Ariana wouldn't know the sweet lady had ever been missing. "Are you finished?"

Her shoulders slumped and she sighed dramatically. "Yes."

"Don't forget our hugs," Dad said.

Alex found Ari's backpack and slung it over his shoulder while she hugged her grandparents.

"See you tomorrow, sweetie." Mom gave her an extra hug.

"Bye," Ari said, pouting.

Alex kissed the top of her head. "I'm sorry to cut this short, but I'll make it up to you tomorrow. Okay?"

"Okay. You can tell me. I'm mature for my age—my teacher says that all the time."

He guided her toward the front door. "I'm sure you are, but Mimi and Papi should be home now, and they want to see you, too. Besides, aren't you still rearranging your bedroom?"

"Yeah, but I want to know what's going on. Please."

Alex sighed and wondered if he'd been this persistent as a kid. He'd probably been worse. He had gotten away with just about everything when it came to his parents, which was why Ariana even stood in front of him now. His parents had no idea he and Zoey were romantically involved, and that had made sneaking around with her all that much easier.

"Please," Ari begged, bringing him back to the present.

He wrapped her in a hug. "Maybe once the situation is resolved, we'll tell you."

She wrinkled her nose at him. "You know, I'll try to figure it out, and whatever I think about will probably be worse than what's really happened. I'll worry more than if I just knew the truth."

Alex ran his fingers through his hair. She actually made sense, but she was still a kid and it was his job to protect her—especially after everything she'd suffered. "We'll talk later. Get your shoes on and spend some time with Mimi and Papi."

Ari sighed even more dramatically than she had a few minutes earlier and then she slid on her shoes.

Alex stepped onto the porch and looked next door. Both Valerie's and Kenji's cars were there, and so was Zoey's. "Your mom is there, too."

"She is?" Ari's entire expression brightened, the mystery of what Alex wouldn't tell her probably forgotten. She hugged Alex. "Bye, Dad!"

He returned the embrace and handed her the backpack. "See you tomorrow, Ari."

"Maybe Mom will tell me what you won't."

Alex shook his head. "She doesn't even know what it is."

"Darn. Well, bye!" She waved and then bolted home.

He watched, making sure she got inside safely. It was tempting to go over there to see Zoey. He hadn't seen her since the previous weekend, but with Lottie missing, he needed to get back inside and tell his parents that yet another person in their family had gone missing.

Phone

CAPTAIN NICK FLESHMAN squeezed the arm of his chair so hard he was sure he would rip the leather right off. He gritted his teeth and took a deep breath, focusing on the picture of his kids next to his laptop. He needed to calm down before he spoke.

There were few things in life he liked less than speaking with his ex-wife on the phone at work, and yet she always insisted on calling him then. Always. He counted to ten silently.

"You still there, Nick?" Corrine's voice grated on his last nerve.

"Of course I am." It took every ounce of self-control to keep his voice steady.

"Well, I'm waiting for your answer."

He squeezed the chair tighter. "No, you will not take them to Disney World for spring break. That's *my* week, and you know it."

"But they want to go!"

"You already told them?" he exclaimed. "Before talking to me?"

"It may have slipped out accidentally."

Accidentally, his butt. "How dare you?"

"They've always wanted to go." Her tone dripped of syrupy sweetness.

"You had mid-winter break, and you have half the summer!"

"Well, I had to work during mid-winter break and Dave—"

"Who's Dave?" Nick demanded.

"Is Dave coming over?" Hanna asked in the background.

Corrine cleared her throat. "That's a conversation for another day. About spring break—"

"Have you started seeing someone and introduced him to the kids before talking with me?" Nick's blood pressure was rising by the moment.

"I can see whoever I want. I don't have to ask your permission. That's the beauty of divorce."

"You never did when we were married, so I wouldn't expect you to now." Nick was dangerously close to yelling, and he didn't want anyone in the department to overhear this conversation. "Why don't you fill me in now? Tell me about this Dave character who's now in my children's lives."

"You have nothing to worry about. He treats them like gold and has no desire to replace you. He's a flight attendant, and he adores the kids."

"So, you're dating a stewardess?" It was petty, but Nick didn't care.

"Nice." He could practically hear her roll her eyes. "Look, he can get us free flights to Florida."

"How about he use those for the court-ordered visitation with me? I haven't seen them since the beginning of the year!"

Corrine huffed. "That's not my fault."

"How is it not?" Nick demanded. "You divorced me, yanked them from my home, and moved across the country."

"Your real wife has always been the police department, Nick. When did you ever see them more than twice a week when they did live under the same roof as you?"

The phone on his desk rang.

"Look, I have to get back to work—"

"Don't you always?"

"You'd better put those kids on that plane for spring break in two days."

"Nick—"

He ended the call and practically threw his cell phone on the desk. The phone continued ringing. Nick stared at it, taking deep breaths. He was in no mood to deal with anything, but he had to push aside the argument. It was part of the job.

Nick picked up the phone in the middle of the last ring before it went to voicemail. "Captain Fleshman."

"Captain, this is Macy Walker. Alex Mercer's sister."

"Macy, hello." He drew in a deep, silent breath trying to focus. "How are you? Alex says you've completely healed from the accident."

"I have, but that's not why I'm calling."

He grabbed a notepad and a pen. "Is something the matter?"

"We think my mother-in-law is missing."

Nick wrote that down. "What makes you think that?"

"She *always* calls us every other day, and she didn't yesterday. Plus, her neighbor hasn't seen her car."

He scribbled more notes. "Is there anywhere she may have gone to?"

"She hasn't been to the shelter she volunteers at. They haven't seen her, either."

"What about work?"

"She's retired, and it isn't like her to take off without telling us. We're her only family."

"Okay." Nick continued taking notes. "What's her name and address?"

"Lottie Mills." Macy told him her home address.

"Mills? Your married name is Walker."

"She goes by her maiden name."

"Any chance she's worried about her ex?" Nick asked. "Is that why she didn't keep his last name?"

"No, he died when Luke was a kid."

"A current husband or boyfriend?"

"No. She lives alone and keeps busy taking care of the house and yard, and also volunteering at the shelter. They almost ended up on the streets after her husband died, and I think that's why she likes to help out there."

"Okay, this is good info," Nick said. "Do you know if she had any trouble with any other relationships? Any reason to think of that she may have fled on her own volition?"

"Um..." Her voice trailed off. "No. We're both really close to her. If anything was wrong, she'd have told us—and she didn't."

Nick rose from the chair. "I'd like to have a look around her house. Do you have keys?"

"Yeah, we're here now."

"Oh, good. Stay there until I arrive." He slid on his jacket. "Is her car there? Is anything disturbed in the home?"

"Her car's gone—the neighbor hasn't seen it—and the house is spotless, as usual."

"What about her mail? Has it been picked up recently?"

"I don't know. Hold on." Her voice grew quieter. "Hey Luke, go check her mail. Okay, Captain, he's going to check."

"Just a couple more questions before I leave. Does she take any medications, or does she have any conditions—medical or psychological—that would put her survival at risk if she doesn't have them?"

"No, I don't think so."

"She isn't prone to wandering off? No early signs of dementia?"

"Lottie's as sharp as a thirty-year-old."

"Okay. While I'm on my way, check for anything missing—clothes, luggage, medications, purse, cell phone, and anything else that would indicate she left purposefully. Also, think of anything you can regarding her disappearance, whether it could be intentional or otherwise. And if you can, gather what you can to help identify her, such as a picture and license plate number, so I can send out a BOLO alert."

"Luke's back with a stack of mail. It looks like it could be a couple days' worth."

Nick's stomach tightened. If Lottie had been missing a couple days already and she hadn't left of her own free will, their chances of finding her alive and well were low.

Dizzy

MACY'S HEAD SPUN. The detective had just asked her and Luke the same questions—albeit in a different order—that the captain had asked before. They'd given them a couple pictures of Lottie, and she'd dug up her license plate number from the home office. Several police were there looking around, and Nick was currently outside, talking with neighbors. He'd already issued the alert and the rest of the force was keeping an eye out for her.

Luke sat next to her on the couch and put his hand on her knee. "Are you okay?"

"I should be asking you that." She sighed and squeezed her hands together. "I'm a psychologist, Luke. I should be handling this better. I can't think straight."

He ran his hands through his hair. "Babe, you're a *child* psychologist, and it's always different... harder... when it's someone you love. You're not just her daughter-in-law, you're her daughter."

Tears blurred Macy's vision. Luke put an arm around her and they sat in silence, watching the police walk around, looking at things and talking on their cell phones and radios. In a way, it didn't feel real. Or maybe she didn't *want* it to be real. She just wanted to see Lottie walk through the door and say it was all a big misunderstanding.

But she didn't. Macy leaned her head against Luke and tried to think of anything they may have missed. Perhaps some detail that would be the missing clue they needed. They'd told the police everything they knew—her typical schedule, physical description, license plate and description of her car, and even the address of the shelter.

There had to be more. Macy looked around the living room, trying to figure out what they may have forgotten. Nothing came to mind. Lottie led a routine life and rarely did things differently. It was Macy and Luke who always had schedule changes, and that was why they hadn't noticed her missed call the day before.

Her chest constricted and guilt stung. They should've noticed, but they hadn't. Would that cost Lottie her life?

"Macy, breathe," Luke whispered.

She let out some air she didn't realize she was holding. "What if—?"

"We can't ask those questions right now. It won't help."

"What are we supposed to do, then?" Her breathing was shallow. She struggled to take a full, deep breath, but couldn't.

He rubbed her back. "Focus on finding her. That's all we can do."

"But I'm so worried."

"So am I, but we have to keep a level head."

She knew he was right, but she was barely hanging on, feeling dizzy and light-headed.

"Macy?"

The room spun around her.

"You're pale as a ghost."

She blinked several times, feeling the sensation of falling. Luke grabbed her shoulders and rose from the couch, still holding her.

"You'd better lie down." He reached for a throw pillow and put it under her head.

Macy tried to sit up, but couldn't. "I'm having a panic attack."

He kissed her cheek, grabbed a green and blue blanket Lottie had crocheted, and covered Macy. "Just rest. Everything's going to be fine."

"How do you know that? We don't know if—"

"No, but we have to be positive. We *have* to be."

Macy closed her eyes. She couldn't do that. Her mind was taking her to dark places, and it was all she could to do to keep from getting pulled in. Ever since the car accident that had landed her in the hospital nearly six months earlier, she'd started having flashbacks to her kidnapping again.

Walking down the street, she saw Chester's face on strangers. It always took a few seconds too long for her to realize it wasn't really her abductor—the man who had starved her and mentally tortured her. When she should have been focused on boys and learning to drive, she'd been at the mercy of a lunatic.

Would she ever fully move on from that experience? She'd been safe for more than ten years, and he was still in jail. He shouldn't ever get out after everything he'd done. Chester Woodran had killed his wife and then had spent months preparing to kidnap Macy. His sights had been set on *her*. He'd wanted to replace his lost family, and Macy was unfortunate enough to be nearly identical to his daughter.

Macy pushed the thoughts from her mind. "I'm safe. I'm safe now." And aside from that, the entire experience hadn't been *all* bad. She'd actually met Luke while under Chester's tight reign. Luke hadn't known she'd been kidnapped, but he'd saved her sanity all those years earlier. It looked like he would be again now.

"Is she okay?" Captain Fleshman's voice broke through Macy's thoughts.

"I think she's flashing back to her kidnapping," Luke said.

How did he know?

"Does that happen often?" asked the captain.

"She's been having nightmares since the accident."

Macy sat up. "I have? No, I haven't."

Luke kissed the top of her head. "At least once a week."

She stared at him. "Why didn't you tell me?"

"I didn't want to add to your distress."

Fleshman gave Macy a sympathetic glance. "Why don't you two head home? We're done here, and we've got this."

Macy shook. "We should stay here. What if she comes back?"

"Officers are going to patrol the area, checking on the house every hour. If she shows up, I'll call you personally."

She turned to Luke, giving him a questioning look. He held out his hand for her to take. Macy took his hand, and he helped her up.

Captain Fleshman handed Luke a card. "If you think of anything else, call me directly."

He took the card. "I can't thank you enough. Really, we didn't expect all this. I wasn't even sure if it was too early to report her missing."

Fleshman shook his head. "Hollywood perpetuating myths. Sooner is *always* better. We'll do our best to find her."

"Again, thank you." Luke put his arm around Macy. "Let's go home."

Awkward

ALEX GLANCED BEHIND his laptop. He'd been waiting outside on the bench for Zoey for nearly an hour now. The sun had given away to gray skies and light showers which had finally turned into a dull drizzle. Having lived his entire life in the Seattle area, Alex found the rain comforting. He'd always enjoyed watching it from the covered porch of his childhood home.

A door slammed shut nearby. Alex sat taller, craning his neck to see if Zoey was leaving her parents' house. Instead, across the street Nathan Willows crossed his yard to a car parked on the curb.

Sighing, Alex turned his attention back to his blog post. He'd written up everything he knew about Lottie and her disappearance, even uploading some pictures he had of her with Macy, Luke, and Ari on his phone. The post was as good as he could get it for the time being. He rubbed his short beard as he ran a spell check on the post and then pressed publish.

Hopefully, it would help. His blog had played a part in a couple kids being found alive. More and more people were visiting daily. Alex hoped that one day soon it would not only pay for itself but allow Alex to stop working as Dad's assistant. He wanted to be able to get a place of his own—one that wasn't falling apart like his last apartment.

Another door closed nearby and then a car alarm beeped. Alex jumped up. The lights on Zoey's turquoise car flashed along with the beeps. He closed his laptop, set it aside, and jumped up.

"Zoey!"

She turned his way. "I have to get going!"

He jogged over to Zoey's parents' house. "This'll only take a minute. It's important."

"What is it?"

Alex nodded toward her car. "Let's talk in there."

She sighed and then opened the driver's side door. He climbed into the passenger side and brushed some rain droplets off his pants. Zoey looked at him expectantly.

"I don't want Ariana to overhear."

"Okay."

"Lottie's missing."

Zoey's brows came together. "Who…? Wait, Luke's mom?"

Alex nodded. "I don't know the details, but yeah. Nobody knows where she is, and it's totally out of character for her. Nick's got half the force on it, and I just posted about it on my blog."

Her face paled and she let out a long, slow breath. "Crap. Well, is there anything I can do?"

"I think the best thing we can do is to keep Ari from finding out. Hopefully, Lottie will come home with a funny story about what happened. Ariana is doing so well, I don't want her to start thinking about her ordeal, you know?"

Zoey nodded. "I hope they find her soon. Does she have dementia or anything like that?"

Alex shook his head. They sat in silence. He wanted to ask her a million questions now that he finally had a moment alone with her, but he didn't know where to start. Things were so complicated between them.

He studied her. She was deep in thought and as beautiful as ever with her long, thick dark hair and equally dark eyes. She was half-Japanese and had the best features of both her parents. His heart fluttered. He wanted to lean over and kiss her, but he was giving her the space she seemed to want—not that he could blame her. Six months earlier, her engagement had been broken off. Then there was the fact that he felt the need to prove himself to her, and the fact that he was living with his parents didn't help anything.

He'd been a screw-up when they got together as kids, and she'd been drawn to that part of him back then. But she wasn't fifteen anymore, and he wasn't thirteen. They were adults now, trying to have a part in the life of their daughter that her parents were raising. She had a college degree and an important job in a huge department store chain, and Alex was a recovering alcoholic who still drove a beater and slept in his childhood bed.

Zoey turned and met his gaze. They stared into each other's eyes for a moment before she spoke. "Thanks for helping Ari with her homework. I still hate math."

"It's kinda fun if you think of it like a puzzle."

"I don't like puzzles, either."

Alex smiled. Some things never did change—like him being in love with Zoey. He'd used alcohol and moving away to try and push his feelings away, but it hadn't worked out on any level. All he'd done was drive a wedge between him and his one true love, and he'd nearly lost her to her ex-fiancé.

She cleared her throat. "So, uh…"

Something inside him screamed to ask her on a date. But he couldn't do it. Not living under his parents' roof, driving his beat-up, gold Tercel, working as his dad's secretary. If he was making less money helping his dad and optimizing his blog, he'd go back to the long, hard hours of roofing just to look better for her.

"I should get going," Zoey said.

"Same here." Alex cleared his throat. "I need to see how Luke and Macy are doing."

Zoey nodded. "Tell them to let me know if they need anything. And tell Macy she can call me anytime."

"I will." He held her gaze again. Her luscious lips parted, like she wanted to say something. It took every ounce of his self-control not to lean over and place his mouth on hers.

She didn't look away. It was almost like she wanted the same thing. But they hadn't shared a romantic moment together in so long. Plus he needed to get out on his own and prove to her that he was good enough for her.

Alex cleared his throat. "So, I'll tell her."

She averted her gaze. "Thanks. I'll, uh, let my parents know what's going on. They won't say anything to Ari, but I'll tell them not to, just to be safe."

"Thanks."

A moment of silence passed.

He opened the door and stepped outside. "Take care."

"You too."

Alex closed the door and walked toward his parents' house while she pulled out of the driveway and headed to her own place. He still had so far to go if he wanted to win Zoey back.

Box

LOTTIE'S EYES FLEW open—not that it helped remove her from the darkness. She gasped for air. The air was hot and heavy. It was hard to breathe in deeply. The shallow gasps barely made it past her chest. Something smelled bad. Ammonia and feces. Her eyes watered.

She tried sitting up, but hit her head on something wooden just above her.

Where was she?

Lottie felt around, the rough wood surrounded her. Her head hurt. Was it from the bad air quality and the smell or from hitting her head? Or something else entirely? Her neck hurt, too. She rubbed it and tried to figure out how she'd gotten in the box.

Soft, muffled conversation sounded from somewhere outside the box.

She froze, fearing the worst. Who was out there, and how had they gotten her in the box?

Her heart thundered against her chest as the fear of being buried alive raced into her mind. What if they thought she was dead, and they were digging her grave?

Lottie pounded on the wood above with her fists and knees. "Let me out of here!"

She continued until her voice and hands both grew raw. The muffled voices didn't move any closer or grow any louder. She sifted through her memories, trying to figure out what had happened.

Why couldn't she remember? Did it have anything to do with her headache? If someone had slipped her something, it might. But who would've done such a thing, and why?

Lottie rubbed the top of her head where it hurt the most. What was the last thing she remembered? She'd been home, working on her garden. It was spring, and soon the flowers would bloom and the fruits and vegetables would ripen.

What had happened next? Had she gone to the shelter? No. It hadn't been her day. She'd taken some food to the homeless and to Sydney's family, hadn't she?

She had. Lottie remembered Sydney's kids running around and little Reyna, who'd lost a tooth.

Her pulse raced. She was close to figuring out what had happened.

Lottie had dropped off the food and then left. She hadn't made it to her car, though.

Why not?

Something had to have happened, otherwise she'd have gone back home and called Luke and Macy.

The voices outside the box grew slightly louder. Lottie strained to hear what they were saying. Everything was still too muffled. She couldn't make out any words. Only that the voices belonged to men.

She froze, terror gripping her.

Lottie knew exactly who had put her inside the box.

Her pulse pounded all throughout her body, and she struggled to breathe. She also fought to hear the conversation outside. She only made out a few words, but she recognized the tones.

Voices she could never forget.

People who had threatened to make her pay as they were dragged away in handcuffs by the police.

They had to have been released, and they'd found her. Not

only found her, but captured her.

Lottie swallowed and tried to control her breathing. She listened as Jonah, Abraham, and Isaac spoke with other former leaders of the community—the cult she had been naive to join when Luke was young. It had been shortly after she'd been widowed, and she was about to lose their old house. They had promised to save her and her son from having to live on the streets.

What were they planning to do with her now? She hadn't even heard of their release from jail.

The community leaders never let anything get in the way of what they wanted. And that was the big question—what did they want?

Memories from her years in the cult flooded her mind like waves crashing over her. One event in particular clung to her mind. A young man had managed to escape the nearly impenetrable fence, but the leaders had caught him. They'd gathered the adults in the community together in the main meeting hall and put him on trial.

The poor young guy hadn't stood a chance. He'd disobeyed the leaders and tried to escape. He *had* escaped. Jonah made sure everyone knew he wouldn't be defied again. The entire community had watched as the young man burned at the stake for his crimes against the leaders. Crimes far less than the ones that had sent the leaders to jail for more than ten years. Things they might blame Lottie for, and they would definitely blame on Luke and Macy.

Overwhelmed

LUKE BOLTED UPRIGHT in the bed, gasping for air. "It was only a dream."

Or was it? He'd dreamed of his mom tied up and tortured.

He took a deep breath and his chest constricted. It *was* only a dream. He had no way of knowing where she was or what she was doing. For all he knew, there was a perfectly good explanation for her disappearance. Not that he could think of a single reason.

Luke pushed the covers off himself and climbed out of bed, wiping sweat from his brow. It was still dark outside, but there was no way he was going back to sleep. He was surprised he'd managed to fall asleep at all.

As his eyes adjusted to the little light in the room—Macy had always insisted on a night light—he noticed she was twisted up in the blankets. He leaned over and pulled them out from under her. She rolled over, mumbling but not waking.

He selfishly wished she'd wake, so they could talk. He let her sleep, though. She'd had a harder time falling asleep than he'd had, finally taking some of her anxiety medication that she avoided unless she just couldn't carry on otherwise.

Luke paced the room, watching as she tossed and turned. Something scratched against the house. He arched a brow. That was strange, especially considering there were no trees on that side of the house.

Another scratch, followed by a bump.

He crept over to the window and lifted a blind, glancing around the backyard. Nothing was out of place.

Scratch. Bump.

Luke glanced down, but didn't see anything. Not that he could see much with only a sliver of the moon casting light outside. He glanced around the yard again, still seeing nothing unusual.

He reached for a flashlight, but then something moved just at the edge of his line of sight. A raccoon ran away from the house toward the far end of the backyard.

Luke breathed a sigh of relief, only to return to the reality of his mom being missing and his wife drowning in anxiety. Macy rolled over, twisting the sheet around her, mumbling something that didn't make sense. He walked over to her, softly kissed her forehead, and went out into the living room.

It was too early to call anyone, but he wanted to get on with the day. He needed to find out if anyone had seen or heard anything. There had to be someone who knew something. It was just a matter of finding that person.

Maybe it wasn't too early to call the police captain. He *had* said to call him. At the very least, Luke could leave a message. He found his wallet on the coffee table, dug out the card with Fleshman's number, and called him. As expected, it went to voicemail.

Luke closed the bedroom so he wouldn't wake Macy and went into the kitchen. "Captain Fleshman, this is Luke Walker. I'm calling to see if you've learned anything new about my mom. Please give me a call either way. Thank you." He left his number and then hung up.

Yawning, he set up the coffee maker to make a pot of strong coffee. He was going to need it. As it started making its noises, Luke leaned over the counter and stared outside. Everything was so peaceful. Too peaceful. He wished some of that would extend into his life. It seemed like he and Macy couldn't catch a break these days. She had only recently recovered from a nasty car accident, and now this.

Why hadn't he checked on his mom the day she missed calling him? He should've noticed she hadn't phoned. What if he could've done something to prevent whatever had happened?

Luke's phone rang next to the coffee maker. His heart jumped into his throat. Could it be his mom? He ran over to see the captain's name on the screen. Luke swiped the screen, accepting the call. "Captain? Have you heard anything?"

"Not yet, Luke. I'll call you as soon as I do."

"Wait. I didn't wake you, did I? I shouldn't have called so early."

"No, I couldn't sleep either. As soon as it's time for breakfast, I'm going back to the shelter to speak with some other volunteers there. Maybe one of the morning crew knows something."

"I can't thank you enough, Captain."

"We're doing everything we can. I hate that your family is dealing with another missing person."

"Is there anything else I can do?" Luke asked. "I feel like I should be doing more."

"From my experience, missing older people tend to show up alive. The best thing you can do, aside from calling anyone who might have heard from her, is to carry on with your life. Go to work, take care of your wife. There isn't any evidence of foul play. She may just show up, having decided on a whim to take a small trip."

"That's not like her."

"I know, but it wouldn't be the first time I've seen someone her age do that."

Luke sighed. He was certain his mom hadn't done that, but maybe there was some other rational explanation. "Thanks again. Call me anytime, okay?"

"I will. Maybe someone at the shelter this morning will know something."

"Let's hope." Luke said goodbye, ended the call, and poured some coffee.

Something crashed in the bedroom. Luke put the coffee pot back and bolted out of the room. He turned on the light. Macy sat up in bed, her hair wild, and some books from her nightstand were strewn across the floor.

"Are you okay?" He ran over to her and untangled her from the sheets.

She gasped for air and shook. "I had a nightmare."

Luke replaced the books, sat next to Macy, and held her close. She continued trembling in his arms. A lump formed in his throat. How was he going to hold it together between his mom's disappearance and Macy's anxiety? He could barely function. How could he take care of her? He rubbed her back and kissed the top of her head. It was all he could do.

"Do you think she's okay?" Macy asked.

"The captain says—"

"What do *you* think?"

He took a deep breath. "I hope she is. It isn't like her to take off without saying anything."

"That's what worries me."

They sat in silence. Luke watched the minutes pass on the wall clock. Macy shook harder. His thin t-shirt dampened from her tears. It was enough to make his own eyes mist. He held her tighter. "Let's get some breakfast."

"I-I can't eat."

"We have to. Neither one of us had dinner last night. What do you think Mom would say about that?"

Macy swallowed. "She wouldn't stand for that."

"Exactly." Luke rose and helped her out of bed. "The captain says the best thing for us is to continue on with life."

She stared at him, her eyes red and bloodshot. "You think we should go to work?"

He pulled a wisp of hair from her face. "What would you tell the kids you work with?"

Macy frowned. "To keep their schedules as normal as possible."

"We should take your advice. Sitting around here will only make us stir-crazy. Let's get some food." He took her hand and led her toward the door.

"Maybe I can speak with one of my colleagues today. I'm sure someone would help me through this."

"That's a good idea." A small amount of relief washed through Luke. He didn't know how to help her with her anxiety. "We'll eat, and then I'll drive you to work on the way to my office."

"You don't want me driving?"

He thought back to her car wreck and her long hospital stay afterward. Though Alex had believed someone else had been behind the accident, Luke had always thought Macy had a panic attack and lost control of the vehicle. She had no memories of the collision or the moments before, so nobody really knew for certain.

He turned to her and kissed her forehead. "I just want you safe."

Macy stared at him like she wanted to protest, but she said nothing.

Looking

ALEX KNOCKED ON his dad's door and went in before hearing a reply. Dad glanced up from the computer screen, took off his glasses, and rubbed his eyes. "Did you send everything to my editor?"

"Yeah. Just got it off to him. Do you mind if I take a break? I want to see if there have been any similar cases to Lottie's disappearance."

Dad frowned, the creases around his eyes deepening. "They still haven't heard from her?"

Alex shook his head. "I just talked to Nick, and he says nobody knows anything."

"Is there anything we can do to help?"

"I've already posted about it on my blog. A lot of people have seen it, but again, nobody knows anything."

Dad twisted his mouth, looking deep in thought. "I'll link to your post on my blog. Somebody has to know something."

"You'd think." Alex stepped toward the door. "Thanks, Dad."

He nodded. "Have you heard from Macy or Luke?"

"They both went to work. That's all I know."

"I'll give her a call in a few minutes."

"She'll appreciate that." Alex headed upstairs to his childhood bedroom which was also his office. He flung himself onto the twin bed and rubbed his temples, worried not only for Lottie but also his sister. Though she was the older of the two, he'd felt the need to protect her since they were teenagers.

The only thing he could do now was to help find Lottie, who was practically Macy's other mom. He'd already written up a lengthy post, telling the world as much as he could about the sweet lady, and he'd included so many pictures, it had slowed the post's load time.

Sighing, he sat up. If there were any other similar cases, maybe that would help them find Lottie. He didn't know how, but it seemed to be the only thing he could do. The police had already talked to all her neighbors and the people she knew at the shelter—other volunteers and the women living there.

Alex grabbed his laptop and started searching. It was kind of sad that he knew what to look for without thinking. Between his searches when Ari had been missing and all the work he'd put into his blog for missing kids, he was practically an expert on the subject.

After close to half an hour, he gave up. There were no similar cases. The only other missing retirement-aged people were those with memory issues who had wandered off, confused. That didn't describe Lottie. They'd played Scrabble recently, and she'd kicked Alex's butt—and he hadn't been going easy on her.

His phone rang. He reached for it, hoping for good news. It was an unknown number. He was tempted to ignore it, but what if it was someone with information on Lottie?

"Hello?" he answered.

"Is this Alex Mercer?" asked a distressed-sounding female on the other end.

"Yes. Who's this?"

"My name is Crysta and my boyfriend is missing. You blog about missing people, right?"

"Yes. Usually kids—"

"But your latest post is about that lady, right?"

"She's family. I—"

"Please help me. I know what you're thinking. He probably ran out on me. But he didn't. I swear. And besides, he's young. Twenty-one. Practically a kid, right?"

Alex didn't reply. She was right about one thing. He *had* been thinking the boyfriend had just left her.

"We're really happy. Once we get on our feet financially, he's going to propose."

"Okay. Tell me what you know about his disappearance." Alex opened a blank note on his computer, ready to take notes.

"Rory went to work last night, but didn't come back. He works as a janitor at night. That's how he pays for his place at the Meriwether."

Alex typed it out. "The Meriwether?"

"It's a low-income apartment. You have to work and pay your rent on time to live there. He's been there for like six months. See? He's responsible. Please write a post about him. I'll email you anything you need. Pictures, anything."

"Okay. You found my unlisted number. I assume you have my email address."

"I do. Thank you!"

"Wait. You've reported this to the police, right?"

Silence.

"Hello?"

"Well, I'd rather not. He has a record. If the police find him..."

"A record or a warrant?" Alex asked.

"He's trying to improve his life! It's for unpaid parking tickets. He didn't kill anyone or anything dangerous like that. You said you'd feature him."

Alex muttered under his breath. "Fine. Send me what you have."

"Thank you!"

"Don't mention it. And when you find him, you should tell

him to pay those tickets."

"I will. Trust me."

"Send me the email, or I can't post anything." He ended the call.

What had he gotten himself into?

Layers

MACY STARED AT the portrait of a mother and baby giraffe hanging behind Lucy.

"Macy?" Lucy asked.

She pulled her attention away from the picture and looked at the woman who was about ten years older than her. "Sorry."

"Don't apologize. Why don't you tell me what's on your mind? You wanted to talk to me, right?"

Macy nodded and then sighed. "I'm experiencing some anxiety because of my mother-in-law's disappearance."

"Understandable." Lucy nodded. She adjusted her turquoise glasses and pulled a strand of black hair behind an ear. "Why don't you tell me about your symptoms?"

It felt like her heart would explode out from her chest, and sometimes she couldn't breathe. How much could she tell Lucy without fearing for her job? Not that Lucy was her boss, but if she felt anything Macy said made her unable to perform as a child psychologist, Lucy had the obligation to speak up about it.

"Macy?" Lucy asked again.

"Sorry. Typical anxiety symptoms—racing heart, shortness of breath, loss of appetite, headaches, the inability to rest."

"Difficulty concentrating?" Lucy smiled sympathetically.

"That too."

"Are you and your mother-in-law close?"

Macy picked at a nail. "In some ways, closer than with my own mom. I can tell her anything."

"Anxiety makes sense in this situation, but I'm sensing there's more."

Macy's pulse drummed in her ears. She'd never mentioned to anyone at work about her own abduction. It hadn't been an issue at the time. Other than some random nightmares and being jumpy when alone in public, it was almost like it had never happened.

Lucy nodded for her to continue.

"My car accident," Macy blurted out. "It was traumatic, and now this."

"Not to mention your niece's abduction. You've been through a lot in the last six months."

Macy buried her face in her palms. She was a mess. They would fire her for sure. Everything was crumbling down around her. Who was she kidding, thinking she could hold down a professional job helping children?

"Is there more?" Lucy asked.

Macy's stomach twisted into a tight knot. Tears threatened. She needed to hold herself together. Her chest tightened. Coming to work had been a horrible idea. She never should've agreed to it. It was Friday, and her boss had said she could take the day off and decide about the following week on Sunday.

A hand rested on Macy's shoulder. "Whatever you say in here is held in confidence. Nobody's going to think less of you. We all have our baggage. That's why we talk to each other when we need to."

Macy relaxed, but the hot tears poured out like a floodgate released.

The chair next to her scraped against the carpeting as Lucy dragged it closer and sat, keeping her hand on Macy's shoulder. They sat in silence until Macy finally finished crying. When she sat up, Lucy handed her a tissue. Macy wiped her eyes and blew her nose. She felt a little better, but her colleague held her gaze, waiting to hear more.

"I was abducted when I was fifteen." Relief flooded through her after finally admitting it.

Lucy's eyes widened and her mouth gaped. "What happened?"

Macy closed her eyes. Even the shortened version could take all day to tell. "I was stupid."

"Really?" Lucy arched a brow.

"I know I was the victim, but there was so much I did wrong. I should've known better." Her cheeks warmed. Even all these years later, it was humiliating to admit how easily she'd walked into the trap. She could've gotten herself killed, and nearly had.

"Did you receive counseling afterward?"

Macy nodded. "That was why I wanted to become a child psychologist. I was inspired to help other kids the way my counselor helped me."

"And you did it. You should be proud of yourself."

She squirmed in her seat as more silence passed between them. It was time she opened up. Maybe not about how she was abducted, but some of the things haunting her nightmares. She swallowed and picked at a nail. "A lot happened after I was taken." Her hands shook, making it impossible to play with the nail. "I-I was restrained and starved. He eventually took me to this place—they called it the community. There was this guy Jonah who pretty much thought he was the savior of the world. It, well I..." Macy took a deep breath. She was talking too fast, and probably wasn't making any sense. "That's where I met Luke."

Lucy gave her a double-take. "Your husband?"

"He wasn't kidnapped, though. Nobody there knew I was. We were all given new identities."

"Wow." Lucy let out a long, slow breath. "I never would have guessed all that. Your anxiety makes even more sense than it did before."

"Should I pack my things?"

"What?" Lucy exclaimed. "No, not at all. But it might do you good to take some time off. You can talk to me anytime you want, okay? Just say the word, and I'll work you into my schedule."

Macy shook her head. "The kids need you more than I do." She glanced at the clock. "In fact, I should get out of your hair. It's time for lunch."

"Not if you need to continue talking."

"I'm spent." Macy slumped down further into the chair. "But I think I will take the rest of the day off. I'm going to have Jennifer reschedule the rest of my appointments for today."

Lucy squeezed her arm. "I'm glad you opened up to me. Remember, I'm here."

Macy forced a smile. "I appreciate that." What she really needed was to go somewhere, but she didn't have her car since Luke had insisted on driving her to work. She forced herself out of the chair, said goodbye to Lucy, and headed back to her office. On the way, she told the receptionist to reschedule the rest of her day's appointments.

Once behind her closed door, she called her lifelong friend. "Hey, Zoey. How do you feel about playing hooky this afternoon?"

Hooky

ZOEY PULLED INTO the parking spot overlooking the lake and turned to Macy. "Do you want to sit here or go out there?"

"I need some air."

"The beach it is." She climbed out of the car and stretched, glad for an excuse to take the rest of the day off. Work had been too hectic all morning, and now she had a headache. She closed her door and remote-locked the car.

The two friends headed for the slightly choppy shore in silence. They'd known each other since they were infants and could read each other like books. Zoey could sense a lot coming from Macy from the moment she climbed into the car—anxiety, annoyance, and sadness all wrapped together.

"Any news on Lottie?" Zoey asked.

Macy shook her head. "It's so unlike her."

"I hope she comes home soon. I've been worried about her ever since I heard the news."

They stopped at a bench and sat, watching the waves. After a couple minutes, Macy turned to her. "What was it like when I went missing?"

The question surprised Zoey. She thought back, trying to remember her initial reaction. She would never forget the morning Alyssa had called and said her daughter was missing. Initially, Zoey thought it was some kind of joke—or maybe she had *hoped* it was a sick joke, not that Chad or Alyssa had ever been ones to pull pranks.

"Do you remember?" Macy asked, her voice softer.

"I'll never be able to forget. It was horrible—I was scared and guilty, and I—"

"Guilty?"

"Well, yeah. We were starting to grow apart, and I was secretly seeing Alex. I'd never hidden anything from you before that, and then you got kidnapped. I felt like I had pushed you into that situation."

Macy nodded, looking out over the water. "I get it. Luke and I both feel like we should've done something differently to prevent whatever happened to Lottie."

Zoey put her arm around Macy and sat in silence with her, staring at the waves. After a few minutes, a few light raindrops landed on them, but neither she nor Macy moved.

"Have you been thinking about your kidnapping?" Zoey asked.

Macy ran her fingers through her hair, pulling tightly. "It's hard not to. I started having flashbacks and anxiety when Ariana disappeared, and now I'm having panic attacks and dreams that feel so real—like I'm right back there again."

"That makes sense. Hearing about Lottie has made me flash back to Ariana's abduction."

"How did you get through that? We didn't really talk much."

Zoey shook her head. "I didn't handle it well. I pushed Kellen away." Not that Ariana's kidnapping could be fully to blame. Zoey had realized her latent feelings for Alex—the very person who had helped her get through Macy's disappearance.

Macy turned to her. "What are you thinking about?"

Zoey's heart raced. She didn't want to admit she was thinking about Alex.

"You can tell me anything. We haven't been close lately, but maybe that needs to change. I'm still the same person, Zo. We're practically sisters."

What did that make her and Alex?

"Don't you trust me?"

Zoey turned and met Macy's gaze. "It's Alex."

"What about him?"

Where to begin? Zoey picked at a piece of lint on her pants. "When you were in the hospital, after Kellen and I broke off the engagement, Alex and I started talking. We worked through some things. It really seemed like we were starting to make progress. But then shortly after Ariana returned, he started pulling away."

Some surprise registered on Macy's face, but she just nodded. "How do you feel about that?"

Zoey frowned. "Don't go all psychologist on me."

"Sorry. What happened?"

"You've got me. It's like he's pushing me away on purpose. Maybe with Ariana back, he just changed his mind. Sometimes it's impossible to tell what's going through his head." She sighed and looked back over the water, ignoring the occasional raindrop landing on her face or hands.

"Maybe he's giving you space to recover from Kellen."

Zoey turned back to her. "Did he say that?"

Macy shook her head. "He doesn't open up to me about his feelings often."

"Has he said anything?"

"Not to me."

Zoey frowned. That wasn't surprising. "Sorry for talking about Alex when you have so much on your mind."

"Don't be. It's actually kind of nice to think about something else. I always thought you two would live happily ever after, and especially now with him back in town."

"Yeah, same here." Zoey's chest tightened. If only she could figure out what was going on in his mind. But that would have to be another day. They needed to focus on Lottie's disappearance.

"What are you guys doing to help find Lottie?"

Macy sighed. "Nick said the best thing we can do is stay in our routine. They're doing everything they can."

"What?" Zoey exclaimed. "You can't just sit around and wait on them! Do you have fliers to hand out?"

"No."

"That's where we need to start. Come on, let's get to your house. Think about what to put on them, and I'll throw something together. Then we'll hand them out. Where do you want to start? The mall? Her neighborhood?"

"You're making my head spin."

"Well, let me go psychologist on *you* for a minute. You're drowning in anxiety because you aren't *doing* anything to help find Lottie. Once you start handing out fliers and telling people to look for her, you'll feel so much better."

"Are you sure?"

Zoey got up and pulled Macy off the bench. "Yes. I've lived through the kidnappings of two people I love more than life itself. I know exactly what I'm talking about."

Macy threw her arms around Zoey and clung to her.

Distractions

NICK HUNG UP the phone and filled out the paperwork for another missing person. He'd never seen so many come in all at once in his entire time on the force. Cases like Lottie Mills were more typical for their small town—retired people wandering away without telling anyone. Although even her case was unusual because she'd never shown any signs of forgetfulness. Macy and her husband had sworn up and down that she had zero memory issues.

Knock, knock.

"Come in." He continued filling out the paperwork for the latest missing homeless person.

Detective Anderson came in. "Got another missing person report. This time, a young mother whose children are in foster care. She's desperately trying to get back on her feet, and her friend says she'd never skip town. Apparently, she'd just gotten a job."

Nick stared at him. "Yeah, I've got another missing person case here. How many are we up to?"

"With this one?" Anderson asked. "I'd say close to ten."

"Something's up." Nick set his pen down. "But what?"

Anderson sat across from him. "Drugs?"

"Only one that we know of was involved with them."

"They're all adults, many are homeless or close to it…" Anderson's voice trailed off. "But really, those are the only similarities. We've got a young mom, a drug dealer, a college dropout, that business owner who lost everything in a fire, the guy avoiding his back child support payments, a—"

"I know." Nick sighed. "They have *nothing* in common other than being down on their luck, other than Lottie Mills."

His office phone rang. Nick sighed. "Probably another missing person. Round everyone up. We need to have a meeting and see if we can figure out what's going on."

Anderson rose. "Let's hope. This is spreading the force pretty thin."

"Don't I know it." Nick picked up the receiver. "Captain Fleshman."

The woman on the other end of the line spoke too fast to understand. Anderson left, closing the door behind him.

Nick cleared his throat. "Slow down, ma'am. I need you to repeat what you just told me."

She took a deep breath, breathing out into Nick's ear. "My roommate—she's gone!"

He grabbed some more paperwork. "What's her name? Where do you live?"

"Kinsley Paine. We live in the Meriwether apartments."

The woman answered all of his questions, and he scribbled down the information. This time, they were dealing with a missing eighteen-year-old from a low-income apartment building. Not homeless, but one step away. Also, being eighteen, she was barely an adult. They would have to start handling these cases differently if they began involving minors, and they turned out to be related.

He finished questioning her, and then asked her to email him a couple pictures of the missing woman before ending the call.

Knock, knock.

"Come in!"

The door opened and Anderson poked his head inside. "Everyone's in the conference room."

Nick finished scribbling the notes about the latest missing person. "Start debriefing everyone, and I'll be right there."

"Got another one?"

"Eighteen years old."

Anderson swore. "We're going to be dealing with minors soon."

"It's beginning to look that way. I'll be right in."

"Okay." Anderson closed the door.

Nick flipped through his paperwork, looking for any similarities he may have missed before. If there were any, he couldn't find them. He rose from his chair and picked up the stack of papers. His cell phone rang. It was Corrine.

He accepted the call. "You'd better be helping the kids pack."

"The kids really want to go to Disney World."

"Of course they do! What do you expect?"

"Daddy, can we go to see Mickey?" came Hanna's sweet voice from the other end of the line.

"Why don't you talk to her?" Corrine asked.

Nick wanted to punch something. "Oh, no you don't! You never should have brought it up with them. *You* can be the one to crush the hope you planted."

"You're so inflexible!"

"And you've lost your mind." Nick struggled to keep his voice low enough that no one in the hall would hear him. "You knew spring break is my time with them, and you told them you'd take them to Disney World."

"They want to go, Nick. Can you blame them? They never see you anymore. It's—"

"And why do you think that is?" Nick asked, sarcasm dripping from every word. "Because you moved them across the country?"

"Would you quit bringing that up? It's old news. Get over it. You wouldn't see them much more if we still lived in Washington."

Nick had been furious plenty of times, but never before had he felt rage as strong as he did that moment. "Put them on the plane tomorrow, or you'll regret it."

"Is that a threat?"

"It's a promise. Don't bother calling me again. If you feel like discussing taking time away from me and my kids, call my lawyer." Nick ended the call.

The door opened. Anderson came in. "Hey, are you…?"

Nick glared at him.

"I'll just head up the meeting. Join us if you can." The door slammed shut behind him.

"How dare she?" Nick glared at the stack of paperwork on his desk, tempted to chuck it all across the room. He took a deep breath. *Time to pull yourself together.* He knew how to stay cool when criminals and punks got in his face, trying to get under his skin. He could deal with mouthy cops. But his ex-wife could send him into a rage with just a sour glance or a word—even from across the country.

He closed his eyes, took several deep breaths, and counted to fifty. It was time to focus on the rash of missing people. If Corrine gave him any more trouble, he would simply call his attorney. He didn't have the energy to focus on her immature games.

Clue

LUKE WANDERED AROUND the dilapidated cafeteria, handing out fliers.

A woman about his mom's age with short, graying brown hair took one from him and read it over. "Oh, no. I didn't know Lottie disappeared."

He nodded sadly. "Two or three days ago, we think."

She frowned. "I hope they find her." She studied him. "Are you her son?"

Luke took a deep breath. "I am."

"I can tell. You have the same eyes and mouth."

"Everyone says I look like her. So, do you have any ideas where she may have gone? Anywhere that might have gotten her into trouble?"

She folded the flier and scrunched her face. "I wish I could think of something. When we talked, it was never about her, regrettably. Lottie always wanted to find ways to get me out of here. Not sure I ever will—not with my bum leg and no income. My husband left me and took our retirement fund with him."

"I'm sorry to hear that. Well, if you think of anything that might help us find my mom, please call the number on the flier."

The woman unfolded the paper and studied it. "Sure. I hope I can help."

"Thanks. I better get more handed out." Luke hurried to the other side of the room, where a new group of people had come in for their dinner. Maybe one of them knew something that could help. So far, all he'd learned was the same thing he'd just heard—that everyone liked his mom and that she never seemed to talk about herself.

He handed out more fliers but didn't learn anything new. It was tempting to give up, but he couldn't do that. What if the person with a clue they needed was only five minutes from walking into the cafeteria?

Luke's phone rang. It was Macy. He stepped into the hall and answered. "Hi, babe. Any luck?"

"No. Zoey and I have walked five blocks in every direction from her house. Some people say they remember seeing her two or three days ago, but no one has seen her yesterday or today. What about you?"

Pain squeezed around his temples. Even though they had only discovered her missing the day before, they were probably outside of the critical forty-eight-hour period. Their chances of finding her safe were dwindling by the moment.

"Luke?"

"Nobody knows anything around here, either."

"Alex and my parents are handing out fliers around the mall. It won't be long before everyone in town knows to keep an eye out for her."

"That's good." Luke sighed.

"What do you want us to do now?" Macy asked—as though he had any answers. "Should we come over there? Hand out fliers somewhere else altogether?"

Luke's stomach growled. He wasn't sure he'd eaten anything all day. "Maybe we should take a break. You're probably hungry. We can figure out what to do after that. I'm having a hard time thinking clearly, myself."

"That's probably a good idea. My parents have food at their house already prepared."

"I'll meet you there, then."

"Okay, I'll—oh, another car just pulled in. I'm going to talk to them and then head over."

"See you." He leaned against the wall, ended the call, and rubbed his temples. He needed to stay positive, but that was growing increasingly difficult. Maybe some food really would help. It certainly couldn't hurt.

He stuffed the phone into a pocket and went back into the cafeteria. A few new people sat at various tables around the room. Luke clutched the remaining fliers and headed over to them.

The first lady who took one, smiled sadly. "I heard about her on the news. I sure do hope they find her."

Luke's eyes widened. "They mentioned her on the news?"

She nodded. "They showed a picture of her here, actually."

A small amount of relief washed through him. He hadn't known they were going to do that—and that potentially meant statewide coverage, depending on which channel it had been. "That's good news. What else did they say?"

"Just that nobody knew where she was. They urged people to contact the authorities if they saw her."

Luke's heart raced. Had any calls come in? "Thank you so much."

She looked confused. "I didn't do anything."

"You did more than you know." He sprang from his chair and handed two more fliers to a couple women a little older than him. "If you see Lottie, please call this number."

The blonde studied the paper. "You know, I might have seen her a couple days ago."

Luke's breathing hitched. The room spun around him. Two pieces of good news in a row? "You did? Where was she?"

She tilted her head toward the hallway and whispered, "Talk to me over there."

He nodded, hardly able to contain himself. What if she knew

where his mom was?

They went into the hall, and the woman looked around before turning back to Luke. She stepped closer to him and spoke just above a whisper. "I was visiting my boyfriend on Wednesday—but I'm not supposed to see him. He can get violent, you know? But he never *means* to hurt me." She rubbed her hip. "Anyway, he threw a beer bottle against the wall and broke it. I ran over to the window to put space between us, and when I looked out, I swear I saw Lottie walking up to the building with some groceries."

"What building?"

"The Meriwether apartments."

Luke pulled out his phone and opened his notes app, adding all the information. "Wednesday, you said?"

"Yeah, you're not going to tell anyone I was there?"

He shook his head. "I don't even have your name. But can I get it? Are you willing to talk to the police?"

Her face paled. "Part of the agreement for me staying here is to stay away from him. If anyone finds out—"

"If it helps find my mom, I'm sure they'll make an exception. Besides, maybe you *should* stop seeing him. You're pretty. You could do a lot better than someone like that."

"You think so?"

"I know so. Can I get your name?"

She bit her lower lip. "Well, I guess I could say I was there for another reason. I'm Lena Watkins."

He added her name to his note file. "Thank you, Lena. You really should think about dumping him."

"Maybe I will."

"I'll let you go so you can eat your dinner." Luke found Detective Fleshman's number in his contact list and called him as she went back to her table.

"Captain Fleshman." He sounded tired.

"This is Luke Walker. I have some information that might

help."

"What is it?"

"Someone saw my mom at an apartment complex called the Meriwether. She was carrying groceries—or something that looked like it."

"Meriwether..." The captain's voice trailed off. "Why does that sound familiar? I swear I heard that name today. Do you know why she would've been there?"

"She never mentioned it, but she must've been helping someone. Mom probably found someone who needed groceries. I just wish she would've said something to Macy or me."

"Okay, well, this is good. We finally have something to go on. I'm going to look into the Meriwether. I'll be in touch."

"Thanks, Captain." Luke ended the call and sent Macy a quick text.

I might've found something. Tell u when I cu.

Out

LOTTIE OPENED HER eyes to find she was still in darkness. She tried to roll onto her side. Her hips and shoulder ached from laying on her back for so long in the wooden box. There was no room to move around. She shifted, trying to relieve some of the pressure. It didn't help. She only managed to add to her soreness.

Conversation drifted from outside. She breathed a sigh of relief. At least she wasn't buried underground. Maybe they would let her out soon. Even though she would have a whole new set of problems, at least she would be able to breathe fresh air. She tried to ignore the stench and the stiffness of her pants where the urine had dried. Underneath, the wetness remained, pooled near the middle.

Something hit the side. Lottie jumped, holding her breath. Something else smacked the wood. A few more sounds all around. Then her feet rose as the box lifted on that end. Her entire body slid down toward the lower end.

She reached for the sides and pressed her palms against them, scraping her skin against the rough wood. Her head hit the wood and the pee rolled down to her back, soaking into her shirt, cold against her skin. The stale ammonia stench made her gag.

The outside scraped against the ground as her captors dragged her. Lottie shifted down, her neck twisting against the rough wall. She jolted to the left and the right as she went along.

Finally, the movement stopped. The box fell to the ground

with a harsh thud. She managed to scoot herself down and relieve the pressure from her neck.

An array of noises sounded just outside. Scrapes, bumps, jostles, and then a creak. A sliver of blindingly bright light shone from the top.

Lottie covered her eyes, the light an assault on her senses after being in the dark for so long. The air grew fresh, pushing aside the stench and the stuffiness. She squirmed and turned toward the wall away from the light. Voices sounded, a mixture of male and female, but they blended together, making it impossible to tell what anyone said.

"Get up!" a familiar male voice commanded.

Lottie groaned and moved one arm away from her face. The light hurt, but not as bad. She blinked a few times to adjust.

"I *said,* get up!"

She rose slowly. Everything ached and the bright light was still too much. Lottie kept her gaze low as she reached up for the sides and pushed herself to standing. Her knees wobbled and her arms shook. The urine-soaked shirt clung to her back and her hair stuck to her face.

"Look at me," the same man ordered.

Lottie took a deep breath, pulled her long hair from her cheeks, and stared at him. Her eyelids tried to close in protest of the sunlight. She forced them to stay open, even only through slits. "Jonah."

The short, stocky dark-haired man crossed his arms. "So, you remember."

"Yes." Her eyes watered as she fought her eyelids from closing.

"Yes, what?"

"I remember."

He shoved her. "Yes, *what?*"

Lottie held back a cringe. "Yes, sir."

"I think you mean, Great High Prophet."

"Yes, Great High Prophet."

"Good, and you remember your capital offenses against the community?"

Her stomach tightened. If she admitted to anything, he could very well kill her on the spot.

"Not speaking? That's fine. You can wait until your trial." He turned to the right. "Take her away and clean her up!"

Two women wearing all white came over to her. Only their faces were visible, and they kept their gazes lowered. The younger one, who may have been a teenager, stayed behind the older one, possibly her mother or sister. The older one, who couldn't have been older than forty, reached out to Lottie, but didn't touch her. "Follow us."

She climbed out of the box, leaning against the side. Every muscle and joint in her body ached. Her eyes finally adjusted to the light, and she could make out their surroundings. Trees went out as far as she could see on either side of them. The sun shone so brightly because they were in a clearing.

The two women walked to the left. Lottie struggled to keep up with pains shooting out from her left ankle and her right hip. They didn't slow for her. Lottie took deep breaths, taking in as much fresh air as she could—not that she could fully escape the smell of her own urine that clung to her clothes.

After about twenty minutes, the other women stopped in front of a tiny shack and waited for Lottie to catch up. Once she finally did, the older woman looked in Lottie's direction but wouldn't meet her gaze. "Do you remember the cleansing process?"

It had been a long time, but she would never forget her and Luke's first day in the community. She nodded.

"Good. That'll make this go faster." She opened the door, and all three women entered the small unfurnished building. "You know that nothing polluted by the world can enter the community."

"Yes." The stench from Lottie's clothes filled the small room. Putting on the community's garb would be a welcome treat.

"The shower is that way." The woman pointed to a door to the right. "We'll wait while you scrub off the world's evilness and influence. Remember, your skin must be red from scrubbing hard, or you'll have to go back inside and start the process over again."

As much as she wanted to clean herself, the thought of an icy shower and extra-rough scrub brush made her shudder.

"What are you waiting for?" asked the woman. "You'd better hurry. There's a lot to do to prepare you for your trial."

"Do you know what I'm being tried for, exactly?"

"You told Jonah you knew your sins."

Lottie took a deep breath. "I don't know which ones I'm being held accountable for."

"Everything you've done to harm the community."

"I see. What about—?"

"You need to hurry." The woman revealed a long, sharp blade hiding underneath the folds of her robe. "Jonah will be displeased if this takes too long."

"We can't have that."

"And don't try to escape. Some of our best fighting men are outside, also brandishing weapons."

"Understood." Lottie walked toward the bathroom door, tears blurring her vision. She would never see the outside world again.

Connection

ALEX HANDED A flier to a guy with a green mohawk carrying a skateboard under his arm. "Call the number if you hear anything."

The guy nodded walked away, stuffing the paper under his board.

Alex glanced around the mall's courtyard for anyone who hadn't gotten a flier yet. His phone rang. It was his mom.

"Where are you guys?" he asked.

"We went across the street to the senior center. Macy just called and said they're headed to our place to eat."

His stomach rumbled. "Sounds good to me. I haven't found anyone who's seen Lottie."

"Neither have we. Where are you? We'll pick you up."

"The courtyard. I'll head out to the parking lot."

Once he got to the sidewalk in front of the mall, his dad's car pulled up. He climbed in, and other than the music, the ride home was silent. When they pulled into the driveway, both Macy's and Luke's cars were out front.

Inside, the house smelled like chicken and spices.

"The casserole is almost done." Macy poked her head out from the kitchen. Alex kicked off his boots and joined them. She and Luke looked as tired as he felt.

"It seems so quiet here without Ariana," Luke said.

"She's at a friend's house," Alex said. "We're not telling her about your mom just yet. I hope we find her before she ever has to know."

Luke's expression darkened. "Yeah, same here."

Macy opened the oven and peeked in. "Just another couple minutes. I'm so glad Mom made this ahead of time. With as stressed as I am, I couldn't make anything."

Alex grabbed a pop from the fridge and sat at the table. "Did you guys have any luck?"

Luke sat taller in the chair. "I don't know if it'll help us, but someone said she saw Mom at an apartment complex called the Meriwether. The only thing that concerns me is that Mom never mentioned that to us, and I'm not entirely sure I trust the source."

Meriwether… Why did that sound familiar?

"Why not?" Alex took a long swig of the caffeinated drink, hoping it would help with his fatigue.

"The source was there, visiting an abusive boyfriend who she isn't supposed to have contact with. Also, she seemed a little… off. I don't know how to explain it."

Macy pulled the casserole from the oven. Alex's mouth watered. He was so hungry, he almost would've eaten it straight out of the oven not caring about burning his mouth. "Maybe the girl was just nervous. She was probably afraid you'd say something and get her in trouble."

"Maybe." Luke didn't appear convinced.

Mom and Dad came in. Mom looked at the food. "Thanks for warming it up. I'll grab the salad."

The air was somber, and they ate in silence. Macy and Luke didn't stay long after eating. Mom and Dad also bolted from the kitchen as soon as everything had been cleaned. Clementine, the orange tabby, sat looking at him in expectation, his tail twitching.

Alex picked a piece of chicken from his plate and held it out for the fluff ball. The cat stretched before ambling over, taking his time before running off with his prize. Alex chuckled and then headed up to his room to check on his blog. He had a bunch of new comments, but none were helpful. Just as he was about to close the tab, he pulled his hand away from the mouse.

The missing janitor he'd written about had lived in the Meriwether. That was the same place Luke said someone saw Lottie. His palms grew clammy as he read over the blog post again and thought back to his conversation with the girlfriend. He couldn't find a connection between Lottie and anything else Crysta had said. The fact that both of them were missing and had been at the Meriwether had to be more than a coincidence.

He pulled out his phone and called Nick. It went directly to voicemail. Alex didn't bother leaving a message. He stuffed the phone into his pocket and headed downstairs.

Dad came up just as Alex slid into his coat. "Going somewhere?"

He grabbed a stack of fliers from the table. "I'm going to hand out some more of these."

"This late?"

"Yeah. See ya in a while."

"Well, I'm sure Luke appreciates your dedication."

Alex nodded and headed out to his car. His mind raced, trying to find a connection between Lottie and Rory. On the surface, they had nothing in common at all besides being living, breathing human beings. They had both been at the same apartment complex before disappearing. That had to mean something.

He found the address and plugged it into the navigation system. It was in the poorer section of town—not surprising, given what Crysta had told him.

It only took him about fifteen minutes to get there. He parked his Tercel against the curb between a dirty white van with three busted windows and a rusted red convertible with bullet holes in the passenger door and hood. He stared at the Meriwether across the street. It wasn't in any better condition.

Alex made sure his pocket knife was easily accessible in his jacket and headed for the walkway. As he opened the front door, the strong odor of dirty diapers and something rotting stopped him in his tracks. He gagged and covered his mouth, his eyes watering, and headed for the elevator. Nothing happened when he pushed the button.

A girl about sixteen stopped. "That's broken."

He turned around and showed her the flier. "Have you seen this woman?"

She studied the paper and then shook her head.

"Do you know Rory… what was his last name?"

"The janitor? He's hot."

"I wouldn't know about that. His girlfriend is Crysta."

"Yeah, she's totally annoying."

"Have you seen him?"

"A few days ago. Why? Is he missing, too?"

Alex nodded.

"Does she live here?"

"No, but she might have been here."

"Huh. Well, hopefully they show up. People come and go around here, you know? If they lose their job and can't pay, they're gone."

"It's not like that with these two. Be careful, okay? I don't know why people are disappearing."

She shrugged. "I can ask around."

Alex handed her the flier. "Call the number on here if you hear anything. No matter how small it seems."

"Okay." She shoved it into her purse and pulled out a joint. "I gotta get going."

"You'll call that number?"

"Sure." She headed outside.

Alex frowned and walked toward a stairwell. Hopefully someone else in the building knew more than she did.

Entrance

EVERY INCH OF Lottie's skin ached from the vigorous cleansing. After showering in the icy water with the pungent soap and horribly rough sponge, the two women had examined her skin to make sure she'd washed well enough. It took three times, and by then, her skin was raw and bleeding in places. That was in addition to the aches and pains from being trapped in the box for so long.

As she walked down the narrow pathway with the two other women, the rough, stiff material of her robe rubbed against her skin. Lottie cringed, but didn't dare slow. The older of the two other women walked in step next to her, hand over the hilt of her hidden weapon.

Lottie couldn't see much because the white head covering only allowed her to look out through a small slit. Despite the ridiculous outfit—that she had once accepted as normal for outsiders to wear when entering the community—she still managed to see Jonah's men positioned in various places behind trees and shrubbery.

There would be no escape. Attempting to run would lead to a certain death. Waiting out the trial at least bought her time to try and figure out a plot to get away. People had gotten out of the community's clutches before, and she was determined to find a way out herself. Though it was certain to be more challenging now. Given the cult had been broken up before, Jonah and the others were bound to be especially determined to keep that from happening again.

The path curved around a bend and Lottie squinted, trying to see what kind of fence Jonah had commissioned his people to build this time around.

"How much longer?" she asked.

"Hush," the knife-bearing woman demanded.

Lottie frowned. "I'm thirsty and hungry."

"Denying your body will make you more spiritual," said the younger woman.

"Don't talk to her," the older one scolded.

Lottie sighed. She'd long since pushed all the community's rules and regulations from her mind. Now she needed to remember all of them again. How had she ever thought they held any normalcy?

She'd been smitten by Jonah's smooth words. He'd saved her from the streets and from possibly losing her son to the system. She would have done anything the leader asked. She shuddered, thinking about some of his requests, which in reality had been nothing more than thinly veiled demands.

Lottie stumbled over a rock. The ground came at her before she had time to react. Four hands grabbed her and pulled her up.

The older woman scowled at her. "You need to be more careful. If you dirty your clothes, you must go through the cleaning ritual again."

"I couldn't help it." Between the eye slit and the shapeless, long robe, she had no way of seeing the ground below.

"Well, you'd better figure out how." She squeezed Lottie's arm and yanked her forward. "We need to hurry. If we don't reach the fence by the time it's fully dark, we'll *all* be forced to sleep outside the wall."

Lottie glanced up. Stars were already appearing in the sky. "How much farther?"

"Stop talking," she snapped.

"I'm not going to do anything to get you in trouble. I'm well aware of Jonah's rules."

"Then be quiet!"

Lottie took a deep breath and lowered her gaze to the ground, keeping a lookout for anything that might trip her up. After about a half an hour, the enormous fence came into view. Her mouth gaped. It was nearly ten feet tall and black, like it had been covered in tar. Spikes loomed at the top of each thick post.

Was it larger than before, or did it seem more intimidating now that she wasn't there of her own free will? Neither would have surprised her.

They walked in silence until they reached the large structure. Rustling and muffled conversation sounded from the other side.

Lottie's heart thundered against her chest. She was about to enter, never to leave again. Everything in her screamed to run. She would have, too, if she thought she stood a chance of getting away. But armed guards patrolled the periphery, and the older woman had taken the knife out from the folds of her robe and pointed it toward Lottie.

One wrong move, and she'd be dead. Maybe that would be for the best—if Jonah was planning to put her on trial, who knew what torture he had in mind? He'd had over ten years to think of new ideas while he sat inside a jail cell. No doubt he blamed Lottie because her son had been one of the ringleaders in what had happened that fateful night.

She shuddered at the thought. Hopefully no one knew where he and Macy lived.

"Open the gate!" shouted the older woman. She squeezed Lottie's arm. "It is Mary and Ruth! We have the prisoner, Lois."

Lottie's stomach twisted at hearing the name Jonah had given her so many years earlier.

"And James and Asher!" shouted a man from right behind them.

Lottie's heart felt like it would burst through her chest.

A loud squeaking sounded before the gate in front of them groaned in protest as it slowly opened.

Tired

A CRASHING NOISE woke Macy. She sat up, trying to figure out where she was and what had just happened. It took a moment to realize she was on the couch in her living room. Her cell phone had just fallen on some empty glasses and plates on the floor. Luke sat at the desk in front of his laptop.

She picked up her phone and wiped it off. The screen showed it was close to eleven. She rubbed her sore neck and rose to her feet. "Maybe we should go to bed, babe."

Luke didn't respond.

"We're not going to be able to help find her if we're too exhausted to function."

He still didn't say anything.

She picked up the plates and glasses from the floor and headed for the kitchen. That's when she realized he was sleeping on the keyboard. Macy took the stuff and put it in the kitchen sink before returning to him. She placed her hands on his shoulders and rubbed. "We should go to bed."

Luke sat up. "What? What's going on?"

She continued massaging. "It'd be more comfortable to sleep in the bed. Come on."

"No, I need to post about her disappearance on more sites."

"There are hundreds, and you've already fallen asleep at the desk. We can do this in the morning."

"That's valuable time lost," he snapped. "I have to do this

now."

"A lot of people have gotten the word out. It was even on the news. Those missing person forums are all filled with people looking for their own loved ones."

"Someone could've seen her. I need to post the flier on as many sites as possible."

"I'll help you in the morning. We'll work twice as fast after getting rest."

"I don't care about rest." His eyes narrowed. "Get some if you want. I'm going to do everything I can to find her."

Macy bit her tongue. He wasn't usually so short with her—not that she could blame him. "I'd help you now, but I can't stay awake."

"Great." He turned back to the laptop and started typing.

"Okay. I love you."

"You, too."

She sighed and went into the bedroom, not bothering to change out of her clothes. The bed seemed empty without Luke. Her eyelids were heavy, but her mind wouldn't slow down. She tossed and turned for a while before sitting up. She needed to talk to Luke.

He was sleeping at the desk again. She sighed. Maybe it was best that she let him sleep there since he wouldn't go to the bedroom. She grabbed a blanket from the couch and wrapped it around his shoulders. He didn't even stir.

Macy went back to bed, but still couldn't sleep. Between thoughts of Lottie and being alone in the bed, she just couldn't relax. Maybe a walk around the neighborhood would help. Fresh, chilly air and some exercise ought to be enough to push her to exhaustion.

She took several fliers just in case she ran into anyone, folded them, and slid them into her coat pocket. On her way out, she kissed Luke's forehead and whispered, "I really do love you. We've been through so much together, we'll get through this, as well."

His eyelids fluttered, but he didn't wake.

Macy kissed him again, and then went outside. The cold night air clung to her in a way it only did after a good rain. She zipped her jacket, stuck her hands in her pockets, and headed down the dark street. Clouds blocked the moon and most of the stars, only showing a few patches here and there. The scattered streetlights didn't illuminate much.

Everything was quiet, other than the soft sloshing sounds of her sneakers on the wet pavement. Macy glanced up at the night sky and wondered where Lottie was, and if she was looking at the same stars. Her chest felt tight. Would she ever see her sweet mother-in-law again? The woman would sell everything she had to help others—she didn't deserve anything bad happening to her.

Hairs on the back of her neck stood on end. It felt like someone was watching her.

Scrape, scrape.

Macy froze in her tracks and spun around. Nothing looked out of place. She studied the yards and driveways on both sides of the street before turning around and walking again.

Scrrrape.

Her heart raced, but she kept going, picking up her pace. She glanced over her shoulder, still not seeing anything or anyone. Maybe it was just a dog in someone's backyard. Or kids sneaking out, up to no good—that had to be it. That's what kids did. Macy should know. That's how she wound up getting abducted.

She sped up and turned down the next block. Now she was halfway home either way she went, and she didn't want to head in the direction of the noise.

A crow cawed overhead on a power line. Macy jumped and chastised herself. It was just a bird. She quickened her steps again, now only three blocks until she made it back home.

Scrape.

Her breath caught. Maybe it was only her imagination. She stood taller and increased her stride again—any more, and she'd be jogging.

Two more blocks. She turned down the next road and prepared to scream as loud as possible if need be. At the end of that block, she turned again. Her house was in view.

Scrape, scrape.

Gasping for air, she broke into a run. She slid on a puddle, but caught her balance, and kept going. Four more houses. Three.

Caw! Caw!

Two more houses. She was almost there, and she was in a full run. She cut across her next door neighbor's lawn and made it to her own yard. She reached into her pocket and found her keys. With the push of a button, she unlocked her car and then jumped in, locking the doors.

Macy started the car and pulled out her phone. There was no way she was going to fall asleep now, so she called her brother.

"Is everything okay?" he answered.

"Meet me at that coffeehouse that stays open late on Thirty-Third. You know the one?"

"Yeah. I'll be right there."

Coincidences

ALEX SET DOWN his mint mocha as he sat across from Macy in the back of the dim, quiet coffeehouse. She played with her cup and barely looked up at him.

"Are you okay?" Alex slid his jacket off and rested it on the back of his chair. "You know, besides Lottie."

She glanced up at him, her face pale with dark circles under her eyes.

"Did something else happen?" Worry pumped through his veins.

Macy took a deep breath. "Yes. No. I don't know."

"What happened?"

"It's probably nothing. I couldn't sleep, so I went for a walk. It seemed like someone was following me, but it was probably my imagination. I'm exhausted and stressed. It's the perfect combination for my mind to make up things that aren't there."

"You went for a walk alone at night?"

"It's a safe neighborhood."

"Yeah, but still. It's just asking for trouble."

"I'm not looking for a lecture from my little brother."

"Little? I haven't been smaller than you since I was, what, nine or ten?"

The corners of her mouth twitched up slightly. "Try closer to thirteen or fourteen."

"Tell yourself what you have to." He sipped his hot, sweet

mocha.

"It's kind of nice teasing each other. Makes things feel a little more normal."

"Always happy to help." Alex took another long swig, allowing the liquid to warm him. "How are you holding up? You look like you could use some sleep. No offense."

She sighed and sipped from her cup. "I tried."

"Maybe don't drink covfefe."

Macy laughed and pushed the mug forward to show him the yellowish drink. "It's lemon chamomile tea."

He grimaced. "I've never known how you could drink that stuff."

Silence sat between them.

"How's Luke holding up?" Alex asked.

His sister frowned. "Not well, but what else can we expect? Lottie's gone without a trace."

"Well, maybe this'll help."

Macy's eyes widened. "What?"

"I was just at the Meriwether, asking questions."

"The apartment complex Luke heard about at the shelter?"

Alex nodded. "There's another missing guy, and he lives there, so I thought I'd check it out."

"You should've told the police."

"You think I didn't try? Nick's number went straight to voicemail. I'm gonna call him later, but I wanted to look around myself."

"Why didn't you leave a message?"

"Because I wanted to check things out myself."

"He's a cop, Alex."

"I had to do something, and leaving a message wouldn't help. He'll see my missed call."

Macy paused, reached across the table, and squeezed his hand. "I guess I get that. It wasn't dangerous, was it? I mean, two people are missing from there."

"You're asking me about dangerous? You went walking alone in the dark when people are being abducted left and right."

"Not in my neighborhood." They stared each other down until Macy spoke again. "Was it dangerous?"

Alex gritted his teeth. "I wouldn't want you going there alone, but I was fine. The—"

"Did you find anything out? You said you knew something that would help."

"Something that *might* help. I talked to everyone I came across, and some of them talked my ear off. Anyway, one woman said she'd seen Luke's mom bringing groceries to one family every week or two for a while."

Macy's mouth gaped. "She knew it was Lottie?"

"Yeah. I showed her the flier and got a positive ID."

"But Lottie never told us she'd been going there."

"Maybe it didn't seem like a big deal."

"But nobody saw her get taken?" Macy held Alex's gaze.

He shook his head. "Nobody I talked to. Only the one person even knew she stopped by. One other person thought he saw her leaving earlier in the week, but he wasn't a hundred percent sure. Not that I'd trust his judgment, anyway. The dude was stoned out of his mind."

They sat in silence for a few minutes. "Do you want to head home?"

She shook her head. "I'm not going to be able to sleep."

"What if I follow you there, and make sure you get inside safely? Would that help?"

"Maybe." She seemed to want to say more.

Alex hesitated to ask, but did anyway. "Is everything okay between you and Luke?"

Tears shone in her eyes. "It's just hard, you know?"

He put his hand on top of hers. "I know all too well how hard it is."

She nodded. "You definitely do."

"You guys have to fight to stay together. This stuff can tear couples apart. When you were gone, I thought for surc Mom and Dad would split."

Macy gave him a double-take. "What?"

"Obviously, they didn't, but it wouldn't have surprised me."

She looked like she was going to be sick.

"You and Luke are strong like them. You'll make it. The two of you, you have history. This'll make you stronger. Not like Zoey and Kellen—they were doomed from the start."

"I hope so."

"I know so." He gave her the most reassuring expression he could muster.

She pulled her gaze away and sipped from her mug again. "What about *you* and Zoey?"

The question shocked him. "What do you mean?"

"You guys seemed like you were close before, but now… it's different."

Alex sighed. He didn't feel like getting into that—not even with Macy. Zoey deserved more than he could give her, and it would take time before he was able to get on his own two feet. "I'm going to call Nick again."

This time the captain actually answered. "Alex?"

"I found someone who thinks he saw Lottie around the time she disappeared."

Shuffling sounded in the background. "Tell me everything. Don't leave out a single detail."

Alex told him everything he'd just told Macy about the two people who'd seen Lottie at the Meriwether.

"Where did you say you went?" Nick asked.

"The Meriwether apartments."

"That's right. Luke mentioned them—and I have another

missing person from there. An eighteen-year-old."

"A third person?" Alex exclaimed. "What does it mean?"

"Third?" Nick demanded. "Who else?"

"Someone contacted me to put it on my blog about her missing boyfriend."

"Email me what you've got. I'm heading over there now. And Alex?"

"Yeah?"

"Let us handle this from here on out."

"Right."

"I'm serious. We don't know what we're dealing with. It could be dangerous."

"Okay." Alex had no intention of backing away. Not with three missing people who were all connected to the Meriwether. It was too much to be a coincidence. Way too much.

Plotting

EARLY MORNING LIGHT poked through some of the beams in the chilly meeting room. Though the building was new—everything was—little particles of dust danced around in the slender rays of light. A mist also moved around amongst the air.

Jonah tapped his thick fingers on the newly stained and polished table as he looked around at the other robed men. "We need to have someone re-tar the outside of this building."

"Consider it done," Isaac said. "I'll make sure it's fixed by lunchtime."

"Good. All the people sleeping outside the wall can come inside once we adjourn this meeting."

"I'll see to it," Abraham said.

"Make sure the prisoners receive water and nothing else."

"Already did." Asher gave a quick nod.

"About Chester and Elijah…"

Isaac leaned forward. "Chester is still in the world's jail, with no chance of parole. Elijah has left his worldly life and is making his way here."

"And Chester? *No* chance of parole?" Jonah narrowed his eyes, staring down the younger man.

"H-he's still locked up with no chance of parole." Isaac cleared his throat. "He has those extra charges, Great High Prophet."

Jonah clenched his jaw. "Right. He failed to mention those before joining. It's no matter. We'll get him out. The trials cannot start without him. Not that we have all of the rebels yet. We need the rest of them, as well."

"It will all come together, Great High Prophet." Abraham gave him a reassuring nod. "We just need patience—and you have more than anyone I know."

"True. We're going to have to think outside the box to get him and find the rest of the rebels."

Isaac cleared his throat. "Great High Prophet."

"What?" Jonah snapped his attention to the younger adviser.

"I know someone on the inside."

"We all do."

"Someone with connections. He might be able to help us with Chester."

Jonah rapped his nails on the table. "In maximum security?"

"You said to think outside the box, right?"

"Yes. What are you thinking?"

"I'm not entirely sure yet, Great High Prophet. But the guy I know—he's not afraid to bend rules."

Jonah nodded, deep in thought. "We do need the help of those who don't respect the false authority of the outside world. Next time you go out to find more of our rebels, you'll reach out to your contact?"

"Most assuredly. I can make that happen this morning if I leave early enough."

"This is good news, indeed." Jonah turned to Asher. "Get an update on Elijah. We need to know where he stands—how close he is to arriving."

"I'll have news when I return tonight."

"Do we have any more information on the rest of the rebels?"

Abraham frowned. "We've got a few more in the area to snatch, but it's harder to find the ones who moved away."

"Find them!" Jonah slammed his fists on the table, making everyone else jump. "We can't pick up where we left off until every single rebel has been properly charged and punished."

"Of course," Asher said. "We're getting closer every day."

"Not close enough." Jonah glared at each man individually. "You will all feel the pains personally if this drags on too long. Do you understand?"

They exchanged worried glances, but nodded to Jonah.

"Good. I'm glad we're at an understanding. This time next week, the trials need to begin."

Held

"WAKE UP!"

Something hard struck Lottie in the back. She groaned and rolled over on the hard floor.

"Get up. Now."

Lottie readjusted the head covering so she could see out from the eye slit and rose. The only thing she could see was a small fireplace. Something boiled from a pot hanging above it. Despite the heavy facial covers, the aroma of a hearty stew drifted to her. Her stomach growled and her mouth watered, reminding her it had been days since she'd last eaten—though she couldn't remember how many. Everything blended together into one horrifying blur.

She turned to get a better look, but all she saw was a rugged shelf built into the wall, holding jars of food—jams, pickled items, and more. If allowed, she would have run over, opened any of them, and eaten. She didn't care what it was as long as she could swallow it.

A hand gripped her arm, squeezing tightly, nails digging into her flesh but not quite piercing the skin through the thick robe. "Come on."

She followed the two women outside the tiny house and down a muddy pathway to a dirt road filled with a variety of tire marks—ones that were all too familiar. The community used wheelbarrows, wagons, and horse-drawn carriages to carry goods and travel through their immense property.

They walked along the side of the road for a full twenty minutes. Little, sharp rocks dug into the soles of her bare feet, cutting through the skin like miniature knives. The pain at least distracted her from the cold. Lottie's stomach hadn't stopped growling. The older of the two women turned and glared at her each time, but she didn't say anything.

Community members stopped and stared at her. It was always a curiosity when someone new joined them—and it was obvious given the typical garb with only the eye slit. Since she had been brought in as a prisoner, she likely had a letter of shame on her robe after she had entered the community. Lottie wondered with the letter might be. *D* for deserter? The possibilities were endless.

They stopped in front of a long, rectangular building. It reminded her of the former meeting hall, except the door had five locks.

"We're here with a prisoner. Lois, the rebel!" The older woman squeezed Lottie's arm.

Rebel? If that's what they were calling them, maybe Lottie had an *R* on her clothing.

Five clicks sounded—slowly, one after the other. The door opened out toward them. Lottie tried to move out of the way, but the woman held her in place. The door scraped over Lottie's bare toes. She cried out. The older woman smacked her across the face. At least the head covering protected her from the sting.

The woman shoved her inside the building. Lottie stumbled, scraping her heel on a stone in the packed dirt floor. She lost her balance and fell, hitting her chin on a larger rock. A man loomed over her, his hands folded across his chest and his brows furrowed. "Get up."

Lottie rubbed her chin.

He kicked her side so hard that little white dots danced in front of her. "I said, get up."

She grunted and struggled to her feet. The man pulled off her head covering, also grabbing onto her hair. Lottie's head yanked backward.

"You'll join the other prisoners. Follow me."

Lottie looked back for the two women—as unpleasant as the older one was, she was far more tolerable than this man. Neither of the women were in sight. She rubbed her neck.

"I said to follow me!" His brows came together and his nostrils flared. "Don't be insolent, woman. You may have spent the last ten years out in the world's influence, but that's over. Time to relearn some respect and obedience, or get it beaten out of you."

She flinched.

"Thought that'd get your attention. Don't test me."

Lottie lowered her gaze to the floor and followed him. Anger pulsated through her, but she pushed it down. She'd lived long enough to know giving vent to her frustrations wouldn't get her anywhere. Her energies would be put to better use finding a way out. If nothing else, she needed to get out and warn Macy and Luke. The last thing she wanted was to see them back in the community, especially violently abducted as she had been.

Muscles in every part of her body ached as she walked along, careful to avoid rocks in the ground. Even her feet hurt, and she didn't want to add to the pain. She needed her strength for whatever came next.

They stopped in front of another door. Lottie nearly walked into the man, but stopped herself just in time. He unlocked the door's five locks, opened it, and stepped aside. "Ladies first," he snarled.

It took every ounce of her self-control to keep from responding to him as she walked through the doorway. He shoved her, but she managed to keep from falling.

The door slammed with a thud behind her and the five locks clicked back into place.

She looked up from the floor. A dozen others were in the room with her, and they had removed their head coverings. Apparently, the requirements didn't apply to the small prison. She recognized each other person, and they all had an *R* on their robe. Most sat and a few leaned against the wooden walls. There was nothing inside other than the dirt floor. Her throat suddenly felt dry and her hunger hit her with a wave of dizziness.

Nobody spoke to her or to each other. The mood was so heavy, she felt like she was attending a funeral—or maybe an execution. Given they all faced trial with Jonah as the judge and jury, it wasn't all that far from their probable fate.

Lottie leaned against a wall and slid to sitting. Her mouth grew more parched by the moment, and her tongue stuck to the roof of her mouth. Everything turned blurry and the floor rushed toward her. Just before hitting it with her face, she lost consciousness.

Recognition

LUKE'S EYELIDS GREW heavy. He struggled to keep them open, but it was a losing battle. After sleeping so poorly at the computer desk, he'd woken and continued working. He hadn't even known Macy had left until she walked in through the front door, half scaring him to death. At first, he'd thought someone was breaking into the house.

Now he sat on the couch in his in-laws' living room. Everyone was talking about his mom, and he couldn't even stay awake. Some son he was. He needed more coffee so he could push through the fatigue until they found her.

Just as he decided to get up for the brew Alyssa had just made, his eyes closed, wrapping him in a warm, comfortable darkness. When he woke, he was sprawled across the couch, covered in a blanket, his head on a pillow. The room was quiet and he felt rested.

Until he remembered his mom was missing.

Luke sat up and tossed aside the blanket. How could he have slept? He needed to do more—there wasn't time for sleeping. What he needed was the coffee he was about to get before he so irresponsibly fell asleep. Luke rose, stretched, and headed into the kitchen. The pot was cold, but he didn't care. He poured some anyway and stuck it into the microwave.

Chad came in, carrying a mug. He held it up. "Great minds."

Luke nodded and took his mug out from the microwave.

"I see you don't mind stale caffeine, either." Chad poured the cold coffee into his mug. "It all works the same, right?"

"Yeah." Luke mixed some flavored creamer into his cup. "Doubt I'm going to taste it, anyway."

Chad started the microwave and turned to him. "How are you holding up?"

"About as well as could be expected, I suppose."

His father-in-law arched a brow, finished preparing his coffee, and sat at the table. He flicked his head toward the chair nearest Luke. "Have a seat."

Luke felt a talking-to coming, but he sat. The two men sat in silence for a minute, both sipping from their mugs. The strong coffee gave Luke a small burst of energy. Maybe after finishing the whole cup, he'd be up for handing out fliers at the Meriwether. He needed to speak with the residents personally.

Chad set his mug down and met Luke's gaze. "How are you holding up, really? You just spent the morning asleep on my couch."

"I was up late, getting word out about Mom's disappearance."

"How are things between you and Macy?"

Luke nearly dropped the mug. He hadn't been expecting that question. "I—what do you mean?"

Chad took a long, slow sip of his coffee, holding Luke's gaze. "I've been where you're at, son. Twice. A missing relative can wreak havoc on a marriage."

Luke swallowed. If he was being honest with himself, and he hadn't thought much about it until that moment, he'd pretty much shoved Macy aside as he laser-focused on finding his mom.

"I'm not trying to find fault." Chad set his mug down. "I'm the last one to point fingers after some of the things I've done. But the fact that I've made some pretty big mistakes means I know what I'm talking about when I say be careful not to neglect your marriage. No matter what happens, your wife is the one you're going to spend the rest of your life with. You two have already been through so much—hang onto that. You'll need each other to get through this, too."

Luke sipped his coffee, giving him some time to let Chad's words sink in. He took a deep breath. "You're right. Thanks for the wakeup call."

"I wish someone had given me one long ago. It would've saved me a lot of heartache." Chad pressed his fingers together and glanced off to the side, looking lost in thought.

Luke wondered what had happened with Chad and Alyssa, but didn't ask. If Chad wanted to talk, he would. But some things were better left unsaid.

Macy walked in. Her eyes widened in surprise at Luke. "You're up. Did you get enough rest?"

He nodded and finished his drink.

Chad rose. "We're just taking a coffee break. I need to get back to work. I've got a deadline quickly approaching." He left the room, giving Macy's shoulder a squeeze on the way out.

She sat next to Luke. "Did I interrupt? Things felt a little tense when I came in."

Luke shook his head and wrapped an arm around her. "Not tense. We were just talking."

"That's good." She turned and looked at him, her expression serious. "I want you to come look at something."

His stomach dropped. "What is it?"

"Just come and see."

"This doesn't sound good." He rose and put the mug into the sink.

"I'm not sure whether it's good or not, but it might be the clue we've needed all this time."

Luke's stomach churned acid. "You won't tell me?"

"You need to *see* what I'm talking about."

"Okay." He laced his fingers through hers and walked with her to Alex's room. He sat at the desk, typing a mile a minute, fully focused on the screen.

Macy cleared her throat. Alex turned to them.

"You found a clue?" Luke asked.

"I have no idea." Alex turned the laptop toward Macy and Luke. "She won't tell me what's going on."

"Guess that makes two of us."

Macy let go of Luke's hand and scrolled through Alex's blog. "This is one of the missing people from the Meriwether. Take a look."

Luke leaned over and studied the picture. It was a guy a few years older with a five o'clock shadow and dark circles under his eyes. He turned to Macy. "Okay?"

"Scroll down. Keep looking at the pictures."

"We need to focus on finding Mom," Luke muttered, but he scrolled, anyway. The next photo of the man was with a slightly younger woman, and the same guy from the earlier picture was now clean-cut, bright-eyed, and smiling widely. Luke was about to scroll down when he paused. There was something about those eyes…

Luke studied the man's face and was suddenly transported back ten years. He snapped his head toward Macy. "Is that…?"

She nodded, her eyes lighting up.

He turned back to the blog and scrolled up and down, staring at all five of the pictures. "It is him."

"What are you two talking about?" Alex demanded.

Luke turned back to Macy, his palms growing clammy. His mind raced with possibilities of what this could mean.

"Well?" Alex tapped the desk.

Macy looked at her brother. "We know him from the community. He didn't go by Rory then."

"He went by Isaac," Luke said.

Waiting

NICK CLIMBED INTO his Mustang after walking around it several times to make sure there were no scratches or other marks. If he'd have been thinking straight, he would've brought a police cruiser to the Meriwether. But all he'd considered before leaving was that a marked vehicle would scare off anyone who would otherwise talk to them.

"That was next to useless." Anderson snapped his seatbelt.

"We did confirm that Lottie had been there giving groceries, and that Rory and Kinsley are both missing."

"All of which we already knew." Anderson shuddered. "I feel like I need to shower off that stench."

Nick couldn't deny that. He was going to pick up his kids from the airport in a few hours, and he had to get rid of the smell from his clothes and skin. It clung to both of them, stinking up his beloved car. He turned the ignition and pushed a single button to roll down all the windows. "Now we need to figure out what the connection is between a retired lady, a janitor, and a young college dropout."

"Lottie Mills loves volunteering. Maybe she was helping the other two, also."

"But if she was, someone would know, right? Nobody mentioned a connection between them and her." Nick pulled out from the spot and squealed the tires as he made his way out of the neighborhood.

"Maybe they didn't know Lottie was helping them," Anderson pointed out. "Her own kid didn't even know she was going to the Meriwether, and it sounds like she's been doing that for a while."

Nick tried to think of what would lead to all three disappearing. "Maybe Rory and Kinsley were involved with something, and it turned bad. They went to Lottie for help, and that led to whatever happened."

"Maybe." Silence rested between them for close to a minute. "Unless Rory was into something, and he kidnapped both Kinsley and Lottie."

"Why, though?" Nick turned onto a main road. "If he took two older women, that would make sense—or if he took two eighteen-year-olds. But to take both of them?"

"They might've seen something they shouldn't have."

"That could be." They discussed other possibilities until Nick pulled into the station's parking lot.

Anderson unbuckled. "We'd better debrief everyone. Maybe we can even find a connection between these three and all the missing homeless. You never know."

"Wishful thinking," Nick said. "It'd be great to be able to solve all the cases at once, but we both know it never works that way. Anyway, I'm going to need you to take this one."

"Wait, what?" Anderson gave him a double-take. "It's all-hands-on-deck, Captain. Your orders."

"I know, and I'm going to work remotely. I have to pick up my kids from the airport."

Anderson nodded knowingly. "Corrine actually put them on the plane?"

"She'd better hope so."

"I'll keep you updated."

"My phone will be on."

Anderson left, and Nick closed his eyes. Despite having had the window open, he could still smell the Meriwether—a mixture of weed, body odor, and butt. Great. Now he'd have to not only shower, but find a way to flush the smell from the car, too. Of all the days for it to stink.

Nick hurried home and into the shower. He threw on some slightly-faded jeans and a Pearl Jam t-shirt from a concert he had taken Ava and Parker to shortly before the divorce. Hopefully when they saw that, it would bring back good memories and they could start their time together on the right foot. He knew it would take more than a shirt to distract them from all the bad things Corrine had been saying to them from the moment she served Nick with the divorce papers.

He walked around the condo, making sure everything was ready for the kids. The cupboard was filled with their favorite snacks. The spare bedroom was decorated with the items from the girls' rooms that had been left behind, plus a number of new things he'd purchased since then for them. Nick's room was converted into a double room using dividers, giving Parker the feel of having his own room.

It was far from perfect, but it was the best he could do with a small two-bedroom condo.

On his way out, he picked up his phone to call Corrine *again.* His calls had been going to voicemail all day.

He had a dozen missed calls and texts, but none were from his ex or the kids. Nick grumbled and checked the time. He didn't have to leave for the airport for at least another hour, so he checked the texts first. Alex had left most of them, insisting he had a break on Lottie's case but he didn't say what.

Nick sat at the kitchen table and called him back.

Alex answered halfway through the first ring. "Finally!"

"What's the big break?"

"Luke and Macy recognize the other two missing people from the Meriwether."

"They do?" Nick asked. "What's the connection?"

"You're not going to believe this."

Nick sat taller. "Try me."

"They were both part of that cult from when Macy was kidnapped."

Nick let the news settle. "They're sure?"

"They even know their names—well, the names they went by in the cult."

"Are the cult leaders trying to rebuild what they had before?"

"Maybe, but Lottie wouldn't have left without a word, much less gone willingly with the cult. And what about Luke and Macy? They don't know anything about it."

Nick glanced at the time. "Meet me at the station. I might have to leave in the middle of questioning, but someone else can take over for me. I'll be there in ten."

"Thanks, Nick."

"Don't thank me yet. Let's get to the bottom of this." He ended the call, texted Anderson, and grabbed his keys.

Questions

ALEX SAT NEXT to Macy in the interrogation room while Nick and two other cops questioned her and Luke about the cult and the two missing people from the apartments. Macy hadn't stopped shaking since she saw their pictures. She was pale and kept stumbling over her words. Both he and Luke held her clammy hands.

Alex glanced at the camera recording their every word and movement. That certainly couldn't help her nerves. At least she wouldn't have to keep repeating the story since they'd have it recorded. Hopefully.

The captain kept glancing at the clock. It was supposed to be his day off, and he was picking up his kids from the airport soon. Yet here he was. If Alex didn't know any better, he might think the captain never had any time off. Nick pushed his chair back. "I'm really sorry, but I have to go. Just keep talking with these officers. I'll go over the video, and let you know if I have any additional questions."

Macy nodded but didn't say anything. Luke thanked him and shook his hand. Alex nodded at him, and then the captain left.

Lieutenant Anderson slid his finger around an iPad. "Let me make sure I understand everything so far." He glanced at Luke. "You and your mom joined the cult willingly when you were ten?"

"Yeah." He looked deep in thought for a moment. "I was almost eleven, but my tenth birthday was the last one I celebrated until we got out. It was right after my dad died, and we were about to wind up on the streets. One of the leaders met my mom while I was in school. He promised they'd keep us off the streets, clothed, and fed. They told her I'd always be cared for. She couldn't say no to that."

"And you never felt that anything was wrong? They didn't mistreat you?"

Macy's hand squeezed Alex's so tightly that it reminded him of Zoey on the day Ariana had been born. He patted his sister's hand and tried to give her a reassuring look. She looked like she'd burst into tears at any moment.

Luke cleared his throat. "Mom warned me they had a different lifestyle from what I was used to, but that we'd both grow to like it because they would take care of us, and we'd never have to be homeless."

"And you compare the lifestyle to the Amish?"

"What does this have to do with anything?" Macy blurted out. "How is talking about this going to find Lottie?"

Anderson gave her a sympathetic glance. "I know this is hard, but if they're trying to rebuild the cult, we need to know everything. Who knows what tiny, seemingly insignificant detail can lead us to them? It could be something you tell us today that leads us to your mother-in-law."

Macy took a deep breath. "Sorry."

"Don't be. If you need to step outside for some air, feel free."

"Really?"

"Of course." Anderson turned back to Luke. "Tell me more about the leaders. You say that Rory from the Meriwether was one of them?"

Luke nodded. "Isaac. He was the son of Jonah's right-hand man. We didn't hear from him much, but if someone stepped out of line, he was quick to put them in their place."

Macy turned to Alex. "Will you go into the hall with me?"

He squeezed her hand. "Yeah."

They walked around the table and out into the hall. Macy leaned against the wall and took several deep breaths. "I never thought I'd have to think about the community again."

"Hopefully after this, you won't." Alex stood next to her and leaned his head against the wall. "I hate that thinking about it tears you apart."

She turned to him, tears shining in her eyes. "Thanks. I hate it, too. I'm home, I'm safe—you'd think I could just put it behind me."

"I don't know if I could. You're one of the strongest people I know, Mace. I hope you know that."

A tear ran down her face and she turned away.

"What can we do to help you get through this meeting?" Alex asked. "I can grab you some stale coffee. I hear that works wonders."

Macy cracked a smile.

"Stay right here." Alex headed to the table where they kept coffee and filled two foam cups and added some sugar cubes and cream. It wasn't a mint mocha, but hopefully it would help at least a little.

When he turned down the hallway and saw her, Macy wiped at her eyes furiously. His heart broke for his sister. If he could find anyone who'd hurt her, he would give them some of their own medicine.

Alex handed her one of the cups and noticed the skin around her eyes was splotchy, like she'd been crying especially hard.

"Thanks."

"I wish I could take it all away. I really do."

She shrugged and sipped the drink. "Maybe talking about it will help find Lottie. Then it'll all be worth it."

"But will you be okay?" He sipped his coffee. It was horribly bitter, despite the cream and sugar.

Macy stood taller. "If we find her, yes, I will be. We should get back in there."

Alex opened the door to the interrogation room and held it for Macy. They walked in together and took their seats.

Luke was speaking. "...at school, Teacher Rebekah taught us the basics—reading, writing, and math. Other than that, everything had to do with the community. I had a lot to catch up on in order to graduate high school. Jonah didn't want us discussing, much less learning, about the world."

Anderson nodded at Alex and Macy as they took their seats. Luke held Macy's hand. Anderson turned his attention back to Luke. "Knowing everything you do, what do you think they're doing now? Are they rebuilding now that many of them have finished their sentences? Are they abducting former members? In your opinion, of course."

Luke glanced at the pictures of Rory and Kinsley on the table. "It wouldn't surprise me if they're rebuilding everything. Nor would it shock me to learn they're taking people by force."

Anderson tapped his tablet's screen and turned to Macy. "What about you? What do you think?"

Flashbacks

MACY STARED AT the lieutenant. "R-repeat the question, please."

He nodded. "In your opinion, what do you think the cult is doing?"

The interrogation room disappeared, and Macy found herself in a dark room. No, it wasn't entirely dark. There was a light flicker coming from the candle in her hand. It reflected in the mirrors around her. The whole room was covered in mirrors. Each one reflected the tiny fire, shaking in her grasp. She looked up at one of the mirrors and saw her face—herself at fifteen, wearing all white.

She was locked in the room. They were punishing her for something. She'd wanted to beg to be released but had been too scared. Fighting them would only make things worse for her. That much she knew.

"Macy? Are you okay?"

Her brother's voice brought her back to the present. Macy shook her head and took a deep breath.

"What do you think the cult is up to?" Anderson repeated.

"They'll want to rebuild. And they'll be furious they were stopped all those years ago. They'll be more careful this time."

"Careful?" asked the other policeman. "What do you mean?"

A lump formed in her throat. "They'll make sure nobody gets away."

"Do you think your mother-in-law went willingly? Like she did the first time?"

Macy blinked back tears. She felt small—like the scared, terrorized fifteen-year-old she'd been. "N-no. Lottie changed her last name to stay hidden from them. She l-lives on her own, and she likes her independence. There's no reason for her to want to go back."

Anderson slid his finger furiously around his tablet's screen and then looked back at her. "Is there anything about Rory or Kinsley that you haven't mentioned yet? Rory was one of the leaders, so he probably left on his own. What about Kinsley?"

"I don't know." Macy gasped for air. "She was just a little kid. I saw her around but never talked to her. And who knows how she feels about the community now? I'd think she'd barely remember it at this point."

He turned to Luke. "Is that what you think, too?"

Luke pursed his lips and took a deep breath. "Her mom was extremely dedicated to the community—all the adults were. Jonah saved them all from bad life experiences. It made him easily revered."

"So, we need to look into her parents. See if they know anything—or if they've gone missing as well."

"Like my mom, her mom wasn't married, either."

"Were there a lot of single parent families?" Anderson asked.

Luke glanced over at Macy and squeezed her hand. "Most came in that way, but a lot were given spouses within the community."

"Your mom was never married in there?"

"Briefly."

"Meaning?"

Luke shrugged. "He was kicked out of the community, and we never talked about him after that."

Anderson made some notes and turned to Macy. "What about

you? What were your circumstances?"

A chill ran through Macy. "Chester, he made me pretend to be his daughter."

"He was some kind of leader?"

Macy shuddered just thinking about it. "He was Jonah's highest prophet."

Anderson arched a brow. "The man who kidnapped and tortured you?"

"And killed people," Macy whispered. She closed her eyes, not wanting to think about her abductor anymore. Luke kissed her cheek.

"Right," said the other policeman. "He's never getting out of prison because of his charges."

A small amount of relief washed through her. Chester had been convicted for a great many crimes and had been sent to prison without the possibility of parole. It was the one thing that helped her to actually sleep at night.

Anderson pressed his palms on the table. "We're done asking about the cult, unless you have anything else to add."

Macy shook her head.

"I don't," Luke said.

Anderson nodded toward the other policeman, who pulled out a large manila envelope. "We have some pictures we'd like you to look at. If you recognize any of the people, let us know."

Macy's stomach lurched. She didn't know what they were about to see, but she was sure it would give her nightmares.

The two cops spread out a dozen photos in front of them. Luke leaned over first. Macy's heart raced but she forced herself to take a peek. At first glance, she didn't recognize anyone. But then one of the pictures caught her attention. The man was about her dad's age, and though he wore his hair long and was clean-shaven, she knew who he was upon studying his eyes.

"I know her." Luke pointed to the picture nearest him. "She

was Teacher Rebekah's assistant for a while—before she took over the younger kids' class."

"And him." Macy grabbed the photograph she'd recognized. "He was one of the farmers."

In a matter of minutes, between the two of them, Luke and Macy had identified each of the people.

"Are they missing, too?" Alex asked.

Anderson nodded. "We've had a rash of homeless people disappearing." He exchanged a glance with the other officer. "And there are high numbers of homeless and low-income people disappearing in other parts of the state, too."

"And in parts of Idaho and Oregon," added the other officer.

Macy's stomach twisted in tight knots. "Chester's staying locked up, isn't he?"

"He's in a maximum security prison. There's no way he's getting out."

The lump in Macy's throat grew twice in size. She squeezed Luke's hand. "What if we're next?"

He shook his head. "We won't be. I won't let them take us."

Her mouth went dry. She wished she could believe him. When Jonah wanted something, he got it. If he wanted to take the two of them, he would find a way.

Luke kissed her forehead. "We'll be on the lookout. Now we have the advantage—we know they're probably going to start scoping us out soon."

Macy's blood ran cold as she thought back to the night before. She'd been sure someone was following her. Why hadn't they taken her? They weren't ready yet? Did they worry about witnesses in the neighborhood?

"Are you okay?" Luke rested his hand on her shoulder.

She nodded. "We'll just have to be really careful."

Parched

LOTTIE MOANED AND opened her eyes. Her mouth and throat felt like the desert. She'd managed to sleep, curled against a wall, but it had been restless and it didn't feel like she'd slept long. Her stomach growled. She felt light-headed and dizzy, and a headache throbbed. The people in front of her appeared in doubles.

The leaders were trying to break her. Make her susceptible to whatever they had planned for her. She needed more than the two tiny cups of water she'd received the night before.

She took a deep breath and forced herself to sit up. No matter how hard it would be, she needed to stay mentally tough. It was her only chance. After a few slow, deep breaths her double-vision went away.

Lottie focused on the others, trying to push her bodily needs out of her mind. There were about a dozen others, and everyone stayed to themselves—alone like her. Some sat, but most lay on the ground. That was probably exactly what the leaders wanted.

Something tickled her nose. Lottie sneezed loudly, the force going all the way down to her empty stomach. Several others glanced her way. She made eye contact with one.

Sydney. Her eyes widened, and she clung to Lottie's gaze, unmoving. Then she turned around and faced the wall.

Lottie sighed. She looked around for Sydney's children but didn't see any kids. When had they nabbed her? Had they left her kids at home, or were they holding children separately? That might be the case, given they were putting the adults on trial.

She forced herself to her feet, using the wall to balance. Her dizziness made it hard to walk. She stumbled but made it across the room.

"Sydney."

The younger woman didn't move.

"Sydney," Lottie repeated.

She spun around. "I go by Dinah here. Are you trying to get me in trouble?"

"Of course not."

Sydney glanced around. "You know the rules."

Lottie lowered her voice. "Did they get your kids, too?"

Her eyes narrowed, but Sydney didn't answer.

"Are they here?"

"We're not supposed to talk." Sydney's brows came together.

"When are they going to feed us?"

"Never, if you keep this up."

Lottie frowned.

Click.

Lottie and everyone else snapped their attention in that direction.

"Go back to where you were." Sydney turned her back on Lottie.

Click.

Lottie shook her head, but went back to where she'd slept. She leaned against the wall and slid to sitting. Who knew what would happen? A new prisoner? Some food or water, maybe? Lottie's heart raced at the thought. What she wouldn't give for another small glass of water and especially just a piece of bread. And that was exactly the point—she would be more willing to go along with whatever they had planned if she was desperate for something to eat.

She held her breath as the last three locks clicked. It felt like forever before the door opened, but in reality, it was probably only a few seconds.

The smell of food—soup?—hit her like a ton of bricks. Lottie pressed her palms on the ground to keep herself steady. She shook, eager for some nutrition. Her head wobbled back and forth as dizziness reclaimed her.

A man came in followed by several women and another man who closed the door and locked it from the inside with a key. The women carried trays with small bowls.

Lottie's mouth watered. Would she finally get sustenance? Or would they continue to deny her? She continued shaking but tried to remain steady. The last thing she wanted was to give them any reason to deny her food.

All the other prisoners kept their gazes averted to the floor, so Lottie glanced down. She had to show them she was fitting back in. That she would do whatever it would take for food. Then once she had a little energy, she would look for a way out.

She took slow, labored breaths as she watched them from the corner of her eye. The women came over to the captives and handed each one of them a small bowl. Lottie felt like she might pass out.

Hold on. She pressed her palms harder against the packed-dirt floor.

The women made their way around the room, stopping in front of everyone until finally only Lottie was left.

Were they going to skip her?

Tears stung at her eyes, but she refused to give into them. Even if they refused to feed her, they would never see it get to her.

The two men whispered. The three women milled about. One bowl remained on a single tray. It took all of Lottie's effort not to stare at it. She watched it from the periphery of her vision. The smell of the soup made her mouth water, which at least was something. She didn't feel so parched. Her stomach felt like it would growl, but it didn't. Perhaps it was too much effort.

A woman came over to Lottie and stood a couple feet in front of her. It was hard to keep her gaze averted. Everything in her wanted to jump up and grab the bowl. She didn't care if the soup scalded her mouth and throat—or if it had been sitting out for two days. It was the only thing in the world she wanted at the moment.

She took another deep breath and pressed herself against the wall and the ground.

"Do you want some soup?" The woman's tone held no emotion.

Was Lottie supposed to answer? It seemed like either option could lead to the worst—no soup.

"Do you want some?"

Lottie nodded slightly.

The woman knelt and held out the tray. The aroma grew stronger. Lottie looked up at the small steaming bowl.

"Take it."

Lottie reached for it, praying it wasn't a trick. The ceramic was warm. Comforting. Her mouth watered more. Her stomach twisted. It had been so long since she'd eaten. Would her body reject it? Her stomach twisted in a knot but her mouth watered as the bowl neared.

It was nothing more than broth with a couple noodles and two small pieces of meat—it was heavenly. The bowl came to her mouth and the hot liquid filled her mouth. Her stomach twisted, but she gulped down what she could.

Before she could swallow two mouthfuls, one of the men kicked the bowl out of her hands, spilling the soup onto Lottie's robe and the floor. "Aw, too bad. Maybe next time."

Reconnecting

LUKE PULLED INTO the driveway and cut the engine. His entire body ached. He didn't want to move.

"Do you want to go inside?" Macy asked.

He leaned his head against the headrest. "I want to go to sleep for days and then wake up to find out this was all just a bad dream."

"I wish. We should get inside."

Luke sat up and looked around outside. "First I need to make sure nobody's going to ambush us."

Everything looked normal. Some kids were kicking a ball in the yard across the street and another group was playing chase on the sidewalk. A neighbor mowed the lawn. A typical suburban Saturday afternoon.

Nobody would try to abduct them with so many potential witnesses.

He pressed a button to unlock the doors and then they headed in. Luke made sure to lock the car and set the house alarm in case anyone did try to sneak in.

"Are you hungry?" she asked.

"Maybe. It's so hard to tell what I feel about anything." He frowned.

"Let me warm something up so we can get some sleep on a full stomach. Then maybe you actually can sleep for days."

"I'll help you make something."

She wrapped her arms around him. "I love you for that, babe, but why don't you get a shower while I fix something? It'll help you relax."

A shower did sound good, and he probably needed one. He wasn't sure he'd had once since all this started. Luke kissed the top of her head. "And I love *you* for that."

When he got out of the shower, the house smelled like bacon and spices. His mouth watered. He wondered what Macy was making. Probably something he'd never heard of since she liked trying new recipes she found online. Luke quickly got dressed and went to the kitchen just as she was pulling a glass dish from the oven.

"Just in time." She pulled the tinfoil off the top, causing steam to gush out, and along with it, a fresh new wave of the mouth-watering aroma.

"How'd you make that so quickly?"

She shrugged. "I just threw some vegetables and bacon in with ground beef, then I topped it off with some mashed butternut squash."

Luke's stomach growled. "It sounds wonderful."

Macy grabbed a serving spoon and stuck it in. "Hand me a plate."

A couple minutes later, they sat at the table, eating. The casserole was even better than it smelled. Once he'd overstuffed himself, he leaned back in the chair and took a deep breath. It had been nice to take a few minutes to think of nothing other than the delicious dish, but now it was time to get back to reality. Mom was missing, and he and Macy were supposed to list everyone they could remember from the community. They'd already identified the missing homeless and told the police the names of a dozen more—not that those were particularly helpful since they only knew their community-given names.

Macy grabbed his empty plate and took it to the sink. He

jumped up and followed her. "I'll get those. You cooked, I clean."

She kissed his cheek. "Thanks. I need to throw some clothes in the wash."

Twenty minutes later, Luke sat on the couch with his arm around her. She snuggled close, and he closed his eyes. It was amazing what some food and a shower could do. He felt more relaxed than he had in days, and he felt a food coma coming on. It also helped to know that the police had found a big lead. Now it was just a matter of finding the community's new location, and since they were coming out into the world to snatch former members, it would make it easier to find someone and follow them there.

Luke's head snapped up. "I have an idea."

Macy met his gaze. "What?"

"I can be bait."

"Come again?" Worry clouded her expression.

"To draw out Jonah and the other leaders."

She shook her head. "No."

"Don't you see? It's perfect."

"I can't lose you, Luke. I just can't."

"The cops would be there, hiding. I'd be perfectly safe."

"Please, no. We can come up with something else."

Luke stared into her eyes. The fear and pleading nearly broke his heart. She was already having anxiety and panic attacks. If something happened to him, it would probably send her over the edge. He cupped her chin in his palms. "I won't do anything to hurt you. We'll find another way."

She breathed a sigh of relief. "Thank you."

His heart exploded with his love for her. He leaned in and pressed his lips on hers, tasting mint gum. She responded by pressing her palms against his chest and kissing him passionately. His fingers found her hair, and he raked them through the length of it, pressing himself against her. She ran her fingernails down his sides, giving him the chills. He reached for her top button and undid it, his fingers fumbling slightly.

Macy's hands made their way to his face, and her fingers moved back and forth across his cheeks, over his three-day-old stubble. He unbuttoned the second and third buttons. She moaned and climbed into his lap.

Luke remembered the blinds were open only a few feet away. He pulled away, taking Macy's gum with him. "Maybe we should take this into the bedroom."

Anticipation

NICK PACED THE baggage claim area, glancing at the flight arrival ticker every minute or so. The kids' flight—if they were on it—had already been delayed a couple times, but for the last half hour had showed the same time. If it was right, he had just under another half hour of waiting.

He wished for the days of being able to wait at the terminal to watch them exit the plane. It was tempting to try and get closer by using his badge, but he didn't want to abuse the privilege. He was off the clock and this was personal.

Someone bumped into him—without apology—and Nick realized another group of people were gathering their things. He was tired of pacing the baggage claim, so he went to the nearest coffee stand and grabbed another cup, this time a mocha. Alex was wearing off on him.

Nick sipped the super-sweet drink while watching the conveyor belts from a distance. At least it was a slight change in scenery. He checked his phone. Nothing from Corrine, of course. She was either ignoring him because she hadn't put the kids on the plane or because she wanted him to sweat it out, or maybe both. But he was done calling and texting her. He wasn't going to give her that satisfaction. And to think he'd thought being married to her had been difficult. It hadn't been until she'd left him, dragging all three kids across the country, that he'd seen what she was really made of. It made him sick that she put the kids in the middle like that. And worse yet, that there was so little he could do about it.

He checked new texts and emails about the case. Anderson and some of the other officers had gotten names and descriptions of everyone Luke and Macy could remember, not that Nick expected them to be all that helpful without real names. The crazy cult had given their members new names—they called them "true names." Nick would never forget that from after the group had been broken up. Many forces from around the state had been called in to help with that mess. They had to book some people who refused to give their legal names. It had been next to impossible to return many of the innocent members to their families because they claimed allegiance to the cult by sticking to the new names.

Nick sighed, leaned against a wall, and watched a new wave of people pick up their luggage. He sipped his mocha, lost in thought. They needed more information about the cult, and especially what they had planned going forward. There were things that didn't make sense—like *why* they were abducting former members. Were they trying to recreate the commune in the woods, or did they have more sinister plans?

It was possible—not likely, however—that if they could talk with anyone else from the cult, they might get the answers they needed. Unfortunately, a lot of them had ended up homeless or in low income housing like the ones who'd already gone missing. Being part of the group had messed them up in ways Nick couldn't begin to imagine. Most of them didn't have the social and familial support that Macy, Luke, and Lottie had had. Those three had been some of the most fortunate of the escapees.

Nick's phone rang. His throat closed up, fearing it was Corrine or one of the kids saying he was a fool for hoping they'd be there—that they were already headed for Disney.

It was Alex. Nick released a breath and took the call. "Hey, Alex. How's it going?"

"I think Macy's feeling better. It seemed to help having them look at the pictures and give the names of the people they remembered. They both felt like they were doing something to help the case."

"That's good. I'm glad to hear it." He glanced at the ticker. Only fifteen minutes until his kids' flight was due.

"You okay?" Alex asked.

"Yeah. Just waiting for the plane. It's already been delayed a couple times."

"You taking the week off?"

"As much as I can. I'll either go in at night or work remotely if possible. I haven't seen them in so long, I have to—"

"I'm not complaining. You need to spend time with them. Believe me, nobody knows more about missing time with his kids than I do."

"Maybe we could get our kids together. Ava and Ariana are close in age, aren't they?"

"Ari's eleven."

"That's what I thought. Ava's twelve."

"Okay. Let's make it happen. I'd suggest the Ball Palace, but..."

Nick shook his head. "I'm not sure I ever want to take the kids there. We'll figure something out."

"I'll ask Ari for ideas—she has no shortage of them." He chuckled. "Well, I'll let you go. Just wanted to check in."

"Call me tomorrow. I don't have anything planned to do with the kids, and it'd be nice to start the vacation off with something fun. I've been so consumed with the case."

"No worries. I'll get a list of fun things to do from Ari and give it to you. The kids'll never know you didn't have a fun spring break planned all year."

"Thanks. I owe you a beer."

Alex didn't respond right away. "I'm not drinking, remember?"

"Ugh. I keep forgetting. Coffee?"

"I won't turn that down. See ya tomorrow." The call ended.

Nick slid the phone back into his pocket, and his mind wandered back to the case. They'd already gotten everything they could from Macy and Luke. There had to be someone else he could talk to about the cult.

His head snapped up. Chester Woodran. He was in prison with no chance of parole. He might talk if he was under the impression he might receive a reduced sentence—he never would, but he might *think* there was a chance. Chester knew the ins and outs of the cult more than most anyone else he could talk to. He'd been included in the inner circle of the leaders. They may have even contacted Chester and told him what their plans were.

Nick opened his notes app and scribbled notes to himself. Once he was done, he glanced back up at the ticker. Just as he did, it switched over to *arrived.*

His breathing constricted. Were his kids on that plane?

Grateful

ALEX RANG THE doorbell. Thundering footsteps sounded on the other side and the front door flung open. Ariana grinned widely in her pink and white pajamas and threw her arms around him. "Daddy!"

His heart warmed and he squeezed her back. It was amazing how much he missed seeing her after only a few days. How had he ever gone the better part of a year without seeing her at all, only visiting a couple times a year?

She stood back. "Where have you been?"

"Close the door!" Valerie called from inside the house.

"Sorry, Mimi!" Ari called back. She waved Alex inside and closed the door. "Daddy's here!" She grabbed his arm and dragged him into the living room. Valerie and Kenji sat together on the couch watching a Mariners game.

Alex waved. "Who's winning?"

"The Mariners. By one." Kenji didn't take his attention from the television.

Valerie glanced over at Alex. "How are things going with… you know?"

He gave her an appreciative nod, glad they were keeping Lottie's disappearance from Ariana. Although with all the fliers around town, it probably wouldn't be long before she found out. If she didn't see a flier, then she might hear it from a friend. He needed to tell her before too long. Maybe that night. "Improving, but it might be a while. It might be time to say something." He pointed to Ari from behind.

"I think so."

Kenji jumped up. "Oh, come on! You could've caught that!"

"You would've, Papi." Ari smiled reassuringly.

"Thanks, dove." The now-retired Japanese professional baseball player smiled at Ariana and sat back down next to Valerie.

Ariana grabbed Alex's arm and pulled him toward the kitchen. "Come on. Mimi and I made cookies today."

Sure enough, the counter was filled with an array of cookies. Valerie must've been trying to keep Ari busy at home, away from fliers and social media. Though Valerie still didn't like Alex much, at least they were able to see eye-to-eye most of the time regarding what was best for Ariana. She respected him as a dad, even if he had no legal rights. After hearing about all of Nick's trouble with his ex and kids, Alex appreciated his situation all the more.

"Which kind do you want?" Ari stared at him with wide eyes.

He studied each plate. "That's a tough decision. They all look equally delicious."

She squealed. "I made the peanut butter ones all by myself. I even put them in the oven and took them out. I'm very responsible." She nodded with a serious expression.

"Wow. I'm impressed. I'm pretty sure I couldn't even pour cereal by myself until I was thirteen."

Ariana giggled. "So, which cookies do you want?"

"Hmm." Alex contorted his face excessively, pretending to be struggling deeply over the decision.

"Daddy!" Ari doubled over in laughter.

He straightened up and put his hand to his chin. "In the face of this most monumental choice—" Ari giggled again. "—I choose the peanut butter cookies. I have it under good authority that those are world class."

Ari's eyes widened and she handed him one, watching in expectation. Alex took a slow, exaggerated bite. He took his time chewing, making a new expression each time he chewed. It was hard to keep up the act and not burst into laughter as he watched his daughter. She looked like she was going to explode with anticipation. Finally he swallowed, but didn't say anything.

"Well?" Ariana clenched her fists in front of her chin.

Alex took a deep breath and puffed out his chest, trying to drag on the moment as her eyes continued widening. "After careful consideration, I can only come to one conclusion."

"What?"

"That is, without a doubt, the best cookie the world has ever seen."

She squealed again and jumped up and down.

Alex winked at her and grabbed some milk from the fridge. "Can't have cookies without milk."

"Nope!" She grabbed some glasses and plates. After Alex had taste-tested all five kinds of cookies, Zoey entered from the living room. Strands of hair had come loose from a ponytail and she had dark circles under her eyes.

"Are you okay?" he asked.

At the same time, Ariana said, "Mimi and I made cookies!"

Zoey gave her a tired smile and sat next to her, across from Alex. "That's great, Ari."

"Which kind do you want?"

"I really don't need—"

"Daddy says the peanut butter ones I made are the best ever!"

Zoey yawned. "I'll bet they are. Sure, I'll try one."

Ari jumped up, started talking about the afternoon's baking, and grabbed milk and a cookie for Zoey, who yawned again. Ariana was still talking when Zoey was done with her snack.

Someone's phone rang. Ari pulled out her new phone—so she would always be reachable—and looked at the screen. "It's Emily! I gotta talk to her. Don't leave—either of you!" She bounced out of the room, already talking with her friend.

Alex turned to Zoey. "You okay?"

"Just tired. I worked all day to make up for missing some time during the week. Any news on Lottie?"

"Not yet. There are some new clues, but nothing great. We have no idea where she is."

Zoey sat a little taller. "What kind of clues?"

"Somehow that cult is involved."

She gave him a double-take. "You mean the one they were all in when Macy was kidnapped?"

"Seems they're having a reunion… or worse." He shuddered.

"What do you mean?"

"If they're kidnapping people, I don't see how any good *could* come of it."

"People? As in, more than just her?"

Alex nodded and filled her in on the details. "I also think we should tell Ari what's going on."

"Yeah, that's a—" Zoey's eyes widened.

"What?"

"What if that cult takes Macy? She's already having massive anxiety over Lottie."

"They know to keep an eye out, and they're going to be cautious."

"Man, I hope so. That's scary. I'm going to call her tomorrow." Zoey yawned. "After I get some sleep. I'm half-tempted to stay here for the night."

"You're more than welcome to," Valerie called from the other room.

"Thanks," Zoey called back. She leaned back against the chair and closed her eyes. Alex studied her, his heart fluttering a little. She was just as beautiful as she'd always been with her jet black hair and mixture of Caucasian and Japanese features. Even tired and resting, she was perfection in human form.

Her eyes fluttered, and Alex leaned back in his chair and picked at a nail, pretending it was the most interesting thing in the room.

Zoey stretched. "I didn't mean to doze off. Maybe I actually should stay here."

"Please do."

She tilted her head. "Are you worried about me?"

"Of course. I don't want to see you get hurt." Didn't she know that? He wanted to say more, but stopped himself.

Zoey held his gaze for a few beats and then opened her mouth to speak.

Ariana bounced into the room, holding out her phone's screen. "Emily got a puppy! Look how cute he is."

"Okay," Zoey said. "Then have a seat, because we need to tell you something."

Ari's smiled faded into a frown. "I *knew* you guys were keeping something from me. What is it?"

He patted the seat next to him.

"What?" Ari plunked down next to him.

"You remember Miss Lottie, right?"

"Yeah, Uncle Luke's mom. She's gonna take me so I can help feed the homeless."

Zoey and Alex exchanged a look. Alex cleared his throat. "Actually, that might have to wait."

Ari's eyes widened. "Why?"

His stomach twisted in a tight knot. This conversation had been easier in his mind. "She's missing."

"What?" Ariana's mouth dropped. "Is she gonna be okay? Like I was?"

"We hope so. The police are working really hard, just like they did when you were gone."

Her eyes widened until they couldn't get any bigger. "What about your blog? You have to tell people!"

Alex pulled her close and hugged her. "I have. Now we just have to wait."

"Just wait?"

Zoey and Alex exchanged a worried glance.

"For now, yes. That's all we can do."

Raging

THE GROUND BENEATH Jonah's feet shook slightly from the nearby construction. His pulse raced and his breathing grew fast as he stared at the small building—if it could even be called that. It was more like a few beams sticking out of the ground.

"What's taking so long?" He stopped and stared at Boaz, the lead of construction.

Boaz stepped back, his face paling. If Jonah had been in a better mood, seeing the fear in him would've made Jonah feel better, but now it only served to irritate him further.

"Well?" Jonah stepped closer, narrowing his eyes.

"Great High Prophet, these things take time."

"And you've had plenty of that, now haven't you?"

Boaz stepped back. "It's been difficult to find trees tall enough for your specifications. You want ceilings almost taller than these trees."

"Yes, I want a tall, impressive courtroom that will instill fear into everyone who passes by. Nobody, and I mean nobody, will ever again consider getting away. Trying to shut us down. I want our people to cower in fear when they get near my courtroom."

"And that will take time." Boaz took in a haggard breath. "Right, men?"

His crew scattered, none daring to tell Jonah what he didn't want to hear.

"How long will it take?" Anger pulsed through Jonah. "I want this done!"

Boaz flinched. "It will be. It'll just take time."

Jonah paced, not saying anything. They'd managed to build plenty of houses, the meeting hall, and several other buildings in the time it had taken Boaz's crew to get up three beams. "Make it happen faster!"

"Yes, Great High Prophet. Do you have more men to help look for trees tall enough?"

"You want more people?" Jonah spun around and got in the other man's face. Though he was a full six inches taller, Boaz shook and his breathing grew even more labored.

"I-it would help."

"Well, too bad. You need to get creative. I want my courtroom exactly to the specifications I gave you."

Boaz swallowed. "It could take months."

Fury tore through Jonah. Why couldn't things simply move faster? It wasn't like he was asking them to build an ark! It was just a courtroom and gallows.

Gallows. He'd nearly forgotten.

Jonah turned back to Boaz. "If you're having trouble with the high walls in the middle of the courtroom, at least work on the gallows. I don't even see the start of the platform!"

"I… I thought we needed to erect the building first."

"Use your head!" Jonah exploded. "I want it all. You know where the courtroom is going! You know where the gallows go. Put them up so I can at least admire them while I wait for the beautiful building."

Boaz swallowed and nodded. "I'm on it."

"Will I have the gallows by tomorrow?"

"I-I don't see why not."

"Good. Get to it!" Jonah spun around and stormed away, heading toward the main part of the community. It was amazing how incompetent some people could be. They knew what he wanted. All they needed to do was to give it to him. How complicated was that? Not very. Get orders. Follow through. Simple!

He stomped down main street. Most people scurried away, but a few stopped to pay him proper respects by bowing. Jonah threw open the door of his large, luxurious study—luxurious by the community's standards. He'd seen plenty of impressive, expensive places in the world, but to Jonah, nothing held a candle to his standards. No, he didn't have leather furniture, marble tables, or fancy framed artwork. The community was a place of rustic beauty. The carvings on his walls were more intricate than anything he'd ever seen. They told a story—the story of their history. The way they had once thrived, but then had been taken down. But that was only the first part of the story. The rest told of the upcoming glory days of the establishment.

The new Community would outshine the old one so much that people would forget all about the old days. The only reminders would be in Jonah's study.

He paced around, admiring the carvings. Part of him wanted to calm down, but more of him wanted to remain furious. It was beyond ridiculous that his courtroom still wasn't finished. He'd pictured it being done sooner than even this—look how much of the great and magnificent community had been restored already.

Sure, the courtroom was new, but that wasn't an excuse. At least he would have his gallows the next day. That brought some solace. Even if the building of judgment had to wait, at least the execution platform would drive fear into people's hearts—deep into their very souls.

Only one more day.

Knock, knock.

Jonah groaned. "It had better be someone with good news." He walked over to the window and pushed aside the curtain. Abraham and Isaac stood outside, looking at each other. Jonah flung open the door and waved them in without a word.

The two other men stepped inside.

"What's the update?" Jonah demanded.

Abraham took a deep breath. "The good news is that we got a few more people."

"What's the bad news?" Jonah clenched his jaw.

"It would appear we've exhausted all the homeless in the area. Anyone else who belongs in the community appears to have either blended in with society or moved away."

Every muscle in Jonah's face tensed. "But you know where they are?"

"Some. We're working on it."

"Have you found everyone who needs to be judged?"

"No."

Jonah threw his arms into the air. "Why not?"

"These things take time, Great High Prophet."

"I'm sick of hearing that! I want them here *now!* Yesterday, in fact."

"You didn't build our grand society on impatience. Patience is what makes us strong. Great. Soon everyone will be ready, but not even the courtroom is ready."

"Don't talk to me about the courtroom!"

Both Abraham and Isaac jumped.

"What would help you to be pleased about the events?" Isaac asked.

"Everything moving faster."

"There's still a lot to be done," Abraham said. "Let's focus on what's going right, shall we?"

Jonah picked up a stack of books and threw them across the room. "Let's focus on making things happen faster, shall we?"

Arrival

NICK DROPPED HIS mocha into the garbage as he walked to the conveyor belt full of luggage. People crowded around—all adults and taller than his kids. He scanned the throng of bodies for his three children. There were children intermingled with the grownups, but none were his.

His throat closed up. If his kids weren't there, he was going to buy the first plane ticket he could get and go see them himself. Even if he had to fly to Florida, purchase Disney tickets, and weave his way through all of the parks to find them. Corrine was not going to keep him from his children.

The crowd thinned, and a young flight attendant with a streak of blue in her hair caught his attention. Ava, Parker, and Hanna stood next to her.

Nick froze, staring in disbelief. The kids were actually there. Only the space of about nine yards separated them. He sprinted over.

Little Hanna's face lit up. "Daddy!"

Nick picked her up and spun her around. She giggled and nearly choked him as she wrapped her tiny arms around his neck.

"Um, sir," said the flight attendant. "I'll need to see your ID."

"Daddy, Daddy!" Hanna squealed, squeezing him tighter.

"Sir."

"Hold on, sweetie." He set her down, but she wouldn't let go of him. "I need to show this nice lady my driver's license."

Hanna continued clinging.

"I don't want to let go, either, but I have to." He managed to pull her off, hating that it was necessary. Hanna threw her arms around Nick's leg and then wrapped her legs around his ankles. A lump formed in his throat as he pulled out his wallet and showed her his license. He had to flip his badge away from it first—he kept it that way so anyone seeing his ID would know he was an officer of the law.

The badge didn't impress the woman, however. She scrutinized his license, comparing it to a paper in her hand. Finally, she stepped back. "Thank you. Have a wonderful visit." She walked away, her heels clacking on the floor.

Hanna was still attached to his left leg. He stepped toward Ava and Parker, reaching out for a hug. Scowling, Ava gave him a stiff hug. Parker folded his arms and refused to return Nick's embrace.

Nick's heart felt like it would shatter into a million pieces. He knew from recent phone conversations that those two were growing distant, but it didn't really hit him until that moment. Nick tried to push the disappointment away as he studied his beautiful children. They both had grown so much. Parker was two years younger than Ava, but almost as tall now. And Ava, she really looked grownup. She looked closer to fourteen than twelve.

That's when he noticed the makeup. She had black eyeliner all around her eyes, and it scooped out at the end like cat eyes. She also had long black lashes, shimmery eyelids, and what looked like faded lipstick.

He and Corrine had agreed Ava would be at least thirteen before she could wear makeup, and even then, it was supposed to be a slow, gradual process of starting with one product at a time.

"Are we just going to stand here?" Ava ran her fingers through her long, slightly wavy hair and rolled her eyes dramatically.

"I need some coffee," Parker said.

Nick just about choked on air. His ten-year-old needed *coffee*?

Needed coffee?

Was Corrine trying to completely ruin their children just to spite him? It was beginning to look that way. He cleared his throat. "Let's get your suitcases."

They made their way to the conveyor belt. Hanna kept herself attached to Nick's leg. He didn't complain.

Ava had two extra-large suitcases, and the other two both had three medium-sized ones. He found a cart and loaded it up. Ava dug into one of her bags and puffed out her lips, applying lip color. It crushed him to see his little girl acting like a woman. She was only twelve! Parker pulled out a baseball style hat with a raunchy rapper on the front, and stuck it on backwards.

If Corrine was there, he'd ring her neck right there in the airport. In fact, it took all of his self-control not to say anything to the kids. He knew that if he did, they would only despise him more than they clearly did. At least he had the week to try and win them back. Nick was just grateful that his ex hadn't managed to turn Hanna against him. Perhaps it was time to speak with his attorney about the custody arrangement again.

They made their way through the airport as Nick pushed the luggage cart with Hanna still attached to his leg.

"I said I need coffee," Parker said as they passed a stand.

"It's late, you three are jet lagged. What you need is sleep."

"Dave would let me have coffee," Parker muttered.

"What did you say?"

Parker looked Nick in the eyes. "You heard me."

Corrine's boyfriend was the one behind Parker's newfound caffeine addiction? Had he been the one to suggest Ava start wearing makeup, too?

"We're not getting coffee." Nick clenched the cart's handle so tightly his knuckles turned white. "I don't care what Dave would do. *I'm* your father."

Ava mumbled something Nick couldn't make out.

"What did you say?"

"Nothing." She glared at him, daring him to ask again.

"Can I ride on the cart, Daddy?" Hanna asked.

"Don't be stupid," Parker snapped. "It's for suitcases."

"Don't call her stupid," Nick said.

Parker glared at his younger sister. "Stupid."

Nick stopped the cart and narrowed his eyes at his older children. "We can either have a good spring break or a miserable one. We haven't seen each other in a long time, and I would like to have a good time with you guys, but it's up to you."

Parker folded his arms.

Ava flipped her hair behind her shoulders. "Whatever."

He stepped closer to them. "This isn't a conversation I want to have in the airport while you guys—"

"I'm not a guy." Ava popped her gum. "Neither is Hanna. Maybe you noticed."

Nick ignored her. "—are exhausted. We'll talk about this later. Maybe over breakfast."

Ava looked away and shrugged. Parker stared at him, his expression growing tenser.

"I have some fun things planned, but only if your attitudes change—severely."

"*You* planned?" Ava asked. "What about what we want?"

"I'm certainly not going to force you to enjoy yourselves."

"Daddy, pick me up!" Hanna jumped around, reaching up for Nick.

He glanced back and forth between her and the cart he needed to get to the car—and they'd all be lucky if everything fit into the Mustang with them. His stomach tightened, realizing Corrine had probably done that on purpose, too. She knew that was the only car he drove.

"Piggyback." Nick knelt down, and Hanna climbed on his back. He adjusted her and reached for the cart. "Let's go."

Ava whistled. “He’s hot.”

Nick followed her gaze to a twenty-something skinny punk covered in tattoos. He ignored her and pushed the cart. If it took all of his energy, he would make sure the kids didn’t see how much they were getting to him.

Refreshed

LUKE ROLLED OVER and opened his eyes. Macy lay next to him, breathing softly. He watched as the quilt moved up and down in time with her peaceful breaths. Luke stretched and realized he felt better than he had in days. His entire body was relaxed and a warmth spread through him, starting at his core and radiating outward.

One of Macy's eyes cracked open. "Good morning, babe."

He ran the back of his fingertips along her cheek. "Morning, beautiful."

"Last night was…" She scrunched her face like she was searching for the right word. "Wow."

Luke grinned. "Yeah, it was."

She scooted over and kissed him. He wrapped his arm around her and they lay in silence. Little particles of dust danced around the room through the cracks from the blinds. Luke rested a hand behind his head and took a deep breath, catching a whiff of what remained of Macy's perfume from the day before.

"Do you want some breakfast?" he asked.

She pushed herself up onto her elbows and smiled at him. "If you mean more of this…" She trailed kisses from the corner of his mouth to his ear and nibbled. It was hard to say no to that. He flipped her over and covered her in kisses.

An hour later, they sat at the kitchen table in their robes, eating toast and cereal. Luke thought of his mom and his good mood faded. He felt like he should feel guilty for enjoying some time with Macy, but deep down he knew she wouldn't want him worrying and fretting for days on end.

"What are you thinking?" Macy asked.

"Maybe we should hand out more fliers today."

"Yeah, I was thinking about that, too. What do you think about going to a different town? By this point, I doubt there's a single resident who doesn't know."

"That's a good idea. I'll call the station and see if they still have stacks of fliers. Otherwise, we'll have to get some printed off somewhere. We're low on ink."

"Already?"

He nodded and then sipped his coffee.

Macy picked up their plates and rose. "I'll get in the shower so we can leave soon."

Luke stood and kissed her. "I'll call the station. Maybe they even have some news."

"Let's hope." She took the plates to the sink and headed for the bedroom.

He finished his coffee and thought back to his time in the community and tried to picture his mom back there. It hadn't been horrible, but he had always hoped to find a way out. The strict rules were a lot to deal with for anyone used to society. Shortly after arriving, he'd mistakenly broken their rules and been publicly shamed during a meeting. The entire assembly had chanted about what he'd done wrong, the words echoing all around him for what had felt like hours.

Then once all that stopped, none of the members had been allowed to speak to him for two whole days. It had been quite the shock, but he had never broken any of their rules after that. Not until Macy showed up, that was.

After they met and he saw her determination to escape, it lit a fire in him. By that point, he'd all but given up any hope of escape.

He'd thought his only option was to take on the job of a supply runner or something else that would allow him outside the tall, thick spiked walls. But that wouldn't have been possible until he was done with school.

He snorted. Their "school" had been a joke—merely learning about the commune's rules, prophecies, and history. By the time he got out of the cult, he was so behind the state standards that he'd had to catch up at home. Luckily with Mom's help, he was able to get through the material quickly and he managed to get his GED at nineteen.

Luke heard the shower start, and it brought him back to reality. He needed to call the station and find out what was going on. The captain was out, but he spoke with one of the officers from the day before who told him that they were still looking into the information he and Macy had given them, but there was nothing new besides some more missing homeless people.

"Wait," Luke said, before the officer ended the call. "Do you have fliers we can hand out?"

"Plenty of stacks. Take what you need."

"Thank you." Luke ended the call and washed the dishes, thinking about where he and Macy should go to hand out fliers. There were several bigger towns nearby, and if they went farther, they could go to Seattle. They would have plenty of choices where they could hand out the papers to crowds. Or they could go closer to nature and hand them out in more rural areas, closer to wooded areas—where the new community was likely to be. They would surely return to a forest which provided so many opportunities to hide.

After he finished the dishes, someone outside caught his attention. A man wearing a black coat and gray beanie paused in front of the house.

Chills ran down Luke's back. That was the second time that man had walked by just in the time he'd been doing the dishes.

Luke leaned over the sink and studied him, trying to tell if he could recognize him. He was too far away to make out any details. It could have been a neighbor or someone from the community—there was no way to tell with the distance between them.

The man turned and looked straight at Luke.

Playing

ALEX LEANED BACK in the folding chair and breathed in the fresh beach air. The sun beat down on him and he closed his eyes for a moment, listening to the kids play and the seagulls calling out as they flew overhead. He appreciated the warm spring day, knowing it could turn back to cold without warning—and probably would.

"It's nice to get away from everything, isn't it?" Nick asked.

Alex gave a nod, not wanting to open his eyes yet.

Nick pulled a can out of the cooler, spilling some ice onto the sand.

Tsst. "Want a pop?"

Alex sat up and opened his eyes. "Sure, why not?" He pulled a pop out and opened it while watching Ari help Nick's youngest build a sandcastle. Nick's oldest was off to the side of them, sunbathing. The only boy of the bunch was at the shore, skipping stones. Alex sipped the cherry soda. "This is nice."

Nick held out his bottle, and they bumped them together. "That it is."

"The kids warming up to you at all?"

"Parker keeps complaining about missing Disney World, and Ava's been throwing me snooty looks ever since I picked them up."

"I'm sure they'll chill. They're probably just testing you to see if everything your ex has been telling them is true."

"Maybe." Nick sipped his pop. "I'm beginning to wonder if

it'll take all week to win them over—and then they go right back into the enemy's hands."

Nick's phone rang for the fifth time since they'd arrived.

"You gonna get that?"

He shook his head. "I told the station I'm unreachable for the afternoon and as far as Corrine goes, I'm returning the favor. I let her know the kids got in safely, which is more than she deserves after everything she's pulled with me. She needs to leave me alone and let me have my time with the kids."

A group of middle school kids ran by, kicking sand onto them. They shouted and laughed loudly at each other.

"Ava!" called a skinny girl with a big afro.

Nick's oldest jumped up from her towel and ran over to the group, shrieking and hugging everyone. She followed the group down the beach, just barely in the line of sight without a word to her dad. The kids brought out a Frisbee.

"At least she's finally having some fun." Nick set his empty bottle down and opened bag of chips.

Alex nodded. "Looks like Ari and Hanna are, too."

"Ariana's so good with her."

"She can't wait to start babysitting. There's a babysitting certification course at the Y she's begging to take. I think it's only a matter of time before Valerie and Kenji cave."

"I've heard good things about it."

They sat in silence for a few minutes. Alex's mind wandered, and it only took a minute before he found himself mulling over Lottie's disappearance. "I know we're trying to get away from anything, but have you heard anything new on the case?"

Nick raked his hands through his hair. "There are some new missing homeless people, but nothing that points us to where the cult is, or any of the leaders."

"Maybe we need to go in and talk with them. Somebody has to know *something*. I can't believe that with all these missing people, no one else saw or heard anything."

Nick opened a pop can. "Have you ever considered becoming a cop?"

Alex gave him a double-take. "Me?"

"Yeah. You were the one who made the connection between Lottie and the Meriwether—though you shouldn't have gone there alone. Your detective work is impressive. We could use someone like you on the force."

"You don't want me."

"Why not?"

Alex shook his head in disbelief. He was an unemployed roofer with no education beyond barely graduating high school. It was a miracle that his own dad had hired him as an assistant.

"You were also a big help when Ari was missing."

"The only reason I've made any difference in either case is because I'm related to the missing people—I have the motivation. Why would you possibly want me as an officer? I haven't been to college. Heck, I still live with my parents." Alex looked down and ran his fingernail along the indents on the pop can.

"For one thing, you have street smarts. That can't be taught in a classroom. You also care—your blog proves that much. None of those people are related to you, but you're advocating for them."

Alex shrugged. "I guess."

"Think about it. I'd be proud to hire you."

"I don't have any experience."

"Well, obviously you'd have to go to the academy, but that doesn't take too long. A hundred bucks says you'd be the top student."

"Right." Alex snorted.

"Like I said, think about it."

"Thanks, but no thanks. I'm gonna go check on Ari." He got up and helped the two girls with the sandcastle. He gave it enough time for Nick to forget about Alex being a cop.

When he sat back down, Nick was on the phone. He ended the call and turned to Alex. "Tomorrow I'm going to drop the kids off with my mom. She's dying to see her grandkids."

"What are you going to do?"

Nick didn't answer right away. "I'm thinking about questioning Chester Woodran."

Alex's blood ran cold. "The psycho who kidnapped Macy? Why?"

"He's the only former cult member still in custody. There's a chance he knows something. I'd bet money they've been in contact with him."

"What makes you think he'd tell you anything?"

"If he's under the impression that it could reduce his sentence."

"Have you lost your mind?" Alex exclaimed. "He needs to rot in there after what he did!"

Ariana and Hanna turned and stared at them.

"It's okay," Nick called. "Keep working on that castle. I'm going to take pictures in a few minutes."

The girls turned back to their masterpiece.

Nick leaned closer to Alex. "I said Chester might talk if he was *under the impression* he could get out—he's in there with no chance of parole, remember."

"The dude has lawyers working on that, you know."

"I do know. They've also had no luck whatsoever—nor are they going to."

Alex scowled. "I don't like it."

"He's not getting out."

"What if he won't talk unless his sentence is actually reduced? Or he lawyers up? This could just make everything worse. If he *is* in contact with the others, he'll tell them you guys know they're behind the kidnappings. What if they hurt Lottie? Or decide to make Macy their next target? What then?" Alex clenched his fists.

There was no way it could end well if Nick paid Chester Woodran a visit.

Desperate

LOTTIE CRAWLED ALONG the wall, looking up and down. She'd made it all around the perimeter of the building and had made it back to her spot without finding any hope of escape. No loose boards, nowhere to dig out, no unlocked doors. They had been sealed inside.

Not that she was surprised. Or that she had any energy to try and get out. She collapsed onto the hard ground—hard because the dirt was only there for show. The actual floor was made with wood, sealed tightly against the walls. The soil was only there to get the prisoners covered in filth, and possibly to lessen their morale.

She closed her eyes. Everything ached. It had taken what remained of her energy to pull herself around the building. If there had been a means of escape, she'd have found it. Instead, she was more exhausted and sleepy than ever.

It had been hours since the guards had come in with breakfast—not allowing her any since she'd made a mess of her dinner the night before. What made that even more ironic was that the man who had told her that was the same one who'd kicked the soup from her grasp.

Lottie's mouth and throat cried out for something to drink. Her stomach had quit grumbling sometime over the night. She was still weak and in dire need of sustenance, but her body seemed to have given up hope that food would come anytime soon.

Tears welled in her eyes. She wasn't going to give into their mind games. They wanted her to give in and succumb to the community's rules and way of life. If it came down to it, she might pretend to slip into old roles but it would be nothing more than a farce so she could get some food and water. She would pretend to be just about anything at this point. If they asked her to pretend to be a house cat, she'd muster the strength and do just that.

Click.

Click.

Click.

Click.

Click.

The others turned toward the door. Lottie didn't so much as move her head. Instead, she focused on her tongue, which was stuck to the roof of her mouth.

Footsteps and masculine voices sounded. The aroma of soup wafted over.

Lottie's mouth watered, freeing her tongue. Her stomach tensed, but it didn't growl. She kept her eyes closed, having no interest in watching the others eat.

Something pressed against her back. "Sit up."

She tried, but nothing happened. Not even her eyes would open.

A hard shoe dug into her rib. "I said to get up."

Lottie pushed on the floor and tried to force herself up. Every muscle in her body ached. A sharp pain shot through her temples. Her eyes fought to stay closed. Finally, she made it to a sitting position and leaned against the wall for support.

"Look at me when I'm talking to you."

Her eyelids were as heavy as a car. She fought to open them. They fought against her.

A fist struck her cheek, the knuckles grazing her nose.

She managed to open her eyes. The man's face wasn't even a

foot away from hers. His bushy brows furrowed together as he stared at her.

"You'd hit an old woman?" she asked.

His face contorted. "You're no spring chicken, but you aren't old enough to be given the respect of the elderly, woman." He struck her again, making the back of her head hit the wall behind her. "And you know better than to speak to a brother without being given permission. Keep your trap shut."

Lottie used what energy she had to keep from telling him off. How had she ever lived under their ridiculous rules? And for so long, no less?

He held her gaze for a minute before twisting his face and spinning around to join the other men. They passed out bowls of soup to everyone other than Lottie—again.

One of the other men came by. He stopped in front of her, holding a single bowl.

Lottie's mouth watered and her stomach tried to growl but it failed miserably. She kept her gaze on his white shoes so as not to make eye contact and give him any indication of how badly she wanted the soup. Had she been younger and not depleted of energy, she may very well have reached for the bowl and tried to drink it before the man realized what had happened. As it was, she was certain her hands would be too slow and clumsy, and he would only slap them away—or worse.

"Look at me." His tone wasn't as harsh as the other man's.

Slowly, she brought her gaze up to meet his. He had kind blue eyes, sand-papery skin, and a salt-and-pepper short beard.

He held out the bowl. "Take it."

Lottie's heart skipped a beat. Was he really giving her a chance to eat, or was it nothing more than a cruel joke?

He nudged it forward.

She reached for it with both hands. The ceramic bowl was warm in her hands. Barely. She stared at it in disbelief.

"Hurry," he whispered and rose.

Lottie brought the bowl to her mouth and tipped it, allowing the miso soup to fill her mouth. She swallowed slowly, finding her stomach twisting. After having gone so long without food, she couldn't rush this.

Everyone else had already finished their soup. Lottie could only swallow a little at a time. She worried the men would take the bowl—or kick it from her—before she could empty it. Her stomach twisted tighter. She started to choke.

Lottie tried to cover the sounds. If the men heard her, they could take away the sustenance. Somehow she managed to regain control before anyone noticed. Well, not *anyone*. Sydney watched her, wide-eyed. The men were distracted in a huddle, whispering to one another.

Her eyes watering from the silent choking, Lottie continued sipping the soup until all that remained were a few tiny chunks of carrot.

The huddle broke apart and the men turned back toward the captives. Lottie tipped the bowl as high as it would go. The vegetable pieces fell into her mouth. She chewed on one slowly. The men made their way to the prisoners and gathered the bowls.

The man with the blue eyes took her bowl and gave a little nod. Though his kindness was small, it was enough to cause a lump in her throat.

Negotiation

NICK CHECKED HIS texts as he sat in the little room, waiting to speak to Chester Woodran. The tiny room wasn't all that different from some of the rooms at his station, but considering all the security he'd had to go through just to get there, it definitely *was* different. Chester was in the maximum security wing of the prison, housed with other mentally unstable criminals. The man deserved it—there was no doubt after all he'd done.

The door opened, and two officers came inside on either side of Woodran, who was clad in a dark orange jumpsuit and had chains connecting his wrists and ankles. His bald head shone in the bright florescent lights overhead, and his eyes narrowed as he glared at Nick through his thick glasses.

"Sit," ordered the officer on the left.

Chester did, but not without muttering something obscene. The officer on the right shoved him and then attached his cuffs to a bar on the tabletop. He turned to Nick. "Do you need anything before we leave?"

Nick leaned back against the chair, sitting tall. "All I need is Mr. Woodran."

"We'll be right outside the door if he gives you any trouble." The officer glared at Chester before they headed outside.

Nick and Chester stared each other down. His beard reached his chest and the man had gained some scars since Nick had last seen him. He also had a few light bruises around his eyes, and probably plenty hiding underneath his orange attire. People like him—people who abused and murdered women and children—didn't tend to fare well in prison, and more often than not, guards would turn a blind eye. Even after more than a decade of that, Chester still hadn't gotten what he deserved.

He wouldn't until he was dead. At least as far as Nick was concerned. Sure, he knew how frustrating married life could be. Even before the divorce, there had been plenty of times he'd wanted to inflict harm on Corrine, but he never did. In fact, he'd only raised his voice with her a handful of times. When he was angry enough to want to hit, he walked away and went to the gym. He worked out his feelings through weights or a punching bag until he could speak calmly.

Chester leaned over the table, pressing his arms against it. "Did you come to admire me?"

Nick folded his arms and kept his expression void. "You know it."

"Hate to tell you, but this is all you get. I don't kiss on a first date."

"How's prison life treating you?"

"Everyone loves me." He rubbed one of his bruises.

"Ever get any visitors?" Nick rested an elbow on the table and relaxed his pose.

"What's it to you?"

"Just making conversation."

Chester's expression tightened. "What do you want?"

"Just checking up on my old buddy."

"Right." Chester cracked his knuckles.

"Ever see your wife or kids?"

The prisoner flinched. Nick had hit a nerve. Chester's now-ex-wife had never once visited him, much less brought their twins in to see him—he'd never met them.

"No?"

"What's the point of this visit?"

"Like I said, just came to say hi. Am I your first visitor?"

Chester pressed his palms on the table. "And if you are?"

"I'm not."

"All you had to do was look at the visitor log, *officer*."

"Captain," Nick corrected.

"Whoop-de-do." Chester held out his forefinger and twirled it in a circle.

"Who came to give you a big kiss?"

"You'd know."

Nick shook his head. "Your friends used fake IDs, Woodran. The best of the best—even got through the doors of this maximum security prison."

Chester shrugged. "I had nothin' to do with that."

"You know who they really are."

"I know their true names, not their worldly names."

"Why'd they come to see you?"

"I'm one of the great prophets." Chester puffed out his chest.

"Did you prophesy your arrest?"

The prisoner's mouth formed a straight line.

"Guess not. So, your visitors are from the cult. Or does *everyone* have a 'true name'? What's mine?"

Chester tapped his nails on the table and arched his bushy brows.

"What did they tell you? That they're rebuilding?"

Something flickered in Chester's expression, but only for a split-second.

"Not feeling talkative, are we?"

Chester narrowed his eyes and his nostrils flared.

"What's it going to take to get you to open up? You don't kiss on a first date, so how about roses? That's what my ex always liked."

His eyes brightened like he was amused, but the man in chains didn't speak.

"How about your ex?"

Chester's eyes widened.

"Yes. I know about the divorce, ol' buddy. Would you like to talk with her?"

"We aren't divorced. I never signed those papers. Prophets never suffer dissolution."

"You must not be a prophet, then. It's legal."

Chester shook his head. His hands shook.

"The truth hurts."

"Worldly laws have no basis in reality. My marriage to Rebekah extends beyond this world. It's morally unbreakable."

"Try telling that to her husband."

His whole body went rigid. He didn't even blink.

"Woodran?" Nick tilted his head.

Chester made two fists. "Bring her in, and I'll tell you anything you want to know."

"Should I bring in the kids, too? What about her husband?"

He slammed his fists on the table. "I am her only husband and authority!"

Nick smirked.

"You don't believe me?" Chester leaned over the table as close to Nick as he could.

"Hey, it's not my place to judge."

"You've got that right." They stared each other down for a full minute before Chester spoke again. "Actually, I have a better idea, *officer*."

"Oh, yeah?" Nick asked, allowing his smile to show his amusement. "What's that?"

"Forget bringing her in. She won't come all the way over here. Transfer me into a lower security prison. Then I'll talk. Tell ya anything you want to know. Hell, I'll even throw the highest prophet under the bus if you want. Just get me outta here."

Nick paused. Why was Chester being so agreeable all of a sudden? "They have a low security area here. It'd be a snap to have you transferred." Actually, it wouldn't, but it was doubtful Chester knew that.

Chester crossed his arms and shook his head. "Nope. Transfer me closer to home. Somewhere near enough that Rebekah will actually visit."

Ah, so that was his angle. "Sure. I'll see what I can do." Nick pulled out his tablet and scribbled, pretending to write notes. In reality, he was actually watching Chester from the corner of his eye.

"Really? You can do that?"

"Well, a police captain could. Not sure an officer has that kind of pull."

Chester sighed. "All right, *Captain.* What do you want to know? I may need time to gather intel."

Nick held back a snort. Chester really was mentally disturbed if he thought Nick bought into his sudden willingness to team up. "Just trying to find out if the community is rebuilding legally. If they are, we can leave them alone, you know."

"I'll see what I can find."

"And I'll get you transferred to a minimal security prison closer to home."

Chester held up his right hand as high as the restraints would allow. Holding back an eye roll, Nick shook his hand. It was almost believable that the two had struck a deal—especially since Nick had no other choice except to push for the psycho's transfer. It wouldn't last. A minimal security unit would never put up with him. Chester would be back here so fast he'd get whiplash.

The trick would be getting the information out of him before that happened.

Remembering

MACY HANDED OUT the last flier and headed across the busy street to where Luke spoke with an elderly gentleman. Luke put his arm around her, thanked the man, and turned to Macy. "Any luck?"

She shook her head. "Maybe we're too far away from where everyone is being taken."

"The community could be anywhere. We've exhausted our town."

Macy nodded. "True. How many fliers do you have left?"

"None. I've been showing people pictures from my phone."

"Oh, that's a good idea. Do you want to keep talking to people or head back?" Macy rubbed her aching neck.

"I want to tell anyone who will listen, but you're probably tired."

"Exhausted." Pain squeezed her head from the top and radiated down.

Luke kissed the top of her head. "Let's get going. Do you want to stop somewhere to eat?"

She didn't realize until that moment just how hungry she was. "Yeah, actually."

"I saw a little Italian place near where we parked. Want to go there?"

"That sounds good."

Luke took her hand in his, and they headed for the car. Macy's head pounded, and the sounds of traffic only made it worse. Luke squeezed her hand. "Are you okay?"

"I have a headache. I'm sure eating will help."

"We'll go home and rest after dinner. Hopefully that'll help, too."

She nodded, feeling a little of the pressure lift. Just knowing he cared helped so much. They stopped at a crosswalk. She leaned her head against his shoulder. Luke was definitely her rock. He'd helped her through so many of life's challenges, and now he was being supportive of her even when his mom was missing.

The light changed and they crossed. The restaurant came into view. It was a small red building with white siding that looked like it had been a house before being transformed into a business.

By the time they were seated, Macy's head had begun to feel better. After she drank a glass of water and ate the complimentary bread, her head felt even better. Then, once her stomach was ready for ibuprofen, she reached into her purse for some.

As they looked over the menus, Luke told Macy about some of the people he'd given fliers to. Even with her headache getting better, it was hard to concentrate. She nodded along, trying her best to listen.

Just after they'd ordered, her phone rang. She groaned, not wanting to deal with anything else. She dug the phone out of her purse and saw that it was Alex.

"Hey, Alex. Is everything okay?"

"Unfortunately, I have bad news."

The headache squeezed harder. "What is it?"

"I just heard that Chester's ex-wife is missing. You've always said good things about her, so I thought you'd want to know."

The room spun around her. Macy nearly dropped the phone. "She… she…?"

Luke looked at her in concern.

"Macy?" Alex asked.

She handed Luke the phone. A flurry of emotions danced around inside. Her stomach twisted in knots. Luke asked questions into the phone in the background. Macy couldn't make sense of them.

The restaurant disappeared around her, and suddenly she was back at the community with Chester. Macy was scared that she'd never see her family again, especially inside the confines of a crazy cult. She sat, covered in a blanket, in the tiny electricity-free home, as Chester made a fire while telling Macy about Rebekah.

Chester had just dragged Macy into the community that day, and that evening, he was to marry a woman he'd never met—only exchanged letters with.

Macy's memories forwarded to the big meeting hall, where she and Chester stood in front of everyone with Jonah and his wife, Eve. Eve had spent most of the day drilling Macy on the community's rules. Jonah performed a strange ceremony welcoming Chester and Macy into the cult, and then asked for Rebekah to come up.

The woman who joined them was barely older than Macy, and turned out to be one of the sweetest people Macy had met. She and Luke were the two people who, more than anyone, had helped Macy adjust to the cult without losing her mind.

"Macy?" Luke's voice broke through her flashback. "Macy?"

She shook her head and blinked. Luke's face came into view, blurry at first but then clear.

"Are you okay?" His eyes were wide.

"I just… Rebekah, was she kidnapped? Or did she go willingly?"

Color drained from Luke's face. "Her husband heard her scream in the backyard where she was painting something. When he went outside, the can of paint had been knocked over and she was gone."

Macy felt like she was going to be sick. "What about her

twins?"

"They were at her parents' house."

Luke and Macy stared at each other. Macy's mind raced. "They're going to come after us, too. The leaders are taking everyone, aren't they?"

"It would appear so. I wouldn't think Teacher Rebekah would be on their hit list, though."

"I'm not surprised."

He arched a brow.

"Think about it. Everything that happened that night—it all comes back to me. According to them, she was my mother."

Luke nodded knowingly, worry in his eyes. "And responsible for your actions."

Tears blurred her vision. "It's all my fault."

"What? No, it's not."

Macy nodded. "It is. I was the one who wanted to escape, and look what happened. People were hurt—people *died*." She choked back a sob, the events of that night flashing before her eyes.

Luke put his hand on hers. "You didn't kill them. And besides, you were far from the only one who wanted to get out. You were the only one *brave* enough to try. I was waiting for a job that would let me outside the walls so I could run. That was my big plan."

She blinked her tears away. "At least your plan wouldn't have gotten anyone killed."

"How can you blame yourself? It was Jonah's idiotic rules that caused all of this."

Macy frowned. "If I wasn't stupid enough to get kidnapped in the first place, nobody would've gotten hurt."

"Then what? Jonah would've just kept running the community like a tyrant, and we never would've met."

She swallowed and held his gaze. It was true she couldn't imagine life without him—she loved him more than life itself. But at the same time, every day she regretted ever meeting Chester Woodran because of the emotional torment that followed her around. And without having been kidnapped, she never would've met Luke. It gutted her that she even considered taking back the one thing that had allowed her to meet Luke, but if it meant saving so many people such torment, she couldn't help but wish it.

Mistake

ALEX TAPPED HIS steering wheel and stared across the street at the abandoned buildings with broken out windows. Nick's warning to let the cops handle the case rang in his mind. Alex pushed it aside. Between Lottie's kidnapping and the distress Macy was dealing with, Alex couldn't just sit around and wait. No, he had to do something. Tonight, that meant talking with people at a homeless camp on the outskirts of town.

He checked his torn, greasy flannel and mud-stained jeans. Hopefully, it would be enough to fit in and put people at ease enough to tell him what they knew. He pulled down the visor and checked the mirror. For good measure, he ruffled his hair out and smeared the dirt he'd rubbed on in front of his house.

A loud crack sounded. Alex glanced around. Across the street, two men were punching each other. One threw the other against a large window that had once been a storefront.

It was almost enough to make Alex lose his nerve.

Alex got out of the car and took a deep breath. Sadly, his car looked like it belonged there. The only thing that made it stick out was that it had all its windows intact—and leaving it there might fix that by the time he came back.

He took a deep breath and headed across the street. A three-legged black cat ran in front of him and down the street.

"That's comforting." He jaunted across the street and headed for an alleyway. Conversation and scuffling sounded beyond it. He stepped over people passed out and held his breath at the strong odor of urine and defecation. It smelled so bad, he wanted to go back to the Meriwether so he could breathe fresher air.

As he exited the alleyway, the stench was covered by smoke from burning garbage.

He pressed himself against a wall and took in the sights, trying to figure out where he should start. For the most part, everyone was grouped together.

A group of three teenagers entered a building not far away. He followed them, keeping a good distance.

Alex walked inside, acting nonchalant. He scratched his chin—the dried mud really itched—and slowed his pace as the teens stopped at a long-dead escalator and sat on the steps, laughing and shoving each other. They reminded him of the kids he'd seen at the beach earlier. Aside from what had to be horrible life circumstances, they weren't really any different.

Without warning, a boy from the group jumped up and headed toward Alex.

He took a couple steps toward the kid. "Hey."

"Who're you?"

"I'm looking for someone."

The kid folded his arms. "You an undercover cop or somethin'?"

"Not even close. Just trying to find out what happened to a friend."

"I can't help you." He moved to the side.

Alex blocked him. "Maybe you can. Do you know any of the people who've gone missing?"

He glared at Alex. "People come and go around here all the time, dude."

"But are they usually *taken*?"

"I don't know what happens to people. They come, they go. It's not like anyone's tied down to a lease, ya know. Let me by. I have to whiz."

"Do you know a guy named Rory?"

The kid shook his head.

"How about—?"

"Nope." He unzipped his jeans.

Alex moved out of the way. The kid went to the nearest corner and peed. Alex turned away and sighed in frustration. But what had he expected? The first person to open up and tell him everything he needed to know? It was ridiculous, and he knew it.

He wandered through the former department store, still not finding anyone approachable. Near the back, he found a stairwell. Would he have any better luck upstairs? It was worth a shot. He headed up the stairs, avoiding sleepers and yellow puddles.

A skinny dude with four missing teeth sat up as Alex approached. "Got a smoke?"

"Nope. Do you know of anyone who's been kidnapped around here?"

"I do if you got weed or somethin' better."

"How about you tell me what I want to know, and I'll see what I can dig up."

"Right."

"I will. I just don't have anything on me."

"Hey, yo. Weed talks, or I walk."

Great. If Alex wanted information, he'd have to become a drug dealer. Assuming the guy even knew anything. "Forget it. *I'm* walking."

"Your loss, man. I know some guys who been up and kidnapped."

Alex waved at him and continued up the stairs. He'd take his chances on finding someone else. Upstairs, he found more groups of people, but they all eyed him wearily. One man even pulled out a dirty blade, making it clear he didn't want Alex around.

On his way downstairs, Alex avoided eye contact with the guy who wanted pot and rushed toward the door. Just before he made it out, fingers wrapped around his arm and squeezed, pulling him to a stop. The person attached to the hand was a tall muscular guy sporting a torn leather vest and two armfuls of tattoos, most of which appeared to be prison designs.

"Can I help you?" Alex stepped back and yanked his arm away.

"What you so curious about?"

"Nothing you can help with." Alex turned toward the door.

A fist collided with Alex's cheekbone, exploding his face in pain. Dots and colors danced before his eyes. He stumbled back and turned toward the jerk. Alex narrowed his eyes and punched him in the nose. Blood gushed out. His nostrils flared and he shoved Alex into the wall. "Nobody hits me!"

"I think I just did." Alex hit him in the eye and then bolted out of the building.

"Get back here!"

Alex tripped over a broken tricycle. He stumbled, but regained his balance before crashing into a guy who looked to be twice as fierce as the one already after him.

"Stop him!"

About a dozen people turned and stared at Alex. He swore and ran faster, digging into his pocket for his keys. He'd been smart enough to leave his car unlocked, but could he start it in time to get away?

Fingers grazed his back, but didn't grab onto him or his clothes. Swearing again, Alex forced his feet to move even faster. The moist ground didn't help, but he was ahead enough to keep from being caught.

He broke free of the alleyway and gasping for air, bolted for his car. He'd never been happier to see the beautiful beater. He flung open the door, jumped inside, and slammed it shut just as several ugly, burly guys reached it. Alex locked the door and stuck the key in the ignition. The men beat on the car. The back passenger window cracked. One man jumped on the trunk and wailed on the roof.

Heart thundering, Alex started the car and peeled away, not caring if he ran over any of them. They jumped out of the way just in time, all yelling and making obscene gestures.

Breakfast

NICK SAT ON the couch, typing on his laptop. Hanna snuggled next to him, holding a doll that looked like her and a new blanket his mom had given her the day before when Nick had made his road trip to visit Chester. Ava and Parker were both still sleeping, and would be for a few hours.

He kissed Hanna's head and turned to the television. She was watching a cartoon with colorful kid vampires at a fair with normal kids, all of them eating ice cream and cotton candy together. He turned back to his laptop, trying his best to type with Hanna leaning against his arm.

Nick read over his notes from the missing persons cases and then checked to see if there was any update on his request to transfer the prisoner to a closer, lower-security facility. He didn't expect any updates yet, but couldn't stop himself from checking every so often. Normally, it was doubtful that the transfer would be considered much less approved, but with the massive case of missing people, there was a possibility. Especially considering Chester's connection to everything. If he cooperated, it might prove to be the break they needed to crack the case.

After a while, Hanna sat up. "I'm hungry."

He set the laptop aside and smiled. "I have all the makings for chocolate chip pancakes."

"Oh, okay." Her voice was flat.

"You guys love those."

"Yeah, I guess."

"What's wrong?"

"Nothing."

"Hanna…"

She looked to the side. "Well, on Saturdays Dave usually makes us soufflés with whip cream and a special strawberry sauce."

Nick's eyes widened and the room seemed to shrink around them as her words settled in. He took a deep breath. "First of all, it's not Saturday. Today's Monday. Second, I'm not Dave. I'm your dad, and you guys have always loved my chocolate chip pancakes."

"Yeah."

"And lastly, does your mom have him living with you guys?" Their custody agreement had been clear about that point.

"No, but he visits a lot."

"Look at me."

Hanna turned to him.

"Are you sure?"

"Yeah. He visits a lot."

That was the same thing she'd just said—word for word. Nick's mouth curved down. "Did she tell you to say that?"

She reached for her doll. "I'm not so hungry anymore."

Nick let out a slow breath. He had to give it to Corrine—she was good. She'd managed to find many ways to ruin his little time with the kids from clear across the country. Little jabs here and there. Given Dave's job as a flight attendant, even if he did live there, it would be easy enough to convince Hanna that he was only visiting.

Hanna played with the doll's hair. "Sorry, Daddy."

He pulled her close. "You didn't do anything wrong. Nothing at all."

"You don't like it when we talk about Dave."

She was observant for being so young. "What I don't like is

that you guys live so far away."

"Mommy says you see us the same amount, but she's wrong. We saw you a lot more before we moved."

He kissed the top of her head and tried to ignore the lump forming in his throat. "I know, sweetie. I hate that."

"So do I."

They sat in silence for a few minutes while a new cartoon started. Nick sat back. "Do you want to help make the pancakes? You've always wanted to help pour in the chocolate chips. I think you might be ready now."

Her eyes lit up. "Really?"

"Yeah. Go wash your hands, and I'll get everything ready in the kitchen."

"Yay!" She set the doll aside and bounced toward the bathroom.

Hanna skipped into the kitchen just as Nick pulled the bag of chocolate chips out of the cupboard. Her eyes widened. "Are we going to put all of those in?"

"Probably not. There wouldn't be any room for the pancake batter."

She giggled. "That might be fun."

"I don't think it'd cook very well. We'll start with a cup of these. Maybe you can have a few extras while they cook since you're helping."

"Yummy!"

They laughed and had fun as they made the breakfast. Nick relaxed and enjoyed the moment, not letting anything interfere. At last, they had a tall stack of pancakes of varying sizes.

"Did I mention we have three kinds of syrup?"

Hanna's eyes widened. "No."

"Well, we do. And bacon. You don't like bacon, though, do you?"

"Yes!"

"Oh, we should probably make that, then."

"Yeah!"

Nick handed her a pancake while he cooked the bacon in the same pan they'd used for the pancakes. Just as they got the table set with everything, both Parker and Ava came out, rubbing their eyes.

"Have a seat." Nick waved at the table. "I'll grab the drinks. Do you want milk or juice?"

"Hot cocoa," Hanna squealed.

"I can do that. How about the two of you?"

"Coffee," Ava said.

"Yeah," Parker agreed. "Me, too."

"How about a round of hot chocolate?" Nick asked. "I'll have some, as well."

They grumbled, but sat. Nick was tempted to say something about them being too young to drink coffee, but knew it wouldn't do any good. He kept the conversation light and even got all three kids to laugh a few times. Maybe things were actually starting to turn around.

Once everyone was stuffed, Nick leaned back in his chair. "Why don't you get ready? We'll go to the Seattle Center, and you guys can go on any ride you want."

"For real?" Ava asked.

He nodded. "But you have to get ready."

She and Parker exchanged an excited glance, and they scrambled from the table.

After Nick had gotten the breakfast cleaned up, he checked his laptop for an update on the transfer. He froze, staring at the words in disbelief. It had been approved. It would be a while before anything happened, but it had been approved! Once Chester was settled into his new home, he would finally tell Nick what they needed to know—assuming they could keep the news of Rebekah's disappearance from him.

Update

JONAH STARED AT the future courtroom as if that could erect it faster. He took a deep breath, cursing the need to be patient. He'd always extolled the virtues of patience to his followers, but he much preferred other people reap its benefits. He wanted what he wanted right away.

Abraham came over and stood next to Jonah. "It's going to be a magnificent building, Great High Prophet."

Hopefully they would both be alive to see it when it finally completed. Jonah nodded. "It certainly will be. Any news?"

"Rebekah is going through the cleansing as we speak."

"Good. How polluted by the world has she become?"

"She married a non-member."

Jonah crossed his arms. "Chester isn't going to be pleased about that."

Abraham shrugged. "If you didn't marry them, it doesn't count. You married her and Chester."

"Right. Any update on him?"

"Isaac went out to speak with his contact. He's back and is going to talk to you as soon as he cleanses himself."

"Good. You really think he'll be able to pull any strings?"

"If anyone can, it's my son."

"He knows where to find me." Jonah stepped away and headed for his home. Along the way, the residents stopped to bow or kiss his hand.

One woman paused, still holding his hand. She stared into his eyes as though wanting to say something.

"Speak, sister Sapphira."

She smiled. "When does your lovely Eve return, kind Great High Prophet?"

He gave a friendly smile. "Not soon enough for my liking."

She squeezed his hand. "We all wish for your happiness."

Another man stopped after kissing Jonah's hand. "When will we have the privilege of hearing about your latest prophecies, Great High Prophet? Will we return to the nightly meetings soon?"

"Eventually, yes. It will take time, however, to return to the blissful state we enjoyed before we were persecuted by the world and ripped apart from our community."

"Understandably so, Great High Prophet. But it's to your good grace that we are on our way to returning. We will certainly be blessed for our persistence and perseverance—and none more than you."

"Thank you, Abel. It's much appreciated."

He nodded. "Blessed be."

"Blessed be." Jonah shook his hand and then managed to get to his home without running into anyone else. Once inside, he sat on his chair and took a deep breath. "Waiting will only make the payoff all the sweeter."

He imagined the courtroom and gallows built to their full glory. All they would need to do would be to hold the trial and execute everyone who had led to the breakup of the community. Then they could bask in their new, improved group, the majestic courthouse and blood-stained gallows a perpetual reminder to everyone of what happened when someone breaks the rules. They may get away with it for a while—but justice always avenges.

A knock sounded on the door.

Jonah closed his eyes and took a deep breath. "Who is it?"

"Isaac, Great High Prophet."

"Come in!" Jonah sat up tall in his chair and waited as the door opened.

The younger man, who was a spitting image of his father, came inside. "May I sit?"

"Of course."

He pulled a chair over and sat in front of Jonah.

"I hope you have good news."

The corners of Isaac's mouth twitched. "I do, Great High Prophet."

"Speak freely." Jonah waved his hands at Isaac.

"Thank you. I spoke with my friend, but there's a few things you need to know."

"Okay." Jonah stared at him and leaned forward.

"It's practically impossible to break anyone out of the prison Chester's in."

"Even from the inside? Come on."

"Would you like me to recount the security measures in place? I could bore you with the details, but it would take up too much of your valuable time."

Jonah leaned back. "You're convinced it's impossible?"

Isaac nodded. "It is. Especially where he's at."

"Splendid. Now what? I thought you said there's some good news."

"It's going to be tricky—dangerous, even. He's not going to risk it without having some benefit."

"Of course not. What does he want?"

"There's also the matter of what I want."

Jonah groaned. "What do you want?"

Isaac nodded. "A higher rank. I'm in the inner circle, but I don't get half the respect you and the others do. Grant me the power to discipline the lower members, and I can get Chester back for you."

Jonah narrowed his eyes.

"I can do it."

It felt like blackmail, and Jonah hated that. He cracked his knuckles. "How about this."

Isaac leaned forward, his eyes wide. "Yes?"

"If you bring Chester to me, you'll get everything you ask for."

"Thank you, Great High Prophet."

"But..."

The younger man's face paled. "But?"

"If you don't, you lose your place in the inner circle."

They stared at each other, Isaac's complexion continuing to lighten.

"Deal?"

Isaac swallowed. "Okay."

"Now, tell me the plan to free Chester from the impenetrable prison."

He cleared his throat. "Well, we're in luck. A policeman has played right into our plan by requesting Chester be transferred to a lower security prison."

"Good. How is he going to break out of that one?"

"He isn't." Isaac leaned back in his chair, his color returning.

Jonah arched a brow. "Don't leave me hanging like that."

"Chester isn't going to make it to the other jail. He's going to be broken out during the transfer."

A slow smile spread across Jonah's face. "I like it. Good work, Isaac. Should this work, you deserve your promotion."

Balance

ALEX GOT OFF the phone with Dad's editor and rubbed his temples. There was so much to do to help him get ready for his upcoming deadline, but there were things he wanted to do for his own blog, too. He was starting to generate more money with it, but he'd had next to no time to put into it. He really wanted to look more into the homeless camp—the people, not the place itself. That was one place Alex was more than happy to let the police deal with from here on out.

His phone rang. Alex answered without looking. "I told you he—"

"Alex, it's Nick."

"Oh, I thought you were someone else."

"You sound stressed. Want to take Ariana to the Seattle Center? The kids and I are getting ready to leave."

"I wish, but Ari's not on spring break this week and Dad's got a ton of work for me to do for his upcoming book."

"Right. I forgot she's in school this week. Oh, speaking of work, have you thought any more about the police academy?"

Alex held back a groan. "I'm not really sure it's for me."

"You have a knack for this stuff, I'm telling you. You really should consider it."

"Maybe."

Voices sounded in the background. "Hey, Alex, I've got to go. Think about the academy, okay?"

"Okay."

The call ended and Alex took a deep breath. His mind wandered back to the homeless camp and his close getaway. He probably would've had better luck if he'd gone in with someone else. Who knew? Maybe the police academy provided training that would help make trips like he'd made successful.

Alex shoved the thoughts aside and turned back to his laptop. There was a lot of data to enter for his dad. That was what he needed to focus on, not becoming a cop. He opened the two programs he needed and entered numbers back and forth until his vision turned blurry and his stomach was rumbling.

He went to the kitchen and warmed up some leftovers. Clementine walked in and rubbed against his legs as he got his food ready.

"Hey, kitty. You've got the life, huh? Eat, sleep, repeat. I could use some of that." Alex grabbed his food from the microwave and sat. Clementine followed him and stayed under the table, probably hoping for scraps.

Mom came in, rubbing her eyes. "Hey, honey."

Alex swallowed a mouthful of food. "Hi, Mom. How's work?"

"Tiring. I had a full schedule this morning." She scooped out some of the lasagna Alex had left on the counter.

"That's great. I'm glad your salon is doing so well."

"It's doing better than I anticipated. Dad and I are talking about me moving it from the garage to renting a place."

"Really? Wow. Where would you go?"

"I could either rent some office space and have my own salon, or I could join an established one, but I'm not sure I want to do that. I like being able to set my own hours."

"I don't blame you."

She came over and kissed his cheek. "And how about you? How's everything going as Dad's assistant?"

He cringed. "If I'm going to keep doing that, I really need a better title. That makes me feel like a secretary."

"*If* you're going to keep it up?" She arched a brow.

Alex shrugged.

"What do you have in mind?"

"Well, there's my blog—"

"That's how Dad got started." She beamed.

He nodded. "And Nick keeps bringing up the police academy."

Mom stared at him. "Really? You'd be interested in that?"

"I don't know. He seems to think I'd make a good cop."

"I've heard there's a shortage of officers."

"You have? Nick hasn't said anything."

"Maybe not here specifically, but statewide." She took her food from the microwave and sat next to him. "I agree with Nick, though. You'd make a great officer. And you'd look so handsome in the uniform."

"Mom."

"You would. Zoey would love that."

Alex sighed. That was another thing to consider—not Zoey liking the way he would look in uniform, but having a stable and respectable career.

Mom patted his arm. "You should think about it, honey. It would be a great opportunity, especially with the police captain backing you up."

"Maybe."

Alex's phone rang. This time it was Dad's publisher. He pressed ignore and put the phone in his pocket. He'd deal with it later.

Mom gave him a sympathetic smile. "It's always hard when Dad's so close to his deadline."

"I'll be fine." He got up and rinsed off his plate. "I'd better get back to work."

"Don't worry about leaving Dad hanging if you quit to pursue a different career. He could easily hire a virtual assistant, and it would cost him half of what he pays you. Don't let us hold you back. We want you to do what makes you happy. No hard feelings."

"Thanks, Mom." He meandered back to his room with Clementine on his heels, meowing. Alex stopped in the rec room and sat on the couch, his head spinning. He pushed aside thoughts of Dad's editor, publisher, publicist, and all the others.

His mind filled with memories—a lifetime's worth hid nestled in this room. Some of his earliest memories consisted of him and Macy playing with Zoey. They'd laughed, argued, and even fought. One of Alex's first real groundings had been after he had punched Zoey and given her a black eye for something catty she'd said to Macy.

Then there had been the magical and confusing—oh so confusing—moment he realized how deep his feelings were for the girl next door. The girl who was not only his sister's best friend, but two years older than him. And at twelve or thirteen, those two years may as well have been decades.

His heart sped up just thinking about it. He'd never forget that moment, staring at Zoey, filled with an array of emotions and realizing how beautiful and wonderful she was.

Somehow, despite everything they'd been through and all the years that had passed, he still felt exactly the same for her. He wanted to be the one to take care of her, to love her, and to tell her how beautiful she is. He'd almost lost her to Kellen, but now he had a chance. How many people got a second chance after blowing it with their one true love?

It had been six months since her engagement had broken off, and Alex hadn't done anything to try and win her over. What if someone else did, and he lost the opportunity again? He would never be able to live with himself.

Alex knew what he needed to do. He jumped up from the

couch, startling Clementine, who scampered to a corner. Alex ran to the stairs and down to Dad's office. He knocked on the closed door. "Dad, we need to talk!"

Terror

THE SMELL OF soup woke Lottie. She rubbed her eyes and then opened them. Her entire body ached from spending so much time on the floor. Her mouth watered when she saw a small piece of bread next to each bowl—again.

She already felt stronger since her last bowl of soup and piece of bread at breakfast. Though she had a long way to go before feeling her normal amount of energy, she was already leaps and bounds ahead of where she'd been before being served any food.

Lottie scooted herself to sitting and rested her head against the wall. The man with the piercing blue eyes squatted down in front of her. He held her gaze for a moment before holding out the small plate.

"Thank you," she whispered.

He gave a small nod and helped her balance the plate. His fingers brushed hers. The simple human contact startled her, and she nearly dropped the food.

"Easy there." He wrapped his hands around hers and looked back into her eyes. "You got it?"

Swallowing, she nodded.

"Hurry," he whispered, gave her hands a slight squeeze, and rose.

Lottie gasped for air, trying to understand what had just happened. The smell of the soup distracted her, and she brought the small bowl to her mouth and sipped. Delight ran through her when she saw several chunks of meat along with the typical vegetables. Even more sustenance.

The guards were gathered in a circle, whispering to each other. Lottie hoped they would give her enough time to finish her meal. Last time, the one in charge had yanked her piece of bread from her hand before she could eat the last few bites.

She ate as quickly as she could without choking on anything. Her stomach cried out for more, finally adjusting to having some food.

Just as she ate the last bite of the bread, the guards broke their circle and gathered the plates. The man with the blue eyes returned to her. He squeezed her hands again as he took the plate and bowl from her, then gave a quick nod before moving onto the next captive.

Lottie watched him, curious. He was just as big as the other guards, though older. Any of the other men could be his sons, not that they seemed to have an ounce of the caring that he did.

After they had gathered everything, they left, locking the door behind them. Lottie wouldn't give up hope that one day they would forget. She glanced around the room, trying to make eye contact with someone. But as usual, everyone kept their gazes averted.

She sighed and thought about the women and children at the shelter. She missed talking with them and wondered how they were doing. A couple ladies were trying hard to find a job, and one woman was considering going back to an abusive boyfriend. Lottie wished she could do more for them—especially now. Without her being a voice of reason, would Andrea return home, only to end up with another concussion and black eye?

There were so many people who needed her. Lottie *had* to find a way out. Now that she had more strength and her mind was less shaky, maybe she could find something she'd missed before.

She rose to her feet and shook her legs. They ached, and a cold feeling moved through them as the blood began to circulate after sitting so long. Her body sure wasn't what it used to be, and that concerned her about escaping. Jonah had so many young spry men working for him. What made her think she could outrun them? She probably couldn't, but she did stand a chance at outwitting them.

Lottie walked around the room. Most of the other prisoners ignored her, but a couple shot glares her way. They could waste away if they chose, but she wasn't going to let them bring her down. If there was a chance of escape, she wanted to find it.

She walked along the wall, trailing her fingertips over the rough wood. None of the boards were loose as far as she could tell, nor had they built a hidden door. That surprised her. She'd noticed when living in the community before that Jonah built one into nearly every building. She'd been sure it was so he could sneak in and spy on the residents.

Lottie paused near the door and shook her legs. The cold feeling grew stronger as blood flowed down toward her feet. A rhythmic noise sounded from outside. She pressed her ear against the edge of the door where just the tiniest space stood between the door and the wall.

The noise thundered like hammering. Sawing also sounded in the distance beyond the pounding.

Her chest constricted. Whatever it was, it couldn't be good news.

Click.

Click.

Click.

Click.

Click.

Lottie's heart skipped a beat and her mouth went dry. They were back already?

One of the other women cried out. Every prisoner had wide

eyes and paled skin. Terror gripped Lottie.

The two burliest guards entered, both holding black whips, separated into five parts with sharp pebbles tied along the leather. Dried blood covered both. The taller man whacked the handle of his whip against his palm and stared each prisoner in the eyes. Lottie's insides turned to mush when he met her gaze and glared at her with a hatred so strong she could feel it. Finally, he turned away and stepped forward.

"Jonah's had another vision. The devil is in one of you waiting to unleash his evil. Who is it? Who's housing him?"

Nobody made a sound.

"Going to make us beat it out of you?"

"You'd better speak up now, or the torment will be all the worse when we figure out who it is."

Lottie trembled. Should she say it was her? Then everyone else would be spared. She was already weak. The others could save their strength and perhaps find a way out.

"We're going to hand out extra lashes in about fifteen seconds." The guard struck the rocky whip against the wall, leaving deep grooves in the wood.

Lottie opened her mouth to speak.

One of the men jumped to his feet. "It's me. I let him in when I allowed myself to entertain rebellious thoughts."

The guard furrowed his brows. "You know the punishment for that, don't you?"

"Yes, sir." The prisoner nodded. Behind his back, his hands shook.

"Turn around!"

The prisoner obeyed. His expression tensed as he spun around. The other guard loosened the man's robe and it fell loose around his waist.

Lottie couldn't bear to watch. She looked down at the ground.

Someone grabbed her chin, squeezing hard enough to bruise,

and yanked her head to face him. "You will watch the beating, woman!"

Shaking, she obeyed.

The other guard pulled his arm back and struck the bare-backed prisoner. His skin offered no resistance as the whip and rocks sliced through with greater force than on the wall. Blood dripped from the long wounds.

After the third strike, the prisoner cried out. "The devil's gone! He fled!"

"Are you sure?"

"Yes!"

"You'd better be right. Face me, prisoner."

The wounded man turned, flinching with each movement.

"Will you entertain rebellious thoughts again?"

"No, sir."

"Good. Now all of you—keep this in mind! When you think wrong thoughts, you invite evil in. Then it will have to be beaten from you. Do you understand?"

"Yes, sir," everyone else replied.

Lottie was frozen in fear, unable to speak.

The guards left. Once the locks had clicked into place, the beaten man pulled his robe up in the front, leaving the back open, and took his place against the wall.

Gasping for air, Lottie tried to forget the inhumane beating. Escaping was going to be a lot harder than she'd thought.

Hopeless

LUKE ROLLED OVER in bed and pulled the pillow over his face to block the smells of bacon and coffee. He wanted neither. In fact, he didn't want to get out of bed at all. It had been ten days since they'd discovered Mom's disappearance. Ten days. Not only that, but it had been almost a week since anyone else had gone missing. No more clues at all had come in—they hadn't even found her car.

The news hadn't even mentioned her in a couple days and fliers were falling off poles. Basically, life was returning to normal for everyone else. Even he and Macy had to return to work the next day. Not that there was anywhere new for them to hand out fliers. They'd exhausted everything over the last week—including themselves.

The bed dipped down as Macy sat next to Luke. She pulled the pillow from his head. "Oh, you're awake already." She kissed his forehead. "Come and have some breakfast."

He shook his head. "I'm just going to stay here today."

"All day?" She frowned.

"What else is there to do?"

"You could eat."

He shook his head.

"I made bacon, eggs, and French toast."

Luke's traitorous stomach rumbled.

Macy kissed him again. "See? You need food."

"What's the point?"

Her face fell. Luke felt bad, but couldn't muster the energy to apologize. It was his last day off, and if he couldn't be out searching, he wanted to mourn—and that meant not getting out of bed for anything.

"Luke, talk to me."

He couldn't take the hurt in her eyes, so he turned away. "I just need to rest. We have to go back to life tomorrow and pretend like everything is hunky-dory."

She ran her fingers through his hair. "Do you want me to bring the food in here, babe?"

He turned to her. "Do you think they're feeding her?"

Macy swallowed. "You mean the community?"

"Of course I mean them," he snapped. "They're clearly the ones who took her, and they could be anywhere. Who knows what they're doing to her? Jonah's been locked away in prison all these years, and he's probably decided to take out his frustrations on her—a kindhearted old woman!"

They sat in silence.

"I think I need to be bait."

Macy's eyes widened. "Not this again. Please, Luke. Don't."

Luke sat up and glared at her. "The police would be there and—"

"No. Do you think your mom would want you doing that?"

They stared each other down. Deep down, he didn't want either of them going as bait. The moment Jonah felt it was a trap, he wouldn't hesitate to kill whoever played the bait. They had to find another way to locate the commune.

He wrapped his arms around her and pulled her into his lap. Tears stung his eyes, and before he knew it, the floodgates broke. Together they sobbed, clinging to each other. He ran his fingers through her hair and breathed in the fruity scent of her shampoo. She clung to him so tightly it nearly constricted his breathing.

Finally, she pulled away and they stared at each other. He pulled some hair away from her eyes.

She ran her fingertips along the stubble of his jawline. "I'll bring the breakfast in here for you."

"No, I'll get it."

Macy shook her head. "No, you're right. You need to rest today. Let me just take care of you."

He didn't have the energy to argue. "Thanks."

She brushed her lips across his and left the room. He leaned back against the pillow and rubbed his eyes. How were they ever going to get through this? What if they *never* found Mom?

Goodbye

HANNA CLUNG TO Nick. "I don't wanna go, Daddy!"

The little girl knew how to gut him like no other. He cleared his throat, trying to dissolve the lump growing there. "I don't want you to, either, but your mom misses you."

"She gets to see me all the time. Can't I stay longer?"

"I wish you could, but you have school tomorrow."

"When can I come back?"

"You guys will be back for a month in the summer."

"The summer?" Hanna exclaimed.

"Come on, Hanna," Ava said. "The lady's waiting for us."

Nick turned to the flight attendant who was going to walk the kids to the plane. "Can we have a minute?"

She smiled. "Take your time."

He knelt down and put Hanna on the floor. "How about we have a group hug? We haven't done that in a while."

Parker groaned. "In public? Come on, Dad."

Father and son stared at each other. They'd made some headway over the week, but as soon as they climbed into the Mustang to go to the airport, his defenses had shot back up.

"For your little sister?" Nick asked.

"Please, Parker," she begged.

Parker threw his head back. "Fine."

Ava groaned, but the four of them hugged. Nick wanted to hold onto them forever, and even though he knew that was impossible, the older two pulled away too quickly.

"See ya in a few months, Dad," Parker said.

"Yeah," Ava agreed.

"I'm going to call more—video calls—so we'll 'see' each other more. Also, I think I might fly out halfway through to visit you guys. Maybe when you have a long weekend or half-days or something. We'll make it count."

Hanna threw herself against him again.

The flight attendant stepped forward. "You guys are so sweet that I hate to break this up, but we really should head over to the plane."

Nick hugged each of the kids individually and told them how much he loved them. Even Ava and Parker whispered *I love yous* back.

As his kids walked away with the flight attendant, tears stung his eyes. It seemed like they'd just arrived, and really, he'd only just started making progress with the older ones. Hanna turned around and waved every few feet. Nick blinked back the tears, forced a smile, and waved back each time. Then they rounded a corner out of sight.

He waited after they disappeared from sight just in case they turned around and needed something. They didn't return. After about five minutes, he sighed and headed back to the parking garage. He picked up a strong black coffee on the way. He'd need it to get through the day at the station. The night before, he and the kids had stayed up late playing board games. It was the most they'd all laughed since they'd arrived.

Once he arrived at the station, everyone greeted him heartily. He forced cheerful greetings and then locked himself in his office, hoping to be left alone for a while. As expected, a large stack of papers waited for him. Luckily, he'd already worked through much of the email from home.

Nick sat and stared at his desk, his mind reeling from the

week. Part of him wanted to pack up and move across the country to see them more, but what would stop Corrine from moving them away again? It would be a perpetual game of cat-and-mouse. And besides, his aging parents were in town, and he couldn't leave them.

No, he would do like he told the kids. Call them more often to stay involved with their lives as much as possible and then he'd fly out and visit them when he could. He'd been avoiding that, not wanting to see Corrine, but that was a poor excuse. The kids needed their dad more than just a few times a year. Doubling that still wasn't enough, but it was better at least.

He finished off the coffee, threw the cup into the trash, and dug into the paperwork. It kept him busy for hours until his legs ached from sitting so long. He walked around the station, finally in the mood to catch up with people. Someone had brought in donuts, and though Nick usually avoided them, he took the biggest one—a cream-filled one with sprinkles. Hanna would've liked it.

After refueling, he went back to his office and checked on the status of Chester's transfer. It had still been pending when he'd checked that morning. He doubted anything had changed yet, but it was their only hope in a case that was growing colder every minute. He wanted to find and rescue each and every person from that cult.

The page took a moment to load, and then he skimmed the details. There were a few minor updates to the upcoming transfer—no date yet, but things were moving forward faster than expected. He might be able to speak with Chester in days or weeks rather than months!

Beautiful

KNOCK, KNOCK.

Jonah grumbled and then scribbled a few more furious notes onto his parchment paper. "Come in!"

The door opened slowly. He sighed. It had to be Abraham. He was one for a dramatic entrance.

Instead, Eve walked through the door.

Jonah's jaw nearly dropped to the desk. "Eve?"

She stepped inside and closed the door. Jonah's heart raced. He hadn't seen his first and primary wife in over ten years. She wore the same white garb as everyone else and had her hair in a tight bun like every other woman resident. Unlike anyone else, she didn't appear to have aged a bit.

"When did you get released from prison?" He rose and hurried over to her. Even close up, she looked exactly the same.

She reached behind her, removed the hair tie, and shook her head, causing her long black hair to fall freely down her back and over her shoulders. "I told everyone to keep it a secret so I could surprise you, dear husband."

His pulse raced through his body like an out-of-control locomotive. He ran his hands through her hair and pressed a palm on her cheek. She was real and she was there—exactly as he remembered her in every way possible. "How did you hold up? Did they treat you well?"

Eve stepped closer and pressed her soft lips on his. "It wasn't anything I couldn't handle. Persecution makes us stronger, right?"

"Yes." Jonah placed both hands on her soft hair and kissed her greedily. It wasn't until that moment he realized just how much he'd missed her all those years. He reached back and locked the door.

She pulled back. "The elders are expecting a meeting. They're gathering everyone now."

"They can wait." He pulled her over to the couch and looked her over again. "Did you find the fountain of youth? You haven't changed a bit."

Eve laughed. "I wish, darling husband. But I'm glad you feel that way."

"Oh, I do." He went around behind her and kissed her neck. The whole community could wait as far as he was concerned. His wife and best friend was finally back in his arms.

An hour later, a knock sounded. Jonah kissed Eve's neck and sighed dramatically. "The Great High Prophet's work is never done."

"No, it's not. We'd best not leave everyone waiting any longer." She rose and smiled at him.

Jonah walked over to the door. "Who is it?"

"Abraham, Great High Prophet."

"Eve and I will find you in the meeting hall momentarily."

"We need to discuss—"

"I *said* I'll see you in the meeting hall, Abraham."

"Yes, Great High Prophet."

Eve came over, patted Jonah's shoulder. "Let's not keep them waiting."

"They'll be fine. Those sheep will wait three hours for me if it takes me that long."

She kissed his cheek. "Everyone admires you deeply, but let's not take advantage of that. Besides, I'm eager to see everyone."

"Not quite everyone."

Eve nodded. "I hear Chester is still in prison."

"He'll be free soon enough. There are some we can't find and a few we're waiting on."

"Oh?" She arched a brow and pulled her hair back. "Who are we waiting for? This sounds interesting."

"We're leaving a couple community members for Chester to snatch personally. He requested to take them himself."

Eve nodded. "Chester's brat and Luke?"

"Correct. They even married, making it all the easier to take them together." They finished getting ready and headed outside. Jonah turned to her. "Have you toured our new community?"

"No. I told James to bring me straight to you."

Heat blazed through his body. "I want to bring you back in there and never come out."

She held his gaze. "Maybe we ought to have a second honey-moon, but really, our people are waiting for us. We should at least meet with them, and then we can have some time to ourselves."

"Wise as always." He took her hand and threaded his fingers through hers.

"Public display of affection?"

"I don't care." He led her in the direction of the gallows and courtroom. "And besides, everyone is in the meeting hall."

"Abraham told me it was that way." She tilted her head in the opposite direction.

"I have something to show you first."

"If you weren't our enlightened leader, I'd say you were naugh-ty."

"Call me whatever you'd like." They walked down a street lined with homes. Jonah led her through a few yards, taking a shortcut.

"Where are you taking me?"

"You'll see." They cut across a few more homes before finally coming to the fully-finished gallows. The tall wooden platform loomed in front of them like an angel from Heaven. The sun even shone down on it through the trees, giving it an effervescent glow.

Eve gasped but didn't say anything.

"Speechless, my dear? She's beautiful, isn't she? Almost as stunning as you."

"Are we really going to have enough executions to warrant *three* nooses?"

Jonah patted her hand. "We have so many people in our jail that it will take all day to get through them. In fact, I'm sure we'll need to take a lunch break."

She stared at it for a moment before turning to the half-built courtroom. The main beams towered over them, taller than the trees. The walls had yet to be built, but the seats and Jonah's massive judgment desk had already been built.

"Would you like to walk inside?" he asked.

"Let's see you behind the desk."

Jonah grinned and marched down the aisle, his chest puffed out as far as it would go. He stepped up to the platform and around the massive desk. A plank of wood was mounted to the structure, allowing Jonah to stand all the taller. Unfortunately, given his shorter stature, he needed every inch of boost he could get.

Once on the plank, he looked over the desk and to the empty, half-built courtroom. Eve sat front and center, her hands folded on her lap. She smiled at him and gave a little nod, encouraging him.

He picked up the gavel with his name engraved on the side and gave it a solid thunk on the desk. The sound was impressive, but not nearly as much as it would be with walls around to help it echo around the room. He pictured the scene—every bench packed with white robed people hanging on his every word.

Sentencing the executions was going to be glorious, simply glorious.

Newcomer

LOTTIE GLANCED PAST the three other women circled around her. The last five or six days had gone by in a blur as Lottie won over friendships with some of the other women.

She glanced behind them at the others. "I think some of them might suspect what we're doing."

Sydney frowned. "They should help us, then! Escaping is in all of our best interests."

"Not if they're worried about being whipped." Lottie shuddered. Every time she closed her eyes, the beating replayed in her mind and in her dreams.

"Or if they think they stand a chance in court," Sydney said.

"Against Jonah, who will be both judge and jury?" Kinsley shook her head. "Nobody's that stupid."

"We know that," Lottie said, "but they still might trust him."

"Even after he kidnapped us, locked us away, and tortured some of us—forcing the rest of us to watch?" Jayla crossed her arms and twisted her mouth in disgust. "If I'd had any respect left for that man, that would've changed my mind for sure."

Kinsley leaned forward and lowered her voice. "We need more people if we're going to attempt anything."

Lottie nodded. "And I'm afraid I won't be of much use with my hip acting up like it has been. If nothing else, I can serve as a distraction so you three can get out and back to your families."

"Are you kidding?" Sydney exclaimed. "No way are we leaving

you behind. You're the mastermind, and besides, I can't do that after all you've done for my family."

"How many more do we need?" Jayla asked. "Realistically?"

Lottie looked over at the rest of the group. With the new prisoners, they now had an even fifteen, but none of the other eleven seemed to have any interest in escaping. Most everyone else had paired off, and each couple stayed to themselves. "I'd say we need more than half of us—maybe nine? If we have to fight the guards, we don't want to risk the other prisoners turning on us."

"We have to more than double our group?" Kinsley's face fell. "We're never getting out."

"Sure we are," Lottie said. "As long as we stay positive."

"How's that supposed to help?" Kinsley stared at her.

"That's how we'll spot an opportunity and take advantage of it."

"I guess." Kinsley sighed, not looking convinced.

Click.

Lottie sat up taller, eyes wide. Her heart thundered against her chest, nearly breaking through her ribs.

Click.

It was too early for dinner, so that could only mean one thing. "Are they going to beat someone again?"

Click.

Sydney's face paled. "I don't know, but scatter!"

Click.

The four women split up, each scurrying to their own usual spot against the walls.

Click.

The door slid open slowly. Something crashed against the wall. Jayla exchanged a worried glance with Lottie.

Could it already be time for the trials to begin?

Lottie's stomach tightened. Her soup and bread from lunch threatened to make a reappearance.

The door flung the rest of the way open with gusto, hitting the wall. Two guards came in, pulling in a prisoner with a tight bun—another woman. Maybe Lottie and the others could get her to join their little group of soon-to-be escapees.

One guard grabbed the new prisoner around the neck, and she cried out. "That's what you get, you disgusting rebel."

She struggled against him. The other guard struck her across the face. Together, they shoved her against the nearest wall. She landed with a hard thud and crumpled to the ground.

Lottie could hardly tear her attention from the newcomer, curious who had been brought in after what she guessed to be more than a week since anyone had arrived. After a few moments, Lottie turned and exchanged curious glances with her friends.

The new girl still hadn't moved. Her head hung low in her lap, making it impossible to see her face. The white robe stuck out, also blocking the view.

One of the guards brought out a whip with tiny wires twisted around the straps.

Lottie gasped.

Sydney shot her a wide-eyed glare and shook her head.

The guards didn't seem to notice Lottie's lapse in judgment. The other one brought out a rocky whip and kicked the newest prisoner. "Look at me, woman!"

She rolled over, but her face was still blocked from view. Lottie's heart constricted, terrified to find out who it was and what the guards would do to her.

"Unlike the other evildoers, Jonah believes you have potential. Your sins must be beaten from you before you can return to your husband."

It took all of Lottie's self-control not to cry out and run to protect the poor woman.

"Now stand up and turn around!"

The newcomer rose, shaking and using a wall to balance. She

turned her back to him, facing the door, continuing to keep her identity hidden. The guard undid her robe. It fell, exposing her back. She grabbed the robe in front, holding it up to her chest. With the fabric sliding down, it revealed a tattoo on her arm.

"Physical pain brings spiritual blessings to those with good and decent souls."

Both guards raised their whips high into the air. Their backs were to Lottie and the other prisoners—that meant she could look away. Lottie played with a hangnail and tried to ignore the harsh whips lashing the woman, who cried and screamed.

Finally, silence.

"That'll teach you." The two guards stormed out of the room, slammed the door, and locked all five locks. The woman crumpled to the ground, burying her face into her arms.

Lottie exchanged worried glances with her friends, then crawled over to the injured woman and stopped a few inches away. She kept her gaze focused on the woman's head—she couldn't bear to look at her back. "Are you okay?"

She nodded, but didn't otherwise move.

"Do you want some help up?"

She shook her head, still not showing her face.

"Can we do anything to help you? Unfortunately, we don't have anything for your wounds."

She shook her head no again.

"Well, if you do decide to get up and move around, it helps to have friends here. There's a small group of us ladies, and we'd be happy to help you out as much as we can."

The woman sat up and stared at Lottie. Her eyes were red and splotchy and her skin pale, but Lottie would recognize her anywhere.

Rebekah. Chester's wife.

"What can you do to help me now?" Rebekah asked.

Lottie's heart thundered against her chest. She couldn't find her voice.

"Exactly what I thought." She lowered her head again.

Lottie tried to find words, but they wouldn't come. Too many questions filled her mind. Did they have Chester? Were they going after Luke and Macy? After a moment, she cleared her throat. "Well, if you want to talk, I'll be over there."

Rebekah didn't respond.

"Okay, then. Whenever you're ready." Lottie rose and went back to her typical spot against the wall and studied Rebekah, who didn't budge. Jayla, Kinsley, and Sydney all exchanged glances with her—all wanting to know who'd just arrived. Lottie mouthed, "Rebekah."

The same shock and concern raging through Lottie registered on each of their faces.

Decision

ALEX CLOSED HIS laptop and pushed the chair away from the desk. He'd been staring at the screen too long and a headache was starting to form. He squeezed the bridge of his nose and closed his eyes.

It had been about a week since he'd told Dad about the idea to join the academy. He'd taken it better than Alex had expected—telling him to do what was best for him. He'd even brought up hiring a virtual assistant, just like Mom had mentioned.

Dad's support had been a weight off Alex's chest, but he hadn't made a decision yet. He needed to decide either way. His dad had asked him about it a couple times, but now that Alex felt free to make the decision he was torn. It was a huge life change with the potential to change everything.

He might be able to finally win Zoey over and give her all the good things she deserved. But what if she didn't want a relationship with a cop? He might have to work odd hours or weekends. She might worry about him. It seemed like every day he heard about a cop somewhere being shot or knifed.

His heart sped up with excitement. Being an officer would certainly be more exciting than being Dad's assistant. He could actually help people. Kind of like with his blog, but out there in the real world. Every day would be a new adventure. Maybe he'd help a lost kid find his parents one day and then the next find a clue that would lead to solving a huge murder investigation.

The more he thought about it, the more he realized what he actually wanted to do. He chuckled to himself at the irony of it. He—Alex Mercer, the lifelong screw-up—was going to become a cop. Upholder of justice. Defender of the defenseless. The face of the law. Okay, that was probably going a little too far, but it was still the last profession he'd ever expected to consider. But like Nick had said, he *did* have street smarts—not like stunts at the homeless camp did much to prove that. Stuff like that only showed why Alex would be the last one anyone would expect to become a policeman.

Then again, maybe joining the force was just what *he* needed. The discipline it would require could be a great way to put his creative energy to good use. He could still do things like go to homeless camps to question potential criminals, but he'd have to do it legally, keeping him from making stupid decisions like he was prone to making, if he was completely honest with himself.

Alex sniffed the air. Chocolate chip cookies? That could only mean one thing—Ariana had to be over. He jumped up from the chair and rushed to the kitchen. Sure enough, she and Mom stood in front of the oven wearing aprons. Mom wore a red one with lip prints that read *Kiss the Cook* across the front, and Ari wore a pink polka-dotted one with white lace.

"Daddy!" She dropped the spatula on the counter and ran over to him.

Alex wrapped his arms around her and kissed the top of her head. "How long have you been here?"

She shrugged. "Long enough to make cookies."

"Next time let me know when you get here." He ruffled her hair. "Can we eat the cookies?"

"They're hot," Mom said. "We just pulled them from the oven."

"So, that's a yes?" Alex winked at Ari.

She giggled.

Alex grabbed a cookie. It burned his finger, and he bounced it back and forth between his hands.

"I'll get the milk." Ariana ran to the fridge.

He stuck the cookie in his mouth, grabbed a plate, and started piling the cookies on.

"You could use a spatula, you know." Mom arched a brow.

"Real men use their hands. Ow."

Mom shook her head. "If I didn't know any better, I'd think you were still twelve."

He shrugged and brought the plate to the table. They sat and ate cookies with the milk while Ariana talked about a science project she was working on.

The timer beeped. Mom set her glass down. "I'll get those."

A whiff of chocolate chip cookies blew on them as the oven opened.

Ari turned to Alex. "So, when are we going to do something with Mom again? It's been so long since the three of us did something together. Why?"

He took a deep breath. That was a really good question, and he didn't have an answer. "I'm not sure, but we'll definitely have to make that happen."

Ari bit into a cookie and sighed, looking deep in thought.

"What are you thinking about?" Alex asked.

She turned to him. "I just wish Mom was here."

"I think she's busy with work."

"She's at lunch with Casey."

Alex froze mid-bite. Was Casey a dude or a lady? "Who's Casey?"

She shrugged. "A friend. From work, I think. I'm not really sure."

"That's nice." Alex bit slowly into the cookie, trying to act casual. What if Casey was a guy? And worse, what if he was potentially more than a friend?

Alex needed to pull himself together, and fast. He whipped his phone out from his pocket and found the browser app.

"What'cha doin'?" Ari leaned closer, trying to see the screen.

Mom glanced over, her eyebrows raised.

"I'm going to sign up for the police academy."

Shock

NICK ROLLED OUT of bed, his head in a fog. His body cried out for more sleep, but he was determined to make it to the gym before heading into the station. He'd stayed up late video-chatting with the kids. Parker had been so excited to tell him about landing a lead in the school play, and Nick hadn't wanted to interrupt him.

The daily calls after dropping the kids off had really helped to build on the progress he'd made while they had been visiting. Ava had even opened up to him about a guy she thought was hot. Nick knew she was testing him, so he'd just smiled and told her that was great. Anything to keep her talking to him.

He stretched, pulled on some sweats and a V-neck, and then headed into the kitchen for an energy drink. "Breakfast of champions." Once that was empty, he headed for the condo's gym and worked out until he was dripping sweat.

It felt good to get some cardio in after so long. The last week he'd buried himself in work, barely giving himself enough time to eat and sleep.

Once back at his place, he noticed a missed call from Alex. He probably had more questions about the academy. Alex had been calling him daily, wanting to know this or that since he'd signed up for the next session. Nick would call him back later. He needed to get into the station after a quick shower.

Before leaving, Nick sat on the couch with his laptop to check

Chester's transfer. Every morning and night, he looked for an update. Each time, he walked away disappointed. It had been nine days since the transfer had been approved, but who was counting?

He was losing hope for finding Lottie and the others. It had been three weeks since the disappearances started, and there had been no new ones in quite some time. Nick had gone to visit Chester the week before, hoping that the news of moving to a new prison would get the lowlife talking, but he'd just sat there with his arms folded and a smug grin on his ugly face. The jerk wasn't going to tell Nick a thing until he was sitting in a lower-security facility.

Finally, the page loaded. Nick nearly dropped his laptop. It bounced off his lap, heading straight for the floor. He grabbed it and stared at the screen. His mouth dropped open and his pulse raged through his body.

Chester's transfer had been *scheduled.* It was actually going to happen—but that wasn't the surprising part.

He was scheduled to move that afternoon. In a matter of hours.

Nick squinted at the words, making sure he had read them right. He had. The notorious kidnapper and murderer who held the key to potentially solving the huge missing persons case was getting his transfer that day.

If Nick played his cards right, he could possibly talk with the slime ball that very day. It was unlikely with all the paperwork and red tape, but it wouldn't stop him from trying. They had over a dozen missing people! That was more important than anything else.

He closed the laptop and threw all his things into a bag. This would be a busy day, and hopefully the day he finally learned what Chester knew about the cult who had taken all those people.

Realization

"YOU WANT TO join us for lunch?" Lucy smiled at Macy from the doorway. "We're going to that Mexican place off Roosevelt Way."

Macy's stomach turned at the thought of one of her favorite restaurants. "Thanks, but not this time."

"Oh, why not?" Lucy frowned.

She tapped her pen on her desk. "I have a lot of paperwork to catch up on."

"Are you sure?"

"Next time." Macy forced a smile. "I might be coming down with that stomach thing going around. I don't think the food would sit right with me today."

Lucy took a step back. "I don't want to get that. If you need to leave early, feel free."

"Thanks. I might just do that."

"Hope you feel better." Lucy gave a little wave and left, closing the door behind her.

Macy yawned as fatigue squeezed her. Was she actually coming down with something, or was it all the stress she'd been under? In two days it would be Thursday—three weeks since she and Luke realized Lottie was missing. Three weeks Jonah and the other leaders had probably been torturing her, if they'd let her live that long.

Macy's throat squeezed at the thought. Maybe she had her

dates wrong. She flipped through her day planner and counted. Nope. Not wrong. Thursday would be three weeks. The time had gone by in a massive blur, both feeling like it had been much longer than it really was *and* feeling like it had just happened yesterday.

She let go of the pages, letting them fall as they did. A wave of nausea ran through her. From stress or a stomach bug? She glanced down at the planner, which had fallen to the previous week.

Macy froze, staring at her note for that Thursday. Her period should have started that day. She did the math. Five days earlier.

Stress could cause a delayed menstruation, right?

What if her nausea and lack of appetite had nothing to do with either stress or a bug?

Could that even be possible? She and Luke had barely done anything other than snuggle the last few weeks. They'd been under so much turmoil from Lottie's disappearance.

Her head snapped up. There had been that one night they'd gotten romantic. When had that been? She closed her eyes and tried to remember the events of that day. That was when they had gone to the station to identify the missing community members. Then she and Luke had gone home and reconnected. She flipped through pages again.

Sixteen days earlier. The room spun around her. How could this happen now, of all times? They'd been trying when things had been good and nothing had happened. But when they were both stressed out to the max, *then* they'd accomplished it?

Unless she was wrong. Maybe it really was just stress. Either way, she needed to let Luke know what was going on.

She picked up her phone and pressed the button. The screen remained black. She pressed three more times. Then she remembered seeing the low battery warning earlier, but she hadn't been able to plug it in then. It was dead now.

Macy reached for her office phone, but then realized she didn't have Luke's number written anywhere. It was in her phone.

That was probably for the best. She shouldn't give Luke any unnecessary stress—what if she wasn't pregnant? Macy needed to run to the drugstore and grab a test. If—and only if—it was positive, then she'd tell Luke.

She set the phone next to the charger and grabbed her purse. Everything spun around her again. She took several deep breaths and then headed for her car. Her mind raced out of control on the short drive to the store.

After paying for the test, she hurried into the public bathroom not wanting to wait until she got back to the office, or worse, home.

The three minutes in the stall seemed to last an eternity and a half. Time had never moved so slowly while she waited with the stick behind her back.

Finally, she brought it in front of her. Two blue lines formed a cross—no, a plus. It was positive. She and Luke were going to have a baby. At the worst possible time.

The ground seemed to wobble underneath her. Macy pressed her arms against the sides of the stall and took deep breaths until her legs were steady again. Dizziness swept through her.

She needed to call Luke. Macy slid the test back into the box and dug around her purse, unable to find her phone. Right. It was sitting on her desk, still dead. She needed to get back to the office and charge it since she'd forgotten before. Then she could call Luke as soon as it had enough energy to turn back on.

The drive back to the clinic went by in a bigger blur than the drive to the store. She parked in her normal spot, stumbled into her office, and dropped her purse on the floor behind her desk. She reached for the phone, but knocked it onto the ground.

What she really needed was a quick nap. She closed her door and the blinds before crashing onto the couch. Her heavy eyelids closed, allowing her to fall into a deep sleep.

Allies

LOTTIE LOOKED AROUND the circle. Now they had eight in the group, and they still agreed they needed at least nine. They had one of the men and all the women prisoners except Rebekah, who sat not far away watching them from the corner of her eye. Days had passed before Rebekah had moved from the spot where she'd been thrown by the guards. She'd been slowly creeping closer.

One of these days, she would have to make the choice to join. Either that, or she'd have to stop scooting their way. Whichever she chose, she'd have to decide soon. They'd been in there for weeks, some claiming more than a month.

The noises from the construction had dwindled in the last couple days. That could only mean one thing. Soon, the trials would begin. Any escape plan would have to be made before then.

Jayla leaned closer to Lottie. "What if we don't get nine? Is eight enough?"

Lottie glanced around, making eye contact with each of them. "What do you think?"

"We might have to," Thomas, the one guy in the circle, said.

"You can't convince any of the other men to join us?" Sydney asked.

He shook his head. "I've tried. They already think I'm nuts."

"Don't they want to get away?" Kinsley asked.

"We can't tell them that's our plan until after they join us,"

Lottie said. "What if they try to stop us?"

"They might, anyway," Kinsley said.

"But if they know what we're doing, they might want to help," Sydney replied.

Lottie glanced back over at Rebekah, who seemed to have scooted closer again. "They might also join us when they see us trying to make our escape. But that's not a risk we can—"

Click.

Click.

Without a word, everyone scrambled to their places against the wall. Rebekah even moved to a different spot than where she'd been sitting.

Click.

Click.

Click.

Lottie's heart thundered against her chest. She prayed the guards were bringing food and not whips. Beads of sweat broke out along her hairline. It was only a matter of time before she fell victim to a harsh beating.

The door opened, and the guards came in with the trays of food. The smell of the soup wafted over. Lottie was grateful for it—the meager nourishment was what had allowed her to slowly build her strength back up—but at the same time, she really wanted something else to eat. Sure, there were worse things to complain about—the impending trial would lead to their certain deaths, for starters—but eating the same meal three times a day for weeks on end was no easy task. Sometimes it was hard to choke down simply because of the constant repetition.

As the man with the kind blue eyes made his way over, Lottie's stomach turned. At first, she couldn't get enough of the soup and bread. Now she'd almost be willing to eat dirt just for a little variety. That was probably part of Jonah's plan to wear them down and make them more agreeable.

Blue Eyes stopped in front of Lottie and handed her the bowl. His fingers lingered on hers for a moment before letting go. He was sending her some kind of message, but she didn't know what exactly. He glanced around and then spoke in a low voice. "I managed to get extras in your soup this time." He handed her a piece of bread, stood up, and went back to the other guards.

Lottie brought the bowl closer. It was filled with chicken and vegetables. Her mouth watered at the sight. She sipped and took in as much food as possible. If she took too long to eat, the other guards would force her to give the uneaten food back before she could finish. By the time she'd scarfed it all down, she was stuffed. With all the extras, it was about twice as much as she had grown used to eating.

When the guards gathered the empty bowls, Blue Eyes came to her first instead of last. He wrapped both hands around hers and stared into her eyes with a striking intensity. He glanced around and then leaned close and whispered, "I'm working on a way to get you out."

Lottie's eyes widened.

"It's going to take a few more days," he continued. "Jonah has this place—everything in the community—sealed tight. Just don't give up hope."

She nodded, her heart thundering. Part of her wanted to tell him she was working on something too, but she couldn't get her mouth to get on board.

He took the bowl and quickly gathered the others. As he walked back to the other guards, he glanced over at her and gave a slight nod. She blinked twice in response, fearing that even a nod would give away the fact that he was trying to help her. They left quickly, with none of the other guards noticing Blue Eyes giving her any attention.

Lottie kept her gaze averted, not wanting to circle up just yet. She was trying to make sense of what she'd just been told. What was he doing? How did he think he could manage to get her out? What about the others? She didn't want to leave them behind—she couldn't. It wouldn't be right. If anyone should leave, it should be one of the others. Most of them had children at home. Lottie had been given her time with Luke, and now had Macy as a second child.

Sydney, Jayla, Rebekah, and some of the others were the ones who needed to have priority. Not only because of their young children, but because they also stood a better chance of escape. They were young and nimble, whereas Lottie had a lot of aches and pains that could easily hold her up.

Sighing, she pressed her ear to the wall.

Silence. The construction had stopped.

If the courtroom was completed, that meant only one thing.

The trials would start soon. And they would bring worse terrors than any beating.

Anger

"DON'T FORGET TO carry the five." Alex pointed to Ariana's math problem. "Try the next ones on your own, okay? I'll be right back."

She sighed. "This is so *hard*."

He ruffled her hair. "You can do it."

Ari scrunched her face. "We'll see about that."

"Want to make a bet?"

She shook her head.

"Five cookies say you can do the whole row before I come back."

Her eyes lit up and then fell. "You don't have five cookies."

"Clearly, you haven't found my secret stash."

"You have a secret stash?"

Alex whistled and gave her his most innocent expression. "Maybe. Wanna make that wager?"

She stared at her sheet and then back up at Alex. "What happens if I don't get them right?"

"That's not going to happen, so don't worry about it. Get to work." He winked and then headed to his room and returned Nick's call. "What's up?"

"You might want to sit down," Nick said. "Wait, you're not driving, are you?"

"No." Alex sat on his unmade bed. "What's so urgent that you wanted me to call right away, and now sit for?"

"I thought you should know that Chester is in the process of being transferred as we speak."

"Say what? Now?"

"Yes. It's good news, Alex. He's agreed to tell us what he knows about the cult once he's in a prison closer to his family."

"And closer to Macy." Alex's voice was practically a growl.

"He's not going to escape the prison, Alex. It may be lower security than the one he's leaving, but it's still secure. Nobody has ever escaped from there."

A tight knot twisted Alex's stomach, and along with it, a cutting feeling like something was really wrong—or would go wrong. "I don't see how you can do this to Macy. She's already having setbacks because of Lottie's disappearance. I can't imagine what having her kidnapper closer to home will do to her."

"If it helps us find Lottie, I'm sure she'll be glad."

"Then what?" Alex demanded. "Do you send him back to the prison he deserves to be in?"

"That'll depend on him."

"What do you mean?"

"If he acts up, the warden won't hesitate to send him back. He has a reputation for not putting up with anything. The man runs a tight ship, and he's proud of that fact."

"You'd better be right."

"I am," Nick assured him. "Chester Woodran is not getting out of that prison. You have my word."

Alex suddenly felt like Ariana wanting reassurance that she could do the math problems—only this bet had far graver consequences than long division. And the sinking feeling in the pit of his stomach didn't help ease his worries.

"I've got to go, Alex. I'll let you know when Chester's there."

"Just for the record—I have a bad feeling about this. It's not just that I hate the idea. I really and truly feel like this isn't going to end well. We're all going to regret this decision."

"Thanks for the vote of confidence. You'll be singing a different tune once we have a lead that directs us to the cult's new location."

"I'll believe it when I see it. Call me."

"Will do." The call ended.

Alex swore. He wished he could believe his friend, but the gnawing feeling in his gut only grew worse. He'd long ago learned to trust that instinct. *Something* was going to go terribly wrong. If Chester didn't escape the lower-security prison, then something else would happen. Alex would've staked his life on it.

He got up and paced, his mind racing. Macy. He needed to call her. She deserved to know what was going on.

Alex grabbed his phone and called his sister. It went straight to voicemail. Alex swore again. He ended the call and redialed. Straight to voicemail.

"Answer, would you!" He called her again. Voicemail. Alex released a string of profanities as he gave it one last go. He got her message again. This time, he waited for the beep. "Macy, listen to me. This is important. Like, seriously the most important thing I've ever said to you. Do not, I repeat, do *not* go anywhere alone. Chester's being transferred as we speak. That psychotic cult is already after you—we know that—but I'm extra worried now. This might be a sign for them to act. I don't know. They're not going to let Chester talk, or if he does, they're going to be furious. Just be careful. Please."

He ended the call and paced some more, pulling on his hair. There had to be something he could do. Leaving a message wasn't good enough.

Luke. He had to call him. Maybe he knew where Macy was. She might even be with him.

Alex called his brother-in-law.

"Is everything okay, Alex?"

"No. Is Macy with you?"

"She's at work. I'm at work. So, no. Why?"

"I can't reach her."

"What's going on?" Luke demanded. "You're worrying me."

"Chester's being transferred to a closer and less secure prison *right now.*"

"What?"

"Exactly."

Silence screamed between them.

"Does Macy know?" Luke finally asked.

"Her phone is going straight to voicemail!"

"Let me try. Then I'll get back to you."

"Thanks." Alex ended the call.

Knock, knock. Knockety-knock.

He took a deep breath and opened the door. Ariana stood there, smiling with pride.

Alex shoved aside his worry and anger and forced a smile. "Did you complete the problems?"

"Yeah. I double-checked the answers. I think you owe me five cookies."

He pulled her close and held her tight.

Unfolding

JONAH REPOSITIONED HIMSELF behind the large, prickly bush and turned to Isaac, who now wore all-black, including a mask only providing small holes for the eyes. Jonah adjusted his own mask. "When is the truck supposed to be here?"

"Could be five minutes, could be thirty."

"Great." Jonah glared at him. "Where's the truck that's supposed to cause the accident?"

"Like I told you, waiting at the convenience store down the road, listening to the scanner *and* waiting for the call. If one fails, the other won't. Our bases are covered."

The unusually hot May sun beat down on them. "You couldn't have picked a shadier location?"

Isaac's face contorted like he wanted to snap at Jonah. "You could've waited back at the community. In fact, you still can go back."

"I'm not missing this. My newest upcoming high prophet is about to rejoin us."

Isaac nodded and then rose, glancing at the road beyond the bushes. He remained standing.

"Do you see something?" Jonah rose and peeked. The street was empty, but a low rumbling sounded in the distance. He arched a brow at Isaac.

The younger prophet gave a slight nod. The noise grew louder, causing the ground to vibrate slightly.

Excitement radiated through Jonah, starting from his belly. It was about to happen. He would get to witness the accident and then help free his second-hand man.

The rumbling finally gave way to the sight of the armored transport vehicle. It was still far off, appearing smaller than Jonah's fist.

From the other direction, the sounds of multiple engines roared to life. A black van pulled out of the parking lot of the convenience store followed by a large, blue pickup truck and a gray van. If the first vehicle wasn't enough to stop the transport, they had backup.

"It's really about to happen."

"Remember, stay back unless they call us over."

Jonah ignored him and watched as all the vehicles seemed to move in slow motion. He wanted to shout for them all to hurry. *Patience.* They hadn't made it this far by being rash. Before he knew it, they'd be heading back to the community with the last freed prophet.

"Down." Isaac squatted behind the plant.

Groaning, Jonah joined him. He moved aside branches and looked down both directions, though the vibrating ground told him all the vehicles were near.

"It's going to be loud," Isaac said.

"That much I expect."

The transport van was almost directly in front of them, and the other three were nearly there, also. With a sudden jerk, the black van crossed the center line. The transport van swerved and honked. Burning rubber filled the air as it skidded across the concrete. Metal crunched as the two vehicles collided.

The two remaining cars also crossed the line, skidding to a stop. More crunching sounded as the pickup collided into the wreck. Gunfire sounded, and the front window of the armored van deformed but didn't shatter. Two gun-bearing guards came out.

One aimed his weapon at the other and shot him in the neck.

"Now!" someone yelled.

Isaac grabbed Jonah's arm and yanked. "Come on!"

Jonah scurried to his feet. Everything was a blur of yelling and people running around. The guard that had shot the other ran around to the back of the vehicle. By the time Jonah got there, the guard was already unlocking Chester's chains.

Once free, Chester ran over and jumped onto the concrete. "I'm a free man."

The guard turned to Isaac. "Someone needs to beat me."

"What?" Isaac stared at his friend like he was crazy.

"The only way I'll be able to convince them I wasn't part of this is if I'm in bad shape."

Chester turned to him. "I'll be more than happy to help."

The guard grimaced. "At least we'll know it'll look convincing. Make sure I'm still conscious." He stared Chester down. "I still have to disengage the cameras and destroy the recordings. They're already on their way, so hurry."

"My pleasure." Chester rolled up his sleeves and stared at the guard with hungry eyes before punching him across the face. Blood spattered on the van. He hit him on the other side, then shoved him into the side of the door and wailed on his chest.

"Remember he needs to live," Jonah reminded the newly-freed prisoner.

"Fine." Chester squeezed the guard's arms and threw him on the ground next to the road. He slid backward on the dirt and rocks. Part of his uniform tore, and the whole thing was covered in dirt and dust.

Sirens sounded in the distance.

"Run!" The guard pulled himself up. "I need to get the cameras."

"You already disconnected them from being online, right?" Isaac asked.

"Yes. Go!"

Jonah exchanged a quick glance with Chester and then Isaac. They burst into a run, heading for the van that hadn't been involved in the collision.

Fear

LUKE ENDED THE call after getting Macy's voicemail for the fifth time. Maybe she was on an important call or busy with a client or a meeting. There had to be a simple explanation for why her calls were going straight to her message.

What if there *was* a simple explanation, but it was because of something nefarious?

Chills ran down his back. Something had to be wrong.

Luke took a deep breath. He was on edge because of his mom. Macy was probably just in a meeting and didn't want to be disturbed. He could always call the front desk at her work. Then they could set his mind at ease and he could get back to *his* job.

He went to his contacts, found the number, and called. His mind was racing so much that it didn't register when someone answered.

"Hello? Is someone there?"

"Sorry," Luke said. "Is Macy there? This is Luke, her husband."

"Oh, hi, Luke. How are you?"

"Okay. Is Macy there?"

"She left for the day. Lucy said she wasn't feeling well."

Macy had gone home sick without calling him? Not even a text?

"Are you there, Luke?"

"Yeah. Thanks."

"Have a great evening."

"You too." He ended the call, his stomach tightening. It wasn't like Macy to leave work early without telling him. Could she really have been that sick to not think of letting him know? Or was she upset about Chester's transfer?

Or what if his transfer was a signal to the leaders to take Macy? They'd already taken Rebekah, but for some reason had left Macy alone—who Jonah and the others believed to be Chester's daughter, Heather.

He called her cell phone again, but as expected, it went right to voicemail. They needed a landline in their home.

Luke gathered his things and went out to the main desk. "I need to leave early. If anyone needs me, I can work remotely."

The receptionist looked up from her computer. "Is everything okay?"

"I… Let's hope."

Her eyes widened. "Is it your mom?"

Luke shook his head. "No. If Paul needs me, have him call."

"Sure thing, hon. I hope everything's all right."

"I'm sure it is." Luke hurried out of the building and headed to his truck. He drove straight to Macy's work, wanting to see for himself whether she was there. But just as he'd been told, her car wasn't in the parking lot. He pulled into a spot and called her again.

Voicemail.

"Where are you, Macy?"

He called Alex.

"Did you find her?"

"No," Luke said. "She's not at work. I'm going to check at home next, and as soon as I find her, I'm having a landline put in. Have you heard more about Chester's transfer?"

"Not yet," Alex grumbled. "Nick was supposed to call me, but I haven't heard anything. It could be nothing, though. He might've gotten called somewhere about something else."

Luke raked his fingers through his hair. "Okay. If you hear anything, let me know right away."

"You, too. I'm really worried about Macy."

"That makes two of us. I'll call you either way once I get home."

"I'll see if Mom and Dad have heard from her."

"Good idea." Luke ended the call and pulled out of the parking spot. As he drove home, his mind raced, trying to think of anywhere else Macy might've gone. Nothing came to mind.

Luke passed a walk-in clinic and pulled into the lot. Lucy said she hadn't been feeling well. Maybe she'd gone to see a doctor. He drove around the building, looking for her car. There were a couple similar ones, but not hers. Had she gone across town to their family doctor?

He'd check there if she wasn't home. His pulse raced faster with each passing minute. Finally, he made it to their neighborhood. When he neared their house, his heart sank as he saw the empty driveway. They almost never parked in the garage. But maybe she had this one time?

Luke sent a quick prayer up, begging that Macy had parked in the garage. His worry was turning into desperation. He turned into the driveway, squealing his tires and slammed to a stop barely an inch in front of the garage. Heart pounding, he flung open the door, cut the engine, and ran to the side of the house and looked into the garage.

No car.

The desperation clawed at him. Luke ran to the front door and struggled to get the key in the hole. Once inside, he called for her. "Macy! Macy!" He ran through each room, finding them all empty. "Where are you?"

Luke collapsed onto the couch and found the doctor's number in his phone. He could barely speak a coherent sentence, but managed to find out that Macy *hadn't* been in or called recently.

His breathing grew harried. There was no way he could lose his mom *and* Macy. No way.

Luke took some deep breaths and then tried Macy's number again. Voicemail. Just as he was about to try again, the phone rang. He didn't even look to see who it was. He just accepted the call. "What?"

"Luke," Alex said. "You'd better check the news."

Blood drained from his body. "Why?"

"Just do it. I gotta go. You can come over here, though." The call ended.

Fear tore at Luke. What could be so bad that Alex wouldn't even tell him? He reached for the remote. His hands shook, making it hard to push the right button. First, he accidentally turned on the streaming. Then he managed to switch it over to cable and find a local news station.

A woman spoke on the screen. Behind her was a car crash and flashing lights. Police combed the scene. A ticker at the bottom read something about an escaped criminal and a botched prison transfer.

Luke's blood ran cold. An escaped criminal from a transfer?

Chester.

And Macy was nowhere to be found.

Alone

SCRAPE. *SCRATCH. SCRRRRAPE.*

Macy opened her eyes. The room wasn't much lighter than the dark behind her eyelids. She sat up, gasping for air. Where was she?

Scrape-scrape.

Her eyes adjusted and her gaze landed on her desk. She was in her office. On her couch.

She leaned back and caught her breath. The events of the afternoon flooded her mind. After going to the drugstore, she'd come back and fallen asleep on the couch. That must've been some nap since it was now dark outside.

Macy spun around to look out her window. All the lights were off in the main part of the building. Everyone must've left, thinking she was gone. Probably because she'd told Lucy she thought she was coming down with that stomach bug. Only her nausea was because she was pregnant—not from illness or anxiety.

She rested both palms on her nearly-flat belly. It hardly seemed possible that there was a little person growing in there—someone who was half her and half Luke. Sadness washed over her. Would the baby ever get to know its Grandma Lottie?

Macy stretched and rose from the couch. She found her purse on the floor next to the door and rifled through it, looking for her phone.

Scrape. Scratch.

She snapped her attention toward the outside window where she could see the shadow of the tree outside moving back and forth. It must have been pretty windy out there. Macy turned her attention back to her purse and finally realized her phone wasn't in there.

It had died. Hadn't she plugged it in before going to the drugstore? She made her way over to the desk, but didn't see her phone. She opened drawers, feeling around for it.

Her shoe bumped into something. Macy lowered herself and felt around. Her phone. How had that gotten there? She picked it up and pressed the button.

Nothing.

She hadn't charged it? There was nothing she could do about that now. She'd just have to plug it in at home. Speaking of home, Luke had to be worried sick.

Macy stuck the phone in her purse and headed out into the dim lobby. Only a few night lights along the floor helped her see where she was going. Just before going outside, she turned to punch the code into the security system. The pad was completely dark. All of the buttons should've been lit even if the system wasn't set—and it should've been when the last person had left.

Weird.

She tried setting the alarm, anyway. Nothing happened. Well, it wasn't like anyone ever bothered the building. They could have someone fix it the next day. She was too tired to deal with it then.

Macy dug her keys out from her purse, stepped outside, and locked the door. She turned around and froze.

The parking lot was empty. She'd parked her car in her usual spot after returning from the drugstore. Sure, she'd been feeling out of it, but she *had* parked there.

What was she supposed to do now? Call Luke first, or report the theft? She reached into her purse. Just as she wrapped her fingers around the phone, she remembered it was dead.

She'd have to go back inside and make the calls. Macy turned around. The tiny hairs on the back of her neck stood on end and a chill ran down her spine.

Slowly, she spun again and scanned the area. The parking lot was empty. Macy couldn't see anyone, but the crawling of her skin told her someone was watching her. She was as sure of that as she was her own name.

Macy reached into her purse for her keys and turned back for the door.

Footsteps sounded behind her.

She swallowed and studied the window in front of her for a reflection of whoever was there. The outline of a bald man stepped toward her.

Her heart pounded so hard it might explode.

Focus. Macy took a deep breath.

The man took another step toward her. She had two options—fight or flight—and he wasn't leaving much room for the latter choice. Macy wrapped her fingers around the key, pulled her arm out of the purse, and turned around to face the man.

He loomed over her, staring at her with eyes she could never forget behind thick glasses. "Remember me, Heather?"

Macy's voice caught.

Chester laughed like a madman. "Cat got your tongue? Didn't think you'd see me again, did you?"

She glanced around him, hoping she could run. He was too close. Her only option was to fight.

"It's time to set some things right, Heather."

"You know I'm not Heather."

Chester stepped closer. "You're the new and improved version. I always liked you better, anyway."

"That's not a nice thing to say about your daughter."

"*You're* my daughter—my true daughter. Remember the ceremony Jonah performed? Me, Rebekah, you, and the twins—we're family. And soon, we'll all be united."

Macy just stared at him. Chester really believed all that nonsense. He was an even bigger loon than she'd given him credit for. She glanced toward the street. "I married Luke, and he's on his way to pick me up. He's going to be here in just a minute."

Chester shook his head. "If Jonah didn't marry you, it didn't count. You're still under my authority, *Heather*."

"Quit calling me that!" Macy bolted around him, dropping her purse but hanging onto the keys.

He grabbed her arm and squeezed tightly. He smelled like fish and chewing tobacco. The odor made her stomach turn. "You're not going anywhere."

She turned to him and dug a key into his cheek, just below his eye and ran it down his face. The gash bled out and got onto her hand.

His eyes widened, and he let go of her. "Now you've done it!"

Macy ran toward the street, nearly tripping over her own feet. She caught her balance and pushed forward. Her hair pulled, yanking her to a stop.

Chester tightened it around his fist, pulled her against him, and wrapped his other arm around her, pressing firmly against her ribcage. "You're going to regret that."

Macy kicked and squirmed, trying to get away. Then she screamed out, "Help me!"

He covered her mouth and dragged her back toward the building. She bit his hand as hard as she could. The metallic taste of blood filled her mouth. She ignored it and clamped down all the harder.

Chester yelled out and yanked her head back so hard he pulled some hair out. In response to the pain, Macy let go of his hand and spit his blood out.

"Our security system recorded all that!"

"You think we didn't already take care of that?" He dragged

her around the other side of the building. Three men stood in front of a van.

"Hurry up!"

Macy's heart sank. She'd know that voice anywhere. Jonah.

Chaos

THE DOOR SLAMMED shut behind the chief as he left Nick's office. Nick banged his head on the desk. Police Chief Crawford spent most of his time in City Hall dealing with political matters, and when he showed up at the station, it was either great news or horrible. And given the new one Crawford had just ripped into Nick over Chester's escape, tonight's visit was clearly the latter.

Though the escape had been well-planned by a number of people, according to the chief, all official fault lay on Nick for having initiated the transfer in the first place. It wasn't his fault Woodran had made a getaway. All security footage in the transport van had been tampered with, and the only way that could've been successfully accomplished was if someone had been working on the inside—and it sure hadn't been him!

Not that any of it mattered. The chief needed someone to blame, and Nick was the one with the big, glowing target on his back.

His cell phone rang. Nick swore at the caller and then grabbed the phone. It was Alex.

"What do you want?" Nick snapped. "I'm busy here."

"This is related to Chester!"

"If your sister's having anxiety—"

"She's *missing*!"

"What?" Nick demanded. "You've got to be kidding me."

"You think this is a joke?" Alex swore.

"Of course not!" Nick grabbed a pen. "Tell me everything."

"We can't find her!"

"I need specifics if I'm going to do anything, Alex. Where was she last seen? When? By whom?"

"She was at work, seen by her coworkers, and she wasn't feeling well. Her car isn't home, she hasn't been to her doctor's office, and her phone keeps going straight to voicemail."

"That's a lot better. Where does she work? What's her home address? Phone number? License plate?"

Alex answered all the questions except for the license plate. "You're going to have to talk to Luke about that."

"Fine. Send me the latest picture you have of her. Or have Luke do that and give me her license plate. I'm going to head over to the clinic and then over to her house. Is Luke there?"

"I think so."

"Tell him to stay there. I'll need to question him."

"The family's always suspect," Alex mumbled.

"Not with Chester on the loose." Nick scratched down a few more notes. "Stay by your phone in case I call. Send me her picture."

"Okay."

Nick ended the call, grabbed his notes, and stormed out of his office. The entire station was in chaos. Nick stuck his finger and thumb in his mouth and whistled. Everyone stopped and stared at him.

"Macy Mercer—now Macy Walker—is missing. Woodran kidnapped her when she was a teenager. We assume he has her now. Finding her alive is our top priority." He turned to Anderson. "You head this up here. I'm heading over to her work and home."

"Got it."

Nick's phone alerted him to a text. It was Macy's picture. He held it up for everyone to see. "This is what she looks like now. I'll forward it to you, Anderson, along with the other information I have. As soon as I find anything else out, I'll let you know. Just get the word out!"

"Consider it done." Anderson motioned for everyone to follow him into the meeting room.

"Foster, you're coming with me."

"Me, Captain?" The young officer stared at him with shock in her gray eyes. Her black hair fell into her eyes and she pushed it away.

"Yes, you. Come on." He spun around and marched down the hallway.

When they reached the parking lot, Foster headed for a police cruiser.

"I always take my car." Nick remote-unlocked his Mustang.

Her eyes grew wider. "Okay."

As they drove to Macy's clinic, Nick filled Foster in on everything he knew, including everything he could remember from her case more than a decade earlier.

When he turned into the empty clinic parking lot, Foster asked, "Do you mind me asking why you chose me to come?"

Nick parked, taking up two spaces. "Because you've shown me you have a lot of potential." Though new, she'd proven herself to be one of the most reliable officers on the force, and more importantly, she was eager to prove herself. If he was right, she'd prove to be a big help in the case. He flung open his door and headed toward the building, shining his flashlight everywhere, hoping for a clue.

Foster ran up to him, shining her light in the other direction. "I see something by the building. Looks like a purse."

Nick's body chilled. He glanced over to where Foster had her light. Something brownish was on the ground, but he couldn't tell what it was. He pulled gloves out of his pocket as they made their way over and picked up the purse once they got there. His light shone on something red on the ground. "Blood?"

Foster ran over to the red. "Looks like it." She pulled a swab out from her jacket, slid it across the liquid, sealed it in a bag, and wrote on it. "We'd better call for backup."

"Have at it." Nick dug through the purse, trying to find ID. If the sinking feeling in his gut was right, he'd find Macy's picture on it. He came across a rectangular box. At first he thought it was toothpaste, but then he realized what it really was—a home pregnancy test. He swore.

"What?" Foster turned to him, getting hair in her face again. She pulled it back into a ponytail.

He handed her the box, unable to find the words, and continued digging through the purse for a wallet. Finally, he found it inside a zipped pocket.

"It's positive," Foster said. "Whoever took this is pregnant."

Just when he thought his night couldn't get any worse, he opened the black wallet to find Macy's smiling face. He showed the driver's license to Foster.

Her tanned skin paled. "And she's pregnant. Do we know how far along?"

Nick shook his head. "I can't imagine it being very long. I'm not sure she told anyone. Her brother would've told me if he'd known."

She aimed her flashlight toward the side of the building. "Those look like fresh tire marks. Someone fled from here recently."

He ran his hands through his hair. "Looks like we're going to need even more backup. I'm calling for everything—search dogs, helicopters, the works."

Attempt

LOTTIE CLUTCHED THE rock and looked around at the others. "Are you ready?"

They all nodded, clutching rocks of their own. They'd spent the last several hours digging up their dirt floor for the only weapons they could find. Once the others saw what they were doing, they wanted in on the action. Now every single prisoner was on board, and they were ready to fight.

"The evening check should be here any minute," Lottie said. "There should only be three of them. This shouldn't be a problem."

Ruben turned to her. "We'll fight them off, you women run."

"I want to beat them up, too," Jayla said. "They made me miss my art show. I'll never get into the college I want now."

"Just run." Ruben narrowed his eyes. "We need you to find a way out. There won't be much time. The guards will be expected to check in after coming in here. We have maybe ten minutes to find a way out of this fortress. Then we'll have to escape while evading the leadership."

"Fine." Jayla scowled.

Lottie's heart raced. Her entire body felt cold. Would she get to see Luke and Macy again, or would trying to escape be the last thing she ever did?

Click.

Click.

Everyone's eyes widened, and they exchanged a mix of worried and excited glances.

Click.

Click.

"Ready?" Ruben asked.

Click.

It didn't matter if anyone was ready or not.

The door burst open. Guards flooded in. More than a dozen of them—the prisoners were outnumbered.

Had they found out about the escape attempt? Lottie's throat closed up.

That's when she noticed what they were carrying. Chains and ropes. More than enough to restrain twice as many prisoners than were locked up already. They also had guns strapped to their backs.

Next to her, Jayla dropped the rock. Everyone else followed suit.

Thud. Thud. Thud.

The guards didn't even notice.

Gasping for air, Lottie looked around for Blue Eyes. He wasn't in the group. Had they figured out that he was trying to find a way for her to escape? Her breathing grew more ragged. What if Jonah had hurt him—because of her?

She exchanged worried glances with the other prisoners. They had no chance of getting away. Even if they weren't outnumbered, the door was blocked. It was tempting to fight the guards, for the sake of the others, but it would be futile. Maybe they stood a better chance wherever they were going. She had to hope, or she had nothing.

"Now!" yelled one of the guards.

Lottie's heart sank. Whatever was coming would be worse than before. Of that much, she was certain.

One of the guards closest to her wrapped his fingers around

her arms, squeezing until it hurt so bad she cried out.

"Shut up." He pulled her arms behind her back and tied her wrists with ropes. Most of the others were chained. They saw her as less of a threat. She needed to use that to her advantage later. He then roped her ankles together.

They were tying everyone up at their wrists and ankles and then connecting each other together with more chains and rope. Once that was complete, they stuck head coverings on everyone—the ones that had been hard enough to walk in without being tied.

Bang!

Lottie jumped and her ears rang from what sounded like gunfire. Her pulse raced. Had they shot someone, or was that just to get their attention?

"You will follow us," one of the guards commanded. "Act out, try to escape, or do anything otherwise stupid—get yourself shot. This is your one and only warning. Let's go."

The ropes pulled her toward the door. Shuffling sounded all around as everybody walked toward the door in a tangled mess. Lottie walked into someone else's chains and nearly tripped. If she fell, she'd take everyone else with her.

Somehow, she managed to get outside without incident. It was hard to see out of the eye slit, but they appeared to be walking down a residential road. People came out to watch as the restrained, covered prisoners made their way to… wherever they were going. Lottie shuddered.

It was probably the trials she'd heard so much about. It wasn't hard to guess what would happen once those began. Jonah would ramble on about his inflated self-importance for a while before judging them—and they were sure to be some of the least fair trials she would ever see.

Without warning, both sets of ropes yanked her to a stop. Lottie nearly fell, and would have, had she not crashed into a much larger prisoner in front of her.

Once standing up straight, she looked around to see where they were. There were no houses, only a building that loomed in front of them, seemingly taller than the trees.

"The trials will begin shortly," announced a guard near the front of the group. "We will put you in a smaller holding cell until it's your turn."

"Will we be given a fair chance?" called out one of the men prisoners.

The nearest guard hit him in the head with the butt of his gun. "Nobody said you could talk."

That answered his question, not that anyone had doubted the one-sidedness of the upcoming trials.

Lottie's ropes tugged, and she snapped to attention, careful not to lose her balance again. They went around the tall building. Lottie glanced to the side and nearly stopped walking.

Gallows. As in, multiple. There was room for three at a time.

She stared until she rounded the corner. They came to a tiny shack that looked no bigger than an outhouse. The guards shoved the prisoners inside, one by one. Lottie's heart raced.

Her end was coming soon. She'd never again see anyone she loved.

Despairing

THE ROOM WAS a dizzying blur of activity. Luke couldn't bring himself to get off the couch.

Macy was pregnant, and he'd found out from a police captain who'd found blood near her abandoned purse. All while his mom was still missing, and though nobody would say it in front of him, probably dead. He wasn't stupid, but he also couldn't bring himself to say the words.

Could the pregnancy test have been planted there as a cruel joke by whoever had taken her? It was probably Chester—that was what everyone was assuming—but he couldn't let himself think about that any more than he could think about Jonah having killed Mom.

Luke needed to do something, but his body wouldn't cooperate. It was all he could do to keep breathing. His entire immediate family was in dire danger—his mom, wife, and child. Child!

As he struggled for natural breaths, his mind wandered to his romantic night with Macy about two and a half weeks earlier. He hadn't thought about protection, and given that they'd been trying to conceive before his mom disappeared, Macy wouldn't have been taking the pills.

If Macy thought she was pregnant, why hadn't she said anything to him? Was she planning on surprising him with the news?

He closed his eyes, unable to think about anything. It only made his head spin all the more.

The couch cushion sank as someone sat next to him. "Are you okay?" Alyssa asked.

Luke shook his head, unable open his eyes.

"Me, neither." Alyssa's voice shook.

It was enough for him to sit up and pry his eyes open. His mother-in-law sat next to him, her face tear-stained and the skin around her eyes swollen and splotchy. This was the second time she was living through this nightmare of Chester kidnapping her daughter.

His heart broke for her. He tried to say something, but nothing would come. Instead, he wrapped his arms around her and pulled her close. Alyssa broke down and sobbed, shaking. That was all it took for Luke's own tears to break free.

Together, the two sobbed and time ceased to exist. It could've been two minutes, or it could've been two hours. There was no way to tell. Alyssa sat back and rubbed her eyes before meeting Luke's gaze. "We're going to get her back again, right?"

The desperation in her expression matched what raged through Luke's entire body. He nodded. "I'll make sure of it."

Chad came over and put an arm around Alyssa. "The police have more questions for us downstairs." His eyes were as red and tear-stained as his wife's.

Luke choked back another sob. Seeing his in-laws, who were normally so strong, was more than he could take right then. "I'll go with you."

Alex came over, sliding his finger around his phone's screen. "Hold on. Do you have any more recent pictures than these?" Alex showed him the screen, which had a bunch of pictures of Macy.

"We'll be downstairs," Chad said.

Luke nodded to him and took Alex's phone. "Yeah, I've got more. Do you want me to forward them to you?"

"I'll do it. Give me your phone."

"Okay." Luke was too wiped out to protest. His arm felt like rubber as he reached for his phone. He entered his passcode—it took three tries—and handed it to Alex, who slid his finger around the screen, his brows together in stark determination.

Footsteps thundered up the stairs, and Zoey appeared in the living room, her eyes red. "Any news?"

"Not yet," Alex said, his attention still glued to Luke's phone.

"Chester really took her again?" Zoey sank into the couch between Alex and Luke.

Luke nodded, his stomach tightening.

"And she's pregnant?" Zoey stared at Luke with wide eyes.

"It would appear so." Pain squeezed Luke's temples.

Zoey threw her arms around him. "What are we going to do?"

"That's what I'm trying to figure out." He rubbed her back as the second woman sobbed against his chest.

"Got them." Alex put Luke's phone on the coffee table and turned back to his phone. "This post better go viral. I've got over thirty pictures of her."

Zoey sat back. "I'm the worst best friend ever."

"Why?" Luke asked.

"No, you're not." Alex didn't look up from the screen.

"I should've been there for her. If she'd have felt comfortable telling me about her pregnancy, I could've been there with her when Chester showed up. I'd have beat him to a pulp before he could take her."

"Or they'd have taken you, too." Alex shook his head. "That'd be the last thing we need. You can help us get the word out about this."

"You mean like how I did such a great job at the press conference?" Her tone dripped with sarcasm.

"Actually, yes. You did really great."

Zoey shook her head. "I nearly had a panic attack right there on stage, in front of like a million people."

"You could've fooled me."

Alex and Zoey stared each other down, and an awkwardness hung in the air.

Luke pushed himself from the couch. "I need some air."

Neither responded. Luke glanced down the stairs to see Chad and Alyssa talking with an officer. They seemed to have everything under control. He wandered to Macy's old room, which still had a lot of her old things in it. Alyssa liked keeping it as it had been, and so did Ariana who slept in there when she stayed the night with the Mercers.

Luke wandered around, picking up stuffed animals and holding them close. He swore he could smell her. Still holding a brown bear, he sat on the bed and looked around. "What am I supposed to do, babe?"

How was he supposed to hold himself together when his entire world was falling apart around him? He'd barely held on with her there by his side. Now what?

He leaned back against the pillow, squeezing the bear against him so tightly he thought the little stuffed head might pop off. His heartache engulfed him, radiating outward, choking the air out of his body. His heavy eyelids started to close. He didn't bother fighting them. Waves of sleepiness washed through his body. There was nothing in him left to fight it. Or anything.

Just as sleep had almost entirely engulfed him, Luke bolted upright. His pulse raged, pulsating through him.

He knew exactly what he needed to do.

Plan

ALEX SAT NEXT to Zoey, quiet hanging in the air between them like a thick shroud in the living room. After a few beats, he placed his hand on her knee and leaned against the couch.

She turned to him. "What are we going to do? Do you think we'll get Macy back again?"

He nodded, trying to show more confidence than he actually had. "She got away from that psycho once, she can do it again."

"You don't think he'll be more careful this time?"

"Doesn't matter. Macy spent years thinking about what she'd done wrong and what she'd do differently if she could do it all over again. He'll be at a disadvantage."

"He's been in jail all these years, Alex. He's had nothing to do other than think about what *he'd* do differently."

"Doesn't change the fact that Macy's smarter than him—by a long shot."

Zoey sighed, clearly not convinced. She leaned back and rested her head on the couch. They sat in silence for a few minutes before Zoey turned to Alex. "We're going to have to tell Ari about this. There's going to be no hiding it from her this time."

Alex nodded. "She's taking Lottie's disappearance pretty well. This won't be any different."

Zoey frowned. "Hopefully, this won't send her over the edge."

"No. She's strong."

They sat in silence again. Alex's mind wandered back to the

mystery lunch date Zoey'd had before. "This is probably not the best time, but I need to ask you something."

She turned to him, her eyes wide. "What?"

He cleared his throat. "Ariana mentioned…" It sounded so dumb. Why was he bringing it up now?

"She mentioned what?"

"A lunch date with Casey. It's probably none of my business—in fact, it's not. Forget I said anything."

Zoey's expression softened. "Casey's my friend."

Alex nodded and turned to his phone. "I wonder how many shares my post about Macy has. We need it to go viral."

"I was helping her plan her wedding, Alex." Zoey put her hand on Alex's.

He turned and met her gaze. "Oh."

"Were you worried?"

Alex couldn't read her expression. He shrugged and turned back to his phone. "Look, already twenty shares. I'd hoped for more, but it's late. People are sleeping. It'll blow up tomorrow, guaranteed."

Zoey squeezed his hand. "I've been waiting for—"

Luke stumbled into the room, his eyes wild. "I know what I have to do."

"What?" Alex and Zoey asked in unison. Zoey kept her hand on top of Alex's.

"I'm going to make myself bait. Get those jerks to kidnap me so I can break my family out of the community."

"That's crazy." Alex stared at him. "How do you plan on getting out?"

Luke narrowed his eyes. "You're going to follow me."

Zoey's hand tightened around Alex's.

"You think *I'm* going to get you out of that mess?" Alex exclaimed.

"Yes." Luke crossed his arms. "Actually, no. I don't *think* you will, I know you will."

Alex's stomach twisted. "You have too much faith in me."

"You got any better ideas?" Luke stepped closer to Alex.

"I..." Alex's mind raced. He was going to join the academy soon—the *police* academy. He couldn't be pulling stupid stunts like that if he was going to be a cop. But maybe that was his answer. He *wasn't* an officer of the law yet—not even an academy cadet. This might be his final chance to be an idiot—what else would he call following his brother-in-law into a notorious cult that had nearly gotten his sister killed?

"Well?" Luke asked.

Both of Zoey's hands wrapped around Alex's and squeezed. "Alex, don't," she pleaded.

He took a deep breath. "Macy needs us."

"Alex."

"My future niece or nephew needs me."

Zoey turned to Luke. "What's your plan, exactly?"

"Jonah clearly wants everyone who had anything to do with the breakdown of the community before. He's going to be looking for me—probably already has guys watching me outside this house."

She shuddered and moved closer to Alex.

Luke continued. "The moment I'm alone and vulnerable, they'll take me. But they won't know Alex is watching from his car. He'll follow them and at some point let the cops know what's going on." He turned to Alex. "You have to wait a while. The police have to be far enough behind that the abductors don't suspect anything."

Zoey pressed her side against Alex. "I can't believe you're going to put yourself in that position—to let them take you."

"I should've done this sooner." His expression tightened. "If I had, Macy would probably be safe at home right now." Luke turned to Alex. "Are you in, or am I on my own?"

Alex jumped to his feet. “I’m in. Let’s do this.”

“So am I.” Zoey rose and wrapped her arms around Alex.

Luke turned to her. “I don’t think I like that idea.”

“Why not?” she countered. “Because I’m a woman?”

He took a step back. “Well, I… If you want to join Alex, I guess there’s no stopping you.”

“Darn straight.”

A surge of pride and admiration ran through Alex. Zoey hadn’t changed a bit, and he loved her all the more for it—but he couldn’t let her go. Not with as many people as he cared about in danger already.

Reveal

EXCITEMENT ROSE IN Jonah's chest as he looked over the courtroom filled with his people. The scene before him was even more majestic and glorious than he'd imagined. He had more members than seats, and as a result many of the women had to stand. Among the sea of white, every face stared at him, filled with eager expectation.

They couldn't wait to hear what he had to say. It was the most spectacular moment of his life—even topping his time reuniting with Eve—and he held onto the sight and feel, relishing in it and wanting to hold onto the memory for the rest of his days and well into his years in the coming promised land.

His people began to fidget. That was Jonah's cue to carry on despite how much he wanted to enjoy the moment for all it was worth. They would cry out for him to dish out more of his glory soon enough.

The moment would only get better.

Jonah picked up his gavel and hit it on his desk. The beautiful sound echoed all around, capturing the attention of everyone in the room. Gasps and smiles went through the audience.

They were going to hang on his every word. He took a deep breath and let it sink in a little more before speaking.

"Dear community members." Every single person in front of him leaned forward with anticipation. "Today is a special day. This is one we will all remember not only for the rest of our lifetimes, but also in the land beyond. The events about to unfold will stay with us forever. Make sure you pay close attention and keep everything close to your hearts."

Everyone hung on his words. A shiver ran down his back. It was almost like they hadn't been separated for so many years. Almost.

"We're about to begin the trials of those who caused our separation. In the grand scheme of things, those missing years won't seem like much—looking back hundreds of years in the future when we're finally in the great promised land, it will only be a drop in the bucket. Unfortunately, as we're all so deeply aware, having had to *live* through the great separation so recently, it's much more than that. Sins were committed, and they must be paid for." Jonah turned to look at the prisoners.

Shuffling noises ran through the crowd as everyone turned to look, also.

Jonah narrowed his eyes at the evildoers, the very people who had ruined so much of his life. He considered addressing them, but it would be a waste of his breath. He turned back to the adoring crowd and waited for them to focus on him. "Now before we begin the trials, two things must happen."

Eyes widened and people leaned forward.

"First of all, I would like to call up our beloved newest prophet who barely got any time here in our most beloved community. He hasn't even had a chance to receive his true name. Come up and join me, Chester."

The room was so quiet, Chester's every footstep echoed around the room as he made his way up.

Jonah put his arm around the taller man and grinned widely as he scanned the crowd. "You all remember how I had visions before he joined us. Vivid, glorious visions about a man and his daughter who would forever change our beloved community. I shared those with all of you, not leaving out a single detail. Then when I went out into the world to search for him, I found him almost immediately. It was truly a divine appointment. He didn't have his daughter with him, so we had to wait." Jonah paused and took a deep breath.

The silence echoed around him. It was such a beautiful thing, everyone hanging on his every word.

"It was most unfortunate that his daughter's role in all of this really did forever change our family. Every single one of us was deeply wounded by what happened. Many of you were put back on the streets where I found and saved you. Nearly everyone has struggled immensely. The good news is that for those of you who are innocent, you will receive a great reward for your hardships. But for those who are found guilty, a different fate is coming." He turned to look at the prisoners again. "You who played a role in that should be most fearful."

Taking a deep breath, Jonah stepped back, let go of Chester, and turned back to the crowd. "And now what you've been waiting so long for—the revelation of another prophecy."

People leaned forward even more. A giddiness ran through Jonah, and he fought to keep his expression steady. He let the moment build as they waited for the prophecy.

"Usually, I would reveal something so important in our meeting hall, but I'm sure you all understand the importance of having the revelation here."

Heads nodded yes, but nobody spoke a word.

"Give me a moment to prepare." Jonah closed his eyes and shook out his arms and legs. He took several deep breaths and allowed images to run through his mind. Images he'd seen before but now would finally share with his followers. At long last, he opened his eyes. "Today we are given the opportunity to restore things to how they were. How often are humans given the chance to turn back time to the way things once were? To the way they should be? Not often, but today is *our* great gift. We will receive our beloved community fully restored as it should be. It will be exactly as though none of our heartache ever happened."

Applause broke out. People jumped to their feet and called out Jonah's name. It rolled off their tongues and echoed around the gorgeous courtroom like a choir of angels. Their chants grew louder, and though Jonah would have loved to stand there and revel in their worship, he needed to continue with the prophecy. He raised his hands high into the air until the room grew silent again and the people took their seats.

"Now the prophecies have revealed that although today will be gloriously restorative, it will also be a sad day for our beloved Chester. It will work out in his favor, lifting him higher than we ever thought possible, but he will stand a test of will and faith." Jonah turned to Chester. "Are you ready to hear the prophecy?"

Chester bowed low. "I am."

Jonah held his gaze. "Unfortunately, since your daughter was the mastermind behind the breakdown of our beloved community, she must suffer the harshest of penalties."

Chester's eyes widened and his face paled.

"To prove your loyalty to not only me, but to everyone here, you must be the one to carry out her punishment."

He didn't respond except to blink. Beads of sweat broke out where his hairline once would have been.

Jonah cleared his throat. "You must sacrifice your daughter, Chester. Then you will receive your true name."

"I, I… But I love Heather."

A fresh, and stronger, wave of giddiness ran through Jonah. He clapped his hands together. "All the better! That'll make the sacrifice all the more meaningful. Your true name will be of so much more value than usual. You really are a rare gem, Chester. I couldn't be prouder to have you here by my side."

Chester swallowed.

"You will complete the sacrifice, will you not?"

Silence echoed around them as the two men stared off. Tears shone in Chester's eyes. He nodded with determination. "I'll do it."

Thunderous applause erupted from the audience and lasted for several minutes. Once the room grew quiet again, Jonah put his hand on Chester's shoulder. "The fact that it will be so hard for you means your reward in the afterlife will be all the greater. You will truly be lifted up." Jonah turned back to the adoring crowd. "And now, on to the trials."

Lead

NICK FINISHED OFF the stale coffee, not that it helped wake him. After weeding through mostly useless leads all morning, his eyes were fighting to close. The only thing remotely helpful was what they'd found early on—the purse, the blood, and the tire marks. Macy's car hadn't been found—it was probably wherever Lottie's car had been taken. Both missing vehicles must've had their GPS locators removed or destroyed. But the tire tracks belonged to a larger vehicle than hers, so her car wasn't even on the priority list.

Knock, knock.

Nick slapped his cheeks, trying to wake up a little. "Come in!"

The door opened, and Anderson entered. "We just got the footage from a camera down the street from Macy's clinic. It caught a van leaving the driveway around dusk. It didn't capture the time, but it appears to be the vehicle we're looking for."

"Let me see it." Nick followed Anderson to his desk and watched the grainy video on his laptop. "Probably no way to get a license plate from that."

Anderson shook his head. "Not with this video quality."

"Call the Department of Transportation and have them go over all the traffic cams in the area. They have to be able to find something, and if there is a plate, they'll have it."

"I'm on it." Anderson took a sip of his coffee. "Have you found anything?"

"Other than dead-end leads?" Nick asked. "Nothing. Let me know what you find out from the DOT. I'm going to catch some shut eye on my couch. If we do find out where this van went, I'll need at least a little sleep."

"I'll make sure no one bothers you unless it's urgent."

"Have you gotten any sleep?"

Anderson nodded. "I went home for a few hours. Notice the wrinkled clothes."

Nick nodded. "Don't hesitate to wake me as soon as you find anything."

"Sure." Anderson picked up his cell phone and pressed a button. "Call the DOT."

Nick rubbed his eyes and made his way back to his office. He closed the blinds, grabbed a blanket from a box behind the couch, and lay down. He fell asleep as soon as his head made contact with the cushion.

As soon as his eyes closed, another knock sounded. Nick groaned. "Come in."

Anderson rushed in. "They found the van, and a series of cameras showed it heading toward a forest in Kittitas County."

Nick sat up. "Trying to hide in the Cascade Mountains."

"It would appear that way."

"How'd they figure that out so fast?" Nick rubbed his eyes.

"You've been asleep for three hours, Captain."

"I have?" He threw the blanket aside. "We'd better get going."

Anderson nodded. "I've set up a team. Helicopters and K9 units are already headed that way. We just need to find out exactly where the commune is located."

"We'll need all the 'copters and dogs we can get in a thick forest like that."

"Yeah. You taking your car or a cruiser?"

"I don't need to put that kind of mileage on my Mustang." Nick hurried over to his desk.

"I'm heading out with Paine. You taking Phillips?"

Nick shook his head. "Foster. She found some critical clues last night."

"She's got potential. Glad you're taking her under your wing. See you there." Anderson rushed out of the office.

A minute later, Foster poked her head in. "You want me to assist you again, Captain?"

He nodded. "I need you to warm up one of the cruisers. I'll be out in a few."

"Consider it done." She ducked out.

Nick pulled out his phone and called Alex to let him know what was going on. The call went to voicemail. "Your sister's missing, and you're not answering your phone? We have a possible location on the cult. Kittitas County, probably in or near the Cascades. Call me if you want more details."

He stuffed the phone in the inside pocket of his jacket and slid it on before grabbing what he needed and heading out to the parking lot. Two cruisers sat idling. He went over to the nearest one. Anderson and Paine were inside, looking at something on a phone. Nick headed over to the other car. Foster sat inside, pulling her long, dark hair into a ponytail in the passenger seat.

Nick climbed into the driver's seat and adjusted the height down. "You could've driven. I'm no chauvinist."

She shrugged. "You're the captain, so I just assumed you'd be driving."

"Doesn't matter to me." He glanced down at the GPS. It was already set for an address near the Cascades. "All set?"

Foster nodded.

Nick pulled out of the spot. "Why don't you fill me in on what's happened the last few hours?"

"Mostly just more useless tips. Johnson and I waded through most of them. Then Anderson heard back from the DOT, and here we are."

"Here we are. Let's just hope that cult is where we think they are."

"I'd hate to think of all this manpower wasted on a false lead."

"Me, too." Nick pulled into traffic. "Me, too."

Locked

MACY PACED THE tiny, well-sealed shack. She'd pulled on every board, finding them all to be sealed tight. Her skin was still raw from the cleansing process. She hadn't been given the dignity of a private shower. At Jonah's command, Eve had scrubbed every inch of Macy's skin.

She shuddered, just remembering it, and pulled her rough white clothing tighter, not caring that it rubbed harshly against her sore body.

Images from long ago flooded her mind, suffocating her. She'd never been able to forget the community, and now her memories were more vivid than ever before.

Macy leaned against the wall and closed her eyes, trying to think about Luke. She pictured him, smiling at her from the altar. Their wedding day had been the happiest of her life, surrounded by people who loved them both. She had stared at Luke as the music played. Her dad had looped his arm through hers, smiling proudly through the tears that shone in his eyes.

Luke had never been more handsome than that day, standing there in the tuxedo. The excitement in his eyes showed that he was as over-the-moon thrilled as Macy. Alex stood next to him, grinning at her. It had been during Alex's rougher years, but he'd been there for them on that important day.

Scratch, scratch.

Macy's eyes flew open, thrusting her back into reality.

Scratch, scratch.

Her pulse burned as it raced through her. She wandered the little building, trying to figure out what the noise was. Whatever it was, it had stopped.

She quit wandering and stared at a pile of stones. Who had put them there, and what had happened to them? Had they suffered the same fate Macy was about to? Had Lottie been here?

Macy picked one up and studied it. There was nothing special about it. Dirt clung to it as though it had recently been dug up. It fell from her grip and bounced on the other rocks.

Tears blurred her vision. If what Eve had told her was true, Macy would never see anyone she loved ever again. She would stand trial with Jonah as judge—and he blamed her wholly for the breakdown of the community and for his jail sentence.

Macy leaned against a wall, slid down to the ground, and allowed her tears to fall freely for everything she would miss. No more anniversaries or birthdays, no more Christmases or vacations. Never again would she wake up to see Luke smiling at her with the same adoration she had for him. She would never get to meet the child they made together—the beautiful little person who would be half her and half him.

Her hands rested on her stomach, and her tears turned into sobs. "I'm so sorry I got you into this. You'll never get to meet your daddy. He would've loved you so much." She choked on her words. "I wish he could at least know about you. That we had a chance at a family. But that'll never happen now."

Macy pulled her knees up and rested her forehead on them. She sobbed until she had nothing left. Time seemed to stand still. There was no way to tell how much had passed. Had it been hours? Minutes?

Finally, she crawled over to the pile of rocks and found one with a sharp edge. Macy clung to it and scooted to the far back corner of the building. She scraped lines and curves onto one plank of wood, working hard and with intention until she had finished her task.

Choking back more tears, she admired her handiwork.

I'm sorry, Luke. For everything.

He might not ever see it, but at least there was a chance—no matter how tiny.

Macy wandered to the other end of the little building and pressed her ear against the wall. Just as before, she couldn't hear anything.

Despite her worry, her eyelids grew heavy. Between the pregnancy and the stress, it was no wonder exhaustion had claimed her. She sat in a corner, leaned her head against the rough wall, and let her eyes close.

In her dreams, Luke stood by a lake and ran toward her with open arms. Macy cried out with joy and ran to meet him, desperate to hold on forever. He ran his hands through her hair and kissed her passionately. She responded by kissing him desperately.

Click.

Click.

Macy sat up, gasping for air. "No!" She tried to go back to the dream. That would probably be the last time she would see him again.

Click.

Click.

Click.

Her throat closed up as the door flung open with such force that it crashed into the wall with a loud thud.

Two men dressed in the community white garb rushed in and glared at her. One of the men covered Macy's head with a white head piece, but Macy had no slit to see from like her previous time in the cult. She kicked and hit them as she screamed at the top of her lungs.

Something hard hit the side of her head, making her ears ring. Arms wrapped around her, making it impossible for her to hit. She could still kick, and she did in every direction her body allowed. Hands wrapped around her ankles, pinning them together tightly. Together the two men carried her.

Macy yelled out as loudly as she could. A hand covered her mouth on top of the fabric. She bit down on the fingers as hard as she could.

The man swore and hit her in the face. "You'd better start behaving, or Jonah will add to your torture. You'll be begging for death, and he'll only laugh in your face."

Action

LUKE SIPPED THE cold, stale coffee as he wandered back and forth in the lonely field. What else did he need to do to get the attention of the community leaders? He was alone in the middle of a field. He'd driven slower than dirt, making sure that anyone watching him couldn't miss his exit from the house.

Either they wanted to drive him crazy, or they had no intention of taking him. But that didn't make any sense given that he was as involved with the community's downfall as anyone else who'd been kidnapped—more than most, in fact. He'd been working alongside Macy, urging her on.

Why didn't they want him? Was their idea of his punishment to wait, not knowing what was happening to his mom and wife? If so, it was working.

A chilly breeze blew by and gave him the shivers. Cold air coming in meant either rain or wind, or both. That would make it harder to find and fight the community members.

"Why don't you want me?" he called out. "What's wrong with me?"

Silence answered him. He continued circling the field. Another gust of cool air kicked up, ruffling his hair. Luke finished off his coffee and set the cup on a tree stump. He'd pick it up on his way back to the car. He wrapped his arms around himself and continued his path around the field, shivering. The breeze continued, growing slightly stronger and colder. Thunder rumbled in the distance.

Even better.

"Come and get me!" He paused and waited, hearing nothing other than the wind.

Luke's chest tightened. He needed to do something—anything more than walking circles around an abandoned field. It wasn't helping anyone. Nobody in the community cared whether or not he wanted in. His suffering was supposed to be outside the commune.

His mind wandered back to that fateful night... The fire. The gunshots. Running through the cornfields. His dear friend dying in his arms. Tears stung his eyes. No matter how many years passed, that memory was one that never faded or eased. Luke had plenty of injuries himself, but nothing like she'd had. And the look in her eyes as she said goodbye, urging Luke and Macy to go on...

He choked back a sob. All these years later, and it still felt like yesterday.

Luke pulled out his phone and called Alex. "I can't do this anymore. Nobody's watching me other than you. I don't know why, but they're not."

"I just got off the phone with Nick," Alex said. "They think the cult is hiding out in the Cascades."

"Does he know where?"

"They're heading to Kittitas County."

Luke passed the stump, grabbed his empty coffee cup, and headed for his car. "I'm going there."

"All they know is what county!"

"That's enough for me." Luke went to the side of the road where his car was parked and waved to Alex, who was in his car. "I'm going."

"So am I."

"This could be a suicide mission." Luke got in his car, turned on the engine, and cranked the heat. He shivered, unsure if it was from the chilly wind or the memories of the life lost in his arms. Either way, he intended to find them and make sure those crazies didn't kill Macy and his mom—if they were still alive.

"My sister's in there." Determination filled Alex's tone.

"Then you'd better be able to keep up."

Alex snickered. "You clearly don't know me if you think I can't."

"Just call me if you hear any more information." Luke ended the call and pulled into traffic. He glanced in the rear-view mirror. Alex was right behind him.

Luke gripped the steering wheel. It would be a long drive to the woods, but he would do what he could to shave as much time off their trip as he could. He had to get there before anything happened to Macy or his mom. If he had to break inside and pretend to be a faithful member of the community, that's what he would do.

He would risk his own life to save theirs. As a father, with his child's life on the line, he needed to do what he could to make sure he or she had every chance to see the light of day—even if it meant Luke wouldn't.

Rattled

A HEADACHE SQUEEZED Lottie's skull as she listened to Jonah drone on and on. The rope around her wrists and ankles seemed to tighten on their own. Half a dozen gun-bearing guards stood around the prisoners. Each one kept their fingers on the trigger, ready to shoot if necessary.

If only listening to Jonah's long-winded speech was their only punishment, but it was only the warm up session. Back in the days of the original community, he held nightly meetings—attendance required for all residents—where he would talk for hours on end about his daily prophecies. She shuddered, thinking about the days when she'd sat still, excitedly taking in every word he spoke.

Jonah whacked the gavel again—that was probably what was giving Lottie her headache. He'd been hitting it so much it was as though he was trying to rebuild the desk. "...and that concludes today's prophecy. Now to begin the trials."

He turned and stared at Lottie and the others, first staring into her eyes and then moving to the others. She shook as soon as he turned his attention to someone else. Someone placed an arm on her back. Gratitude washed through her at the simple gesture reminding her that they were all in this together.

A crash sounded near the back of the courtroom. The main door flung open and two guards rushed inside, dragging someone whose face was covered. She writhed about, obviously trying to free herself from their hold. Gasps sounded throughout the building.

Jonah hit the gavel close to a dozen times. "Silence!"

The courtroom quieted.

"Reveal the traitor!"

Lottie's stomach tightened. With all of Jonah's talk about Heather—Macy—she had no doubt her sweet daughter was the one struggling against the guards. Tears blurred Lottie's vision.

One guard wrapped his arms around Macy while the other reached for the head covering. Lottie sent up a futile prayer that it was someone else about to be revealed. But who else would she be?

The guard gripped the head covering and waited a beat before yanking it off. Macy cried out and her head twisted as the white fabric pulled away.

Lottie's stomach lurched. It was definitely her sweet Macy.

Jonah clapped his hands. His eyes lit up with glee. "Bring her here and stand her before me."

The room spun around Lottie. Her knees wobbled and her stomach lurched again. Hands clung to her shoulders. "We'll get through this," Jayla whispered in Lottie's ear. "Now that we're out of the jail, we stand a chance at breaking free."

Lottie nodded, though she didn't believe a word of it. Aside from the ropes, chains, and gun-bearing guards, there wasn't a person in the entire building who would let them escape. The prisoners were public enemy number one. The docile members wouldn't hesitate to turn into a murderous mob if Jonah gave the order.

She continued trembling as Macy stood in front of the platform, looking up at Jonah. Though she said nothing, there was a fire in her eyes. She wasn't going to give up without a fight.

Good girl.

Jonah struck his gavel again. "Do you know why you're here, Heather?"

Macy nodded.

"Answer me!"

"Yes."

"Tell me why."

Macy's expression tensed. "For my crimes against the community."

"Which are…?"

Macy took a deep breath. "Breaking out and convincing others to come with me."

"And?" Jonah leaned forward.

"The eventual destruction of the community."

Jonah nodded. "And now once you're sentenced, you can't claim ignorance. You know exactly what you're being executed for."

Lottie gasped out loud. Sydney spun around and covered Lottie's mouth. Her eyes widened and she shook her head, silently begging Lottie to stay quiet.

Jonah turned to the group and glared at the guards. "Keep our prisoners in line."

Several guns cocked.

Lottie froze.

"Good." Jonah turned back to Macy. "You will be tried last and your punishment will also be last. Not only will you watch others die because of your poorly thought-out decisions, but your own death will be the longest and most excruciating of all. You'll have plenty of time to think about what you've done—so much so that you'll beg for mercy. You'll plead. But you know what?"

Macy didn't flinch.

"Do you know what?"

"What?"

"You won't receive any! You'll suffer at the hands of your father." Jonah waved his arms toward Chester. Macy flinched at the mention of Chester being her dad. "The longer your suffering, the greater his reward. You didn't prevent him from becoming a high prophet. No, you only delayed the inevitable. Instead of converting someone from the world, now his duty to become prophet is to sacrifice the one he loves most—you. He's going to find his way to the glorious promised land. You… well, dear. You're going somewhere else altogether."

Macy stared at him, somehow not responding to his lunacy in any way. Lottie was certain she couldn't have remained so strong if she'd been in that position.

Jonah turned to the two guards wrapped around Macy. "Put her with the others." Jonah turned to the audience and spoke about the upcoming executions.

They dragged her over and threw her. Macy crashed into Thomas and Kinsley and fell to the ground. Lottie lunged toward Macy, but Jayla and Sydney stopped her. Thomas helped Macy up. She dusted herself off and looked around, her gaze finally meeting Lottie's. Tears shone in her eyes, and then she hurried over to Lottie.

Lottie made her way over to Macy and leaned against her—the closest she could come to an embrace with ropes tied around her. "I'm so sorry you're here."

"And I'm glad you're still alive." Macy rested her head against Lottie's.

"Not for long, unless something changes."

Macy pulled back and stared into her eyes. "There's a huge search effort."

Lottie frowned. "Not that it'll help us much, I'm afraid."

"It will." Macy leaned closer and whispered in Lottie's ear. "We have to believe it's true. You're going to be a grandma."

She froze and stared at Macy. "You're…?"

Macy nodded.

Lottie took a deep breath. She needed to think of a way to save Macy from the executions, but how?

Lose

ALEX GRIPPED HIS steering wheel. Luke was making it hard to keep up, and it wasn't like Alex was a stranger to driving fast. He used to street race in high school, and even a little after. Despite having the world's crappiest car, he'd won more often than not.

Luke blazed through an intersection and then the light turned yellow. If Alex tried to speed through, he'd run it for sure. He slammed on his breaks and swore. He watched as Luke's car grew smaller and smaller until it finally disappeared from sight.

Just as the light turned green, Alex's phone rang. He answered it, putting it on speaker, and sped through the intersection. "Where are you, Luke?"

"This is Nick."

Of course it was. Alex turned the radio down. "Any news?"

"Helicopters are flying over the forest, but given the size of it, we'll be lucky to find them anytime soon."

"Are you there yet?"

"Still on my way."

"Thanks for the updates."

"No problem," Nick said. "I'll let you know if anything changes."

"Sounds good." Alex ended the call and studied the sky, trying to see any helicopters up ahead, but he was too far away still. At the next stoplight, he called Luke.

"Hey, Alex. Sorry for losing you back there, but I can't slow down. I'm close. I can feel it in my bones."

The light turned green and Alex put the pedal to the metal. "I'm trying to catch up. Anyway, Nick just called and said there are helicopters searching the woods. If you see them, head in that direction."

"Will do."

The call ended. Alex ran a yellow light and narrowed his eyes, trying to see Luke's car up ahead. His brother-in-law had to be going twice the speed limit to stay that far ahead. Alex's respect for Luke doubled.

He turned up the music and bounced his head back and forth, happy to lose himself in the music. Five or six songs played before Alex realized he still hadn't caught up with Luke. But now the forest was in sight. There was a long, winding road in between him and it, but it was at last within reach.

Alex came to a stop sign at a deserted intersection. He grabbed his phone and called Luke. It rang five times before going to voicemail.

"Call me." Alex ended the call and pressed the gas pedal. Had Luke already made it to the woods? Alex grumbled. Why hadn't Luke at least let him know what was going on?

Once he finally reached the thick forest, he studied the side of the road, looking for a turnoff or his brother-in-law's car. Alex turned down the music and rolled down the windows. Helicopters sounded in the distance. He couldn't see them, so his only option was to keep following the dark, narrow road.

His phone rang. Alex picked it up and checked the screen. It was Nick.

"Did they find anything?" Alex asked.

"The helicopters still haven't found anything—it's literally like finding a needle in a haystack, Alex. We could be here all night and not find the commune. Especially if they're actively trying to blend in."

"So, what's the update?" Alex asked. "You wouldn't be calling me if you didn't know something, right?"

"I just got here. The K9 units are heading into the woods as we speak. Just hang tight. I'll keep you updated. Have you heard from Luke? My partner has been calling him, but he's not answering his phone. Strikes me as odd since his pregnant wife and his mother are missing."

"Maybe he fell asleep," Alex fibbed. "He's exhausted, you know."

"Well, if you hear from him..."

Alex slowed as he came to a turnoff. It was a dirt road with *No Trespassing* and *Private Government Property* signs. Exactly the type of place psychotic cult leaders would choose to build a secret commune.

"Are you still there?" Nick asked.

"Yeah. I'll tell Luke to call you. Thanks." He ended the call and went up the steep, narrow road.

More reflective signs warned him away. Alex's heart raced. He had to be getting close—he just had to be.

Judgment

SILENCE ECHOED ALL around the courtroom as Jonah looked at the adoring crowd. All eyes were focused on him, with each person loving him and eagerly waiting for him to speak. He took a deep breath, relishing in the admiration. It was more than that, really. They worshiped him. The venerate crowd would do anything he asked. Anything at all.

It was glorious and exhilarating. The thrill of it all was enough that he almost believed he could soar in the air above them.

He'd waited for more than a decade for this, and it had been worth every moment.

Luckily, he had plenty of time to revel in it because now he needed to carry on with the trials.

Jonah whacked the gavel onto the desk. Several people before him jumped at the sound. Every single person kept their attention on him—fully and wholly. Could anything be more wonderful?

"Trial number one." Jonah rose his heels, standing slightly taller. He turned to the guards standing near the prisoners. "Bring forth Bilhah."

The guard nearest her grabbed her arm. She cried out.

"No, Jayla!" called one of the prisoners.

"We do not go by our worldly names here." Jonah hit the gavel three times as hard as he could. "Not unless, like our beloved Chester, someone has not had the opportunity to receive their true name yet."

"Jayla!"

"Whip her!" Jonah demanded.

One of the guards grabbed Lois, the eldest prisoner, and dragged her away from the group. Heather—who wanted to be called Macy—clung to her, but another guard pulled her off and shoved her into a wall. A third guard pulled a whip from his belt and lashed Lois until red colored the white fabric on her back.

She screamed.

"Now stay quiet," Jonah ordered.

The guard holding Lois threw her to the ground.

Jonah turned back to the front of the room. Bilhah now stood below, held down by two guards. She glared at Jonah.

"Strike her." Jonah narrowed his eyes at one of the guards.

The guard did as he was told, hitting her hard enough to leave his hand print on her cheek.

Jonah bore his gaze into hers. "Do not disrespect me even with your expressions, woman."

Her mouth formed a straight line, but she didn't otherwise react.

"Speak to me, prisoner."

Her nostrils flared. "Yes, Great High Prophet."

"Much better." Jonah banged the gavel until his ears rang. "Now to begin."

She stared at him, shaking, but said nothing.

"What are your crimes against our people?" Jonah leaned forward, holding her gaze.

Bilhah kept quiet.

"Hit her again."

"Attempting to escape with the others," she said quickly.

"And?" Jonah leaned even closer. Any more, and he was likely to tumble off the platform.

Her expression tensed.

"The more you continue to ignore me, the more of a beating

you're inviting." He glanced at the guard on her left.

"I told the authorities about—"

"The *worldly* authorities," Jonah corrected.

Bilhah swallowed. "Yes, I told the worldly authorities the secrets of the community."

"And what did that lead to?" Jonah tilted his head and tensed his expression.

She sighed disrespectfully. "The—"

"Beat her for such insolence." Jonah leaned back and crossed his arms as the two guards struck her several times each.

Gasps sounded from the others awaiting trial.

"Enough." Jonah waited for the guards to stop, then he leaned forward again and bore his gaze into hers. Blood dripped from her nose, and one eye was swelling. "Are you ready to speak respectfully? No sulky sighing and no haughty expressions."

Bilhah nodded, her bruised mouth twisting.

"And what do you say?"

A beat passed. "I apologize."

"I missed part of that. What?" Jonah cupped his ear.

Her eyes widened, and she flinched as though expecting to be hit again—not that Jonah had ordered it. "I apologize, Great High Prophet."

"That's better. Now back to my question. When you broke the trust of every single person here by telling our secrets to the worldly authorities—which are no authorities at all—what did that lead to?"

She swallowed. "The breakdown of the community."

"And?" Jonah furrowed his brows.

"You and the other leaders went to jail."

"But that's not all, is it?"

Bilhah hesitated.

Jonah turned to one of the guards and opened his mouth.

"No," Bilhah said quickly. "It wasn't all. Everyone had to leave their homes and go back to the world."

"And many people were homeless, right?"

"Yes."

"But you weren't one of them, were you?"

"No, Great High Prophet."

"What happened with you?"

"I went back to my family. They found me and took me back."

"And you got to live in a big, expensive home with anything you wanted at any given moment, didn't you?" Jonah leaned forward again.

"Yes."

He leaned back and tapped his nail on the desk. "Did you think by moving away, you would escape your inevitable punishment?"

She swallowed, but didn't reply.

He let that slide. "We found you, though, didn't we?"

Bilhah nodded.

"It never pays to turn your back on your *true* family, does it?"

She shook her head.

Jonah cupped his ear again. "What was that? I couldn't quite hear you."

"No, Great High Prophet."

"What do you have to say for yourself?"

Her eyes widened, but she didn't speak.

"Nothing? This is your chance to defend yourself."

Bilhah's mouth gaped.

"No defense?"

"If I say anything, you'll call me a traitor. I'm already guilty in your eyes."

"Now you claim to know the thoughts of the Great High Prophet?"

She sighed. "See? No matter what I say, I condemn myself."

"You were never this mouthy before. Look at how the world has polluted you." Jonah turned to the guards. "Beat her."

They struck her all over until she fell to the ground, gasping for air and glaring at Jonah.

He picked up his gavel and struck it on the desk. "My judgment is guilty. Take her to the holding area."

The guards hefted Bilhah up and dragged her out of the courtroom.

Jonah turned to the other traitors and tapped his fingernails. "Who should come up next?"

Some of the prisoners leaned against each other. He made eye contact with one, then another until his gaze landed on Heather. "Don't worry, Heather. You won't be chosen for a while."

She clung to the old woman all the more. That gave Jonah his answer.

He struck his gavel again and looked at the old woman. "You're next, Lois. Let's discuss your sins."

"No!" Heather cried out.

"Strike her."

A guard punched Heather across the face.

"Bring the old woman over."

The same guard turned to Lois, grabbed her arm, and yanked her away from the others. He shoved her to the front of the platform, not letting go of his grip on her.

Jonah held her gaze for a moment. "Lois, Lois."

"I go by Lottie—short for Charlotte, my given name."

"You know how we feel about worldly names."

She glared at him.

Jonah found that far more amusing than when Bilhah had done the same thing. "I never thought you'd turn on me, *Lois*. Not after saving you and your boy from the streets. Very few of our residents were ever as grateful to me as you were."

Her nostrils flared and her eyes narrowed, but she remained

silent.

"Tell me, are you still grateful?"

The old woman shook from head to toe, but said nothing.

Jonah turned to the guard. "Hit her."

He punched her in the stomach. She doubled over. Cries sounded from the criminals.

Jonah waited until she stood upright. "Let's try that again. Are you still grateful to me?"

Searching

NICK PUSHED THE branches aside and stepped out of the woods into the gravel parking lot. More cruisers had arrived, practically filling it. Shining his flashlight on them, he recognized police forces from all over the state.

Foster turned to him, tucking some loose hair behind her ear. "Are we going back in?"

"Yeah. I just need some water." He headed for their cruiser, grabbed a couple water bottles from the trunk, and tossed her one.

She caught it and took a swig. "I hadn't expected the trail to be that steep."

"And I didn't expect it to end at the edge of a cliff." Nick shuddered thinking about how close they had come to falling to their deaths. He finished off the water bottle and glanced up toward the helicopters. "It looks like they're headed in the other direction now."

"Let me call in for an update." Foster pulled out her phone and slid her finger around the screen.

Gravel crunched behind them. Nick turned to see a beat-up, gold-colored Tercel driving in. "That's not…?"

Alex waved at him as he drove past and parked in one of the few remaining spots.

"Hold on," Nick told Foster. He jogged over to the beater and opened the driver's side door. "What are you doing here?"

"I'm going to help find my sister."

Nick crossed his arms and furrowed his brows. "No, you're not."

Alex climbed out. "Actually, I am. Luke's already out there." He nodded toward a black sedan not far away.

"Why?" Nick exclaimed. "Why would you two do this to me? I was keeping you updated because of how close you are to the situation! Not because I wanted you involved in the search. It's dangerous out here."

"My pregnant sister is out there somewhere, being held by a murderous cult leader. I'm not going to sit at home twiddling my thumbs."

"This isn't the kind of stunt to pull if you want to join the academy."

"I won't do anything like this once I'm in. Scout's honor." He held up three fingers.

Nick rolled his eyes and shook his head. "Go home, Alex."

Alex slammed the door shut. "I can't—I won't."

They stared each other down.

"You can't make me go home."

"I can arrest you."

Alex leaned against his car. "You really want to do that? I thought you wanted me on the force."

"What am I supposed to do? You keep pulling stuff like this. Part of being an officer is taking orders."

"I know."

"You do?" Nick crossed his arms tighter.

"Yeah, and I'll be the model cadet and officer once I'm there. I'll be the dude everyone uses as an example to the others of what they're supposed to be doing."

"I'll believe that when I see it."

"I thought you wanted to see me on the force? That I had potential."

"Yeah, it's going to take work. You have drive. You care.

You've got life experience that most don't. But you have to stop doing stupid things—and this is one of them."

"You ready, Captain?" came Foster's voice from behind. "Who's this?"

Alex stepped past Nick and extended his hand. "Cadet Mercer. Pleasure to meet you."

She shook his hand. "Officer Foster." She threw Nick a confused glance. "Why did you bring along a cadet?"

Nick slapped his forehead. Yes, Alex had potential—a lot of it—but they were going to have to dig deep to pull it out. "I didn't bring him along, but since he's here, he's going to join us."

Alex's eyes widened and he grinned.

"Let's go." Nick gestured toward a different entrance to the woods. Foster headed toward it. Nick turned to Alex. "Don't make me regret this."

"You won't. I swear."

Nick wasn't half as sure as Alex sounded, but there was nothing he could do to keep Alex out of the woods, and he didn't want to arrest him, so he may as well keep him close. "If anyone asks, I didn't authorize this."

"Authorize what? Who's Captain Fleshman?"

"Glad to hear it." Nick dug into his coat and found his smaller backup flashlight and tossed it to Alex, who caught it and turned it on. "You're going to need that. Watch out for sudden cliffs."

"I've hiked and camped out here before."

"Here? It's private government property."

He shrugged. "That makes it all the better for camping, hiking, and hunting."

Nick shook his head. "Come on."

"So, who's Foster? She's hot." He moved aside some bushes and held them back for Nick, who walked in ahead of him.

"I thought you were worried about your sister."

Alex caught up. "I am. I just thought maybe you and her—"

"She's one of my officers. That's it. Stop talking. We need to listen."

They walked in silence and caught up with Foster, who walked with a very feminine sway to her hips. Nick groaned. Now Alex was getting into his head. He focused his gaze ahead of Foster and listened to the helicopters, following their general direction.

After about twenty minutes, dogs barked in the distance.

Foster turned around and stopped. Nick nearly stumbled into her. Foster's full lips gaped. "The K9 units found something."

Nick looked away from her. "Let's go." He went around her and ran toward the barking. The helicopters and the dogs both grew louder. They came to a steep incline with barely a path up. He turned back to Foster and Alex. "This is going to be tricky. Be careful."

After no more than fifty feet up the path, Nick's legs burned and he was gasping for air—and he was in good shape. He hoped Alex could keep up. Or maybe it would be better if he couldn't, because then he might actually go back home where he should've stayed.

Finally, they all made it to the top. Nick leaned against a tree, gasping for air. Alex and Foster also breathed heavily.

"How did they get an entire cult up there?" Alex wiped his forehead.

Foster pointed across the way, where a group of officers were gathered together. "Looks like they found an easier path."

"Lucky us." Alex glanced up to where the helicopters were. They were all staying in one place, aiming their lights in the same spot.

"Looks like the commune is just beyond those trees." Nick pushed himself from the tree. "Time to bust in."

Inside

LUKE PULLED ON the wide board, ignoring the gashes in his hand and the blood dripping down his arm. He would get through the fence no matter what. The irony wasn't lost on him. More than a decade earlier, he'd worked equally as hard on a similar fence trying to get *out* of the commune, but now here he was fighting to get back in. But it was all for the same reason—to protect Macy.

Everything he did since he'd met Macy had been for her. She was his first and only love, and as before, he was willing to die to keep her safe. And now he had even more at stake with his mother and baby in danger, as well. He couldn't let any harm befall any of them.

The board snapped in half, sending slivers flying in all directions. He ducked and covered his face, barely missing some headed right for him. Luke wrapped his hands around the remainder of the thick wooden plank as best as he could and pulled, pressing both feet against the bottom of the fence. The board gave a little, but not enough.

A shot rang out in the distance.

Luke gasped and let go of the board. He stumbled backward, nearly losing his balance. He reached out and caught himself by pushing against a tree. Heart thundering against his chest, he hurried back to the fence and pulled on the board again. It popped out.

Luckily, he'd lost significant weight over the last month. He'd be able to squeeze through the space. Before, there wouldn't have been a chance. He maneuvered himself through the tight space, scratching himself even more.

Another shot sounded, this time louder. Closer.

He sent up a quick prayer for the safety of his family. Maybe the gunfire was from someone in the helicopters or the cops taking aim at Jonah and the other leaders.

The helicopters circled overhead, shining lights beyond trees and buildings.

That was where Luke needed to go. He pulled up his sleeves and ran, staying near trees as much as possible. He couldn't risk drawing attention to himself—not from the community and not from the police.

He made his way to where the lights shone down. Men and women danced in an open field, but none were any of the leaders.

Luke's stomach sank. That meant they were only a distraction—decoys. He ran away from them, desperate to find the leaders. Wherever they were, his loved ones were bound to be.

Three shots rang out. Luke skidded to a stop and spun around just in time to see one of the dancing decoys fall to the ground.

His throat closed up and adrenaline pumped through his body. He spun back around and ran through a neighborhood of tiny log homes—exactly like the one he'd lived in so long ago.

A dog barked nearby. In the distance, cows, sheep, and horses cried out. Luke ran for the nearest house and threw open the door, knowing there would be no lock. He pressed himself against the door in case anyone tried to come in after him. The barking grew quieter, and Luke's breathing returned to normal. They hadn't seen him.

He peeked out the window to make sure no one was outside. It was hard to see without any lights, but as far as he could tell, nobody lurked in the shadows.

Luke gripped the doorknob, his skin sticking to it thanks to the dried blood. He hurried outside and glanced around. A tall building—nearly as high as the trees themselves—loomed in the distance. That was different. Everything else was almost an exact replica of the old commune, but not that.

He headed straight for it. Shouts and cries sounded just beyond the high structure. Luke slowed as he reached it, and crept around it, staying close to the building. Once he rounded the corner, he froze in place. His blood ran cold and he couldn't breathe.

A group of people dressed in the traditional community white garb stood in front of a platform with three gallows. Each one had a person hanging from the rope.

Someone addressed the crowd—Jonah. Luke would know that voice anywhere. Luke's gaze landed on the group standing behind Jonah. Two women hugging each other caught his attention. Macy and his mom. His throat closed up. They were still alive. There was still time to save them. He had to do something.

Luke ran over to the group. Jonah didn't notice him. Not until Macy cried out.

Jonah turned to him. Luke stood taller.

"Get him out of here."

Two of the robed men, both of whom Luke recognized from years before, marched toward him. Luke stepped away, raking his mind for ideas. He held up his flashlight, switched it over to a rapidly blinking mode and shone it in the eyes of the larger of the two men.

"Hey!" He covered his eyes.

The other man rushed for Luke and grabbed the flashlight. Luke clung to it and tried to shine it in his eyes but the man's grip wouldn't allow that. Instead, Luke punched him with his left hand. It was enough to surprise him into letting go of the flashlight. Luke pulled it away, aimed the flashing light to the man's eyes, and then struck him across the face with it. He stumbled back a step.

Luke jumped back, but the other man had recovered and ran toward him. Before he knew what had happened, he and the other man were both on the ground. A fist struck Luke's jaw. He hit the other man across the face with the flashlight. Blood gushed out of his nose, spraying on Luke.

"Enough!" Jonah shouted. "Bring him to me."

Luke hit the man again as he struggled to get up. Both of the men grabbed Luke, pinning his arms so that he was forced to drop his only weapon. The flashlight bounced on the ground, the light reflecting in the crowd and the gallows. He froze when he realized the three hanging bodies were people he'd grown up with. They'd all attended the community's small school together.

Jonah's men took advantage of his shock and dragged him over to the leader.

"Let him stay," Jonah said. "He wanted in. Let him watch everyone hang—especially his mother and Heather, who he married without my permission or her father's."

"I had her father's blessing!" Luke yelled. He tried to free his arms, but the two men only gripped harder. "Her *real* father."

Jonah shook his head. "Look how far you've fallen—how much you've let yourself become polluted by the world."

"Let them go, Jonah. They don't want to be here!"

"They need to be punished, but your outburst gives me an idea. Take Lois to the platform."

Dread washed through Luke. Lois was his mom's community name. He struggled harder to get free. "No!"

Jonah just laughed.

Two men grabbed his mom and pulled her away from Macy. "Lottie!"

"Stop!" Luke glared at Jonah. "Take me instead. In the place of both Macy—I mean, Heather and Lois."

"No," both women cried out.

"Luke, don't!" His mom turned to him, her eyes wide and begging.

He turned back to Jonah. "Take me."

Jonah raised a hand and snapped his fingers.

Half a dozen men pulled out guns and aimed them at Luke.

"Last chance to walk away," Jonah said.

A sense of calm ran through Luke. He shook his head. "I'm serious. I want to take their place."

"Luke, no!" Macy cried.

He held her gaze. "I need to protect my family."

Her mouth gaped and her hands moved to her stomach.

Luke gave a slight nod, acknowledging he knew about their baby.

Macy's eyes widened, but nobody else seemed to notice the hidden level of their conversation.

"This would almost be sweet," Jonah said. "If you weren't all heathen criminals! Take them all up to the gallows."

Close

ALEX STAYED BEHIND Nick and the others, not wanting to draw attention to himself as the only non-cop. Nick and Foster spoke with a group of officers while others swarmed the enormous fence, looking for a way in. In the distance, helicopters hovered, their propellers kicking up a breeze and making Alex's ears ring.

"Ow!" An officer jumped back from the fence, shaking his hands and swearing profusely.

"What happened?" A couple cops ran over.

"The fence has spikes, and I think they're covered in poison. Look at this swelling."

The three of them rushed away. It was a good thing there was an ambulance already in the parking lot, and that they had an easier way to get there than Alex had taken with Nick and Foster.

Alex turned his attention back to the fence. Nobody was paying attention to him. Maybe he could sneak away and look for another way in. Something less conspicuous that wouldn't be smeared with toxins.

He crept away to go around the fence.

Shots rang out from inside the compound. Alex shuddered. Would they get to Macy and Lottie in time? Did Luke manage to break in? Maybe if Alex jogged around the perimeter, he could find Luke or the entrance he'd made.

Whack, whack!

Alex spun around. A group of firefighters were wailing on the fence with axes. Shards of wood flew through the air, and before he could turn back around, they had broken through the fence.

Nick shouted orders, but from where Alex stood, he couldn't make out what he said. The firefighters pried boards off, throwing them to the side. There was a big enough gap for people to get through. Police ran over and squeezed through.

Before Alex could decide if he would enter there or try to find a different place, yelling came from inside. More cops rushed in, followed by the firefighters. A commotion of yelling and gasps sounded on the other side of the fence.

Terror gripped Alex. He ran for the hole and pushed his way through. Several officers were down—but not just lying on the ground. Two had long rods sticking out from their midsections and another had been impaled by one, and he hung from it, not touching the ground.

Alex's stomach lurched. He covered his mouth. Was dealing with this type of thing something they taught in the academy? His stomach lurched again, bringing up his last meal. He turned away and vomited out the contents of his stomach. So many years of watching violent shows and movies couldn't prepare him for the real thing. The images of the dead cops wouldn't leave his mind, and he threw up again.

"Watch out!" someone yelled.

Alex spun around, wiping his mouth. Spikes rained down from above. Everyone scattered. Alex ran toward a log cabin. Something grazed the back of his head. He jumped to the ground, sliding on his stomach and crashing into the cabin. Alex scrambled to his feet and ran for the door. It was unlocked.

He ran inside and closed the door behind him, gasping for air. He sat in a wooden rocking chair. The cult was far more sadistic than he'd imagined—a poisoned fenced, and rods and spikes coming down from above. What else did they have in store?

Once he caught his breath, he needed to head out and find where they had Macy. A cold chill ran through him, thinking about what they would do to her. Probably something far worse since they'd gone to all the trouble to break Chester out from jail and kidnap her. And would Lottie still be alive after all this time?

Would either of them be alive?

Alex pushed himself away from the chair. He didn't have time to catch his breath. If they were still alive, they probably didn't have much time given the helicopters, K9s, and the police barging in. The leaders would freak out and want to hurt or kill them.

He flung open the door and ran, heading toward the helicopters. They wouldn't be hovering overhead for nothing. Macy had to be close to there. He ran down a dirt road with tiny log cabins on either side until he reached the helicopters.

They shone lights down on a group of people wearing all white. Alex paused, scanning the faces. Neither Macy nor Lottie were in the group. Hopefully that was good news.

Alex ran on, hearing shouts and cries in the distance. He darted across mini-lawns and in between the cabins, following the voices. He came to a group gathered around a platform. But it wasn't just any platform. He rubbed his eyes to make sure he was seeing it correctly. Gallows? These people really were backwards. It was like he'd stepped into a time warp.

Three people hung from the ropes and three more were being led up onto the platform. Each one was tied up.

Alex ran closer, careful to hide behind trees, bushes, and buildings. Once he got close enough, he stopped and watch the scene before him. A short, stocky man with dark hair was yelling to the crowd about the price of rebellion. Alex scanned the crowd for Macy and Lottie, but didn't see them.

Then he looked on the platform. The three people tied and headed for the ropes were Macy, Luke, and Lottie.

He couldn't breathe.

Three men were loosening the nooses of the people who'd already been hanged.

Could he get to them in time? If he did, would he even be able to save them?

He had to try. Alex surveyed the scene before him. If he went around the long way, staying behind a trail of bushes, he could stay out of sight. Then he could surprise them and rush onto the platform. Maybe he could push the men down to the ground below, giving the captives a chance to run.

Alex rushed out behind his hiding place and hurried over to the bushes. Nobody saw him. They were all listening to the short, loud man. Once he got closer to the gallows, he could see his family members clearer. Macy had tears running down her face.

It gutted him. Anger surged through him and he burst into a run, stumbling as he reached the lopsided steps.

Macy's eyes widened and she shook her head at him. Alex ignored her and shoved the man closest to him off the stage. The man reached for Lottie, trying to take her with him. Alex grabbed her and pulled her away. "Run!"

"Stop him!" someone yelled.

People spun around, looking in all directions. Alex took advantage of the confusion and shoved the closest white-clothed man off the platform. He reached for Luke, who he'd been guarding, but Luke jumped back and shoved the man holding Macy. He stumbled, but caught himself before falling.

Bang! Bang!

Alex's ears rang as gunfire sounded. Police swarmed the area.

"Come on!" Alex waved Luke and Macy.

The man who'd been holding Macy jumped up and wrapped his arms around her. Luke punched him in the nose. Alex ran over and hit the man in the back of the head. He stumbled back, reached into his robe, pulled out a rifle, and aimed it at Luke.

"Shoot!" yelled the annoying short man.

Alex shoved Luke out of the way and then reached over and pulled Macy down.

Gunfire sounded from all around. Luke jumped on top of Macy, shielding her from any bullets. Cries sounded. Bullets flew through the air.

Luke turned to Alex. "Find my mom! I'll get Macy out of here."

Alex rolled over and crawled to the stairs. The short, loud guy stood there, aiming a gun at him. Alex's heart skipped a beat. He couldn't let him get to Macy. He jumped to his feet.

The crazy man cocked the gun. Then he pulled the trigger.

Time seemed to stand still as Alex waited for the bullet to release. He tried to move, but his body wouldn't cooperate.

Cease

MACY TRIED TO break free from Luke's hold, but he wouldn't let go. "Alex!"

She couldn't pull her gaze from her baby brother. Images from his short life flashed before her eyes—them playing chase through the yard as kids, birthday parties and Christmases, playing hide-and-seek while camping, fighting as teens, then growing close after her abduction, and finally watching him grow as a dad with Ariana after moving back home.

Macy gasped for air. Her brother still stood at the edge of the platform. He hadn't fallen.

Jonah studied his gun, holding it at various angles. "Empty already!"

Relief washed through Macy. Her body went limp. It was a good thing Luke had such a tight grip on her.

Alex flew through the air, gliding over the steps. He crashed into Jonah, knocking him to the ground. Dust picked up as the two men hit and kicked each other.

"Come on." Luke pulled Macy in the other direction.

"I can't leave Alex!"

"We have to find Mom."

Macy looked back and forth between her brother and husband. How could she choose between Alex and Lottie? They both needed their help. "You help Alex fight Jonah, and I'll find her."

Gunfire rang all around them. A bullet breezed past them.

Macy flashed back to the night they escaped the community before.

Luke pulled her to the ground. "Alex can handle Jonah. I have to get you off this platform."

Police ran toward Alex and Jonah, aiming their guns at them.

"No!" Macy managed to free herself from Luke's protective hold and ran toward her brother.

"Macy!" Luke cried.

"Alex! Watch out!"

He looked up, confused. Then his eyes widened as he saw the guns pointed at him. Alex let go of Jonah and raised his hands into the air. Jonah hit Alex in the temple with the gun. Alex's head rolled back, and then he fell to the ground.

Police swarmed Jonah, pulling him away from Alex. They held him down as Captain Fleshman cuffed him and read him his rights.

"You'll never get away with this!" Jonah shouted. "I'm the Great High Prophet!"

"No, you're the one who won't get away." The captain shook his head.

Two policemen dragged Jonah away.

"I'm the Great High Prophet!"

"Did you prophesy this?" Luke called out.

Macy took his hand. "Come on, let's check on Alex and then find your mom."

Alex was already starting to sit up as they made their way down the stairs.

The captain walked over and helped Alex up. "Let's get you down to the medics."

He rubbed his temple and turned to Macy. "Are you okay?"

She nodded. "Just shaken up."

Alex threw his arms around her and squeezed tight. "I was so worried."

"So was I."

"Come on." The captain waved them over and turned to Luke. "Your mom's already down there. A couple officers escorted her a few minutes ago."

Alex let go of Macy and the four of them walked through the community in silence. More gunfire sounded not far away.

At least they were all safe and the community leaders would be going back to jail—and hopefully they would stay there.

Over

ALEX ADJUSTED HIS tie and squirmed in the uncomfortable wooden pew. On his right, Macy sniffled and dabbed her eye with a tissue. He squeezed her hand and gave her a sad smile. What could he say to make it any better? She'd been kidnapped a second time and watched three people she knew executed by a madman who had almost killed them, too.

The minister concluded the service with a prayer. Then he motioned toward the casket. "Everyone is welcome to come up and say their goodbyes to Sydney. We ask that you allow family the opportunity to go first."

Alex leaned over and kissed Macy's cheek. "Unless you need me, I'll meet you in the reception hall."

She wiped a tear away. "It's okay. Luke's going to walk up with me. I'm sure Jayla and Lottie will join us. I think I saw Kinsley, too. It's almost a reunion."

Luke put his arm around Macy, helped her up, and guided her to the aisle.

Alex waited for the crowd to thin out before rising and making his way back. He nodded to a few people on his way out of the sanctuary and followed the aromas of food to the reception hall.

Nick and the pretty cop stood by a wall, both sipping on coffee. Alex made his way over and poured himself some coffee, too.

She smiled at Alex. "Hey, Cadet."

He held back a grimace, remembering Nick's story, and

glanced at her name tag. "Hi, Officer Foster."

"Soon to be Detective." She grinned and turned to Nick. "Right, Captain?"

Nick gave a nod, his attention focused out the window.

Curious, Alex craned his neck to see what was so interesting. He almost dropped his coffee. Across the street a man stood, staring at the church building. Other than the fact that the man had wavy brown hair and much tanner skin, he could've been Flynn Myer—the man who had abducted Ariana.

Alex shook his head. It couldn't be Flynn. Flynn was in prison without a chance at parole. But then again, so had Chester, and he'd managed to escape—though not for long. He was back behind bars, where he belonged, along with all the other cult leaders.

Gasping for air, Alex turned to Nick. "That isn't…?"

"It can't be." Nick pulled out his phone and headed for the door. "I'll be right back."

"What's the matter?" Foster asked.

Alex couldn't find his voice. The man across the street could have easily been Ariana's abductor. Alex should know—he'd confronted him enough times.

"Okay." Foster threw her paper cup in the garbage. "I'll see you around. I'm going to talk with Detective Anderson."

Alex nodded, still unable to speak.

A couple minutes later, Nick returned. "Flynn's still in jail. That guy's not him."

"He looked just like him." Alex glanced back outside, but the man had left.

"It was just a coincidence." Nick put his hand on Alex's shoulder. "Don't let that rattle you. They say everyone has a doppelganger. That must be his. Let's just focus on the fact that all your loved ones are safe, and you're about to start the academy. What else could you ask for?"

Alex took a deep breath and focused on his friend. "You're right. It's time to look forward. The past is done haunting me." He stood taller. "I'm going to find Macy."

"See you later, Alex." Nick flicked a nod and gave a friendly smile.

Foster waved.

Alex spun around and went into the entryway. He nearly bumped into Lottie.

She embraced him. "It's so good to see you, Alex."

He returned the hug. "And it's great to see you—you really had us worried. You know you shouldn't do that."

Lottie laughed. "I'll try not to." She stepped back and took the hand of a man with a salt-and-pepper beard and striking blue eyes. "Alex, I'd like you to meet Wayne. Wayne, this is Alex, Macy's brother."

Wayne smiled widely and shook Alex's hand, nearly crushing it. "Good to meet you. Macy has told me great things about you and Ariana—I hear she's thrilled to have a cousin on the way."

"Over the moon." Alex grinned. "She hasn't stopped talking about it since she found out."

"I'm sure we'll see you around. Pleasure to meet you."

"You, too." Alex nodded and headed toward the sanctuary. Zoey waved him over. He gave her a double-take. "I didn't know you were here."

She nodded. "I wanted to give moral support to Macy and Luke, but I sat in the back because I didn't know Sydney. Hey, I don't suppose you want to go somewhere else? Maybe grab some coffee? Macy and Luke are pretty busy. I don't think they'll miss us."

His pulse quickened. She wanted to go somewhere with him? This might be a good chance to tell her about joining the academy. At least she would see that he was trying to better his life. "Yeah, sure." Alex glanced over at Macy, speaking with a group of women. "I'll just text her and let her know we left."

They headed outside. Zoey turned to him. "My car?"

"That'd be best. I rode with Macy and Luke. Otherwise, we'll have a long walk to my house."

She laughed. "I've always appreciated your humor."

"Always?" He arched a brow. "I can think of a few times you weren't so happy about it. In fact, I think you left a permanent bruise on my arm when I joked about your cooking setting off the smoke detector."

The corners of her mouth twitched. "You had it coming, and besides, it was just that one time."

"Didn't your mom have to throw away that pan?" He held back a laugh.

She remote-unlocked her turquoise smart car. "Get in."

They joked back and forth over the short car ride to her favorite coffee shop. Zoey tapped the steering wheel but didn't turn off the engine.

"Everything okay?" Alex asked.

She turned to him. "Ever since Lottie and Macy came back, I've been thinking a lot."

Alex's stomach twisted into a tight knot. "Oh?"

"Yeah. About what's important in life, and about not letting important things slip by."

He cleared his throat. "Makes sense. Anything in particular?"

"You."

"Me?" He turned to make sure she didn't mean someone else.

"Oh, stop. Yes, you. What happened? Things were going so well after Ariana returned, but then… Why did you pull away from me?"

Not this conversation. Alex cleared his throat again and tugged on his collar. "Well, you know, I wanted to get my life together."

"What do you mean? You've turned into dad of the year with Ari."

He looked away. "To get a job."

"You have one."

"Yeah, as my dad's—I mean, working for my dad. And I need a better car and a place of my own."

"Wait a minute. Are you trying to impress me, Alex?"

That sounded a whole lot better than trying to be good enough for her. He shrugged.

She grabbed his chin, turned him toward her, and kissed him.

"Wow, and I didn't even tell you about the Police Academy!"

Her eyes widened. "What about it?"

"I'm starting next month."

She threw her arms around him. "That's so great! You're going to make such an amazing cop." She gave him a once-over. "And I can't wait to see you in uniform."

Alex grinned. "Really?"

"Yeah, really. Now let's go inside, and you can catch me up on everything else you've been holding out."

He laughed. "There really isn't anything else."

"We'll see about that." She cut the engine and climbed out of the car. Alex let his gaze linger on her a moment before getting out, too. What a turn of events—first Macy and Lottie made it home safely, then he was accepted into the academy, and now Zoey. Maybe things were actually turning around.

Story Worlds by Stacy Claflin

Stacy is a *USA Today* bestselling author who writes about complex characters overcoming incredible odds. Whether it's her Gone saga of psychological thrillers, her various paranormal romance tales, or her contemporary sweet romances, Stacy's three-dimensional characters shine through bringing an experience readers don't soon forget.

If you haven't yet read the Gone Trilogy (the story of Macy's abduction as a teenager) then you should read that. You'll find out what happened and learn more about Chester and the cult. No Return and Dean's List are standalone spin-offs from that saga. Stay tuned for a third Alex Mercer book in the fall of 2017.

The Gone Saga

The Gone Trilogy: Gone, Held, Over

Dean's List

No Return

Alex Mercer Thrillers

Gone Saga spin-off

Girl in Trouble

Turn Back Time

Curse of the Moon

Lost Wolf

Chosen Wolf

Hunted Wolf

Broken Wolf

Cursed Wolf

Secret Jaguar

The Transformed Series

Main Series

Deception

Betrayal

Forgotten

Ascension

Duplicity

Sacrifice

Destroyed

Transcend

Entangled

Dauntless

Obscured

Partition

Standalones

Fallen

Silent Bite

Hidden Intentions

Saved by a Vampire

Sweet Desire

Short Story Collection

Tiny Bites

Standalones

Haunted

Sweet Dreams (Indigo Bay)

The Hunters

Seaside Surprises

Seaside Heartbeats

Seaside Dances

Seaside Kisses

Seaside Christmas
Bayside Wishes
Bayside Evenings
Bayside Promises
Bayside Destinies
Bayside Dreams

More coming soon!

Visit StacyClaflin.com for details.

Sign up for new release updates and receive **three free books.**
stacyclaflin.com/newsletter

Want to hang out and talk about books? Join My Book Hangout and participate in the discussions. There are also exclusive giveaways, sneak peeks and more. Sometimes the members offer opinions on book covers, too. You never know what you'll find.
facebook.com/groups/stacyclaflinbooks

Author's Note

Thanks so much for reading Turn Back Time. (If you skipped ahead to this first, please stop reading. There are big spoilers ahead!) I hope you enjoyed the second Alex Mercer thriller! I had a lot of fun writing it—so much that I have many ideas spinning in my mind for the following books. I'm eager to get started! Writing this was an interesting experience because I haven't visited with Chester, Jonah, or any of the other community members in so long. It was a really interesting experience climbing into the mind of Jonah for his chapters. His were actually some of the easiest to write. It was almost alarming how natural his point of view came to me!

I hope you enjoyed watching the characters grow and change as much I have. That was one of my favorite parts of the trilogy and now these new books. I'm excited to see Alex join the academy and watch what happens with Nick and his kids. What will come of Lottie and blue-eyed Wayne? Will Macy and Luke's baby manage to avoid the family fate of being kidnapped? We'll all find out soon enough!

If you enjoyed this book, please consider leaving a review wherever you purchased it. Not only will your review help me to better understand what you like—so I can give you more of it!—but it will also help other readers find my work. Reviews can be short—just share your honest thoughts. That's it.

Want to know when I have a new release? Sign up here (stacy-claflin.com/newsletter) for new release updates. You'll even get three free books!

I've spent many hours writing, re-writing, and editing this work. I even put together a team who helped with the editing process. As it is impossible to find every single error, if you find any, please contact me through my website and let me know. Then I can fix them for future editions.

Thank you for your support!
~Stacy

Made in the USA
San Bernardino, CA
07 August 2019